MERLIN APPEARS

King Arthur Chronicles Book 1

TOBY NEIGHBORS

Merlin Appears: King Arthur Chronicles Book 1

Copyright © 2020 by Toby Neighbors

ISBN: 978-1-952260-20-9

Mythic Adventure Publishing, LLC

Post Falls, Idaho

Copy Editors Gabrielle Guarracino

ALSO BY TOBY NEIGHBORS

PROLOGUE

I heard this story from an old man in a tiny village on the coast of Wales. I had booked myself into a hotel for a short holiday between stops on a book tour. It was an idyllic place: towering cliffs over the ocean, narrow streets with eclectic stores, tiny coffee shops and ancient pubs. The people there seemed ancient, too. I can't even remember how I found it, but I vividly recall the details of that place, as well as the people.

The most memorable was an old man wearing short sleeves and drinking coffee on the patio of a tiny restaurant that had a spectacular view of the ocean. I was seated next to him, ordered a coffee, and got out my laptop. It's not unusual for people to notice me writing, but they usually have the grace to be subtle. This old man made no attempt to hide his curiosity.

"Working?" he asked.

"I'm a writer... novels," I replied.

"A bard—how fortunate," the man said. "I've a tale for you."

People often share stories with me, usually one book idea they've

1

been toying with for years but never got around to writing. Fortunately, as a novelist, I've never run out of story ideas or struggled to write myself. In fact, I usually have more ideas than I can work on at once. Most of the time, I try to distance myself from people who want me to write their stories. It's not that I don't respect their ideas, but there simply isn't enough time to write everything. I have to be very selective and balance my art with what the market demands. But there was something different about the old man—something that I couldn't ignore. He was tall and lean; if not for the mass of wrinkles on his face and the mane of white hair on his head, I would have taken him for a much younger man.

He had strange tattoos on his forearms: his right arm had the three letters R-T-C, and his left had the three letters G-N-V. The skin was loose, like an old garment worn too many times, but there were stout-looking muscles beneath the skin, and the tattoos were still readable. His eyes were clear, not cloudy or bloodshot, and his voice was strong. Something about the man was intriguing—charismatic, even. I found myself wanting to hear his tale.

"A story?" I asked.

"Not just a story," he said, turning in his chair so that we were nearly side by side, both staring out over the cliff's edge to the sea. "It's legend, really, of a forgotten time. People today have heard whispers, and some may have seen glimpses of it, but they don't realize what was lost."

"Okay, I'm listening," I said, closing my laptop and picking up my mug of coffee.

"You've heard of Arthur, the great king," the old man said, his voice full of a strange emotion. "But those are just stories, based on events that happened long before—in the time even before the Romans came to Britain, when the Greeks were still just children, and magic was real."

CHAPTER ONE

Merlin glided through the air over the great salt marshes that spread across the border of the southern kingdom. In his falcon form, he could travel much faster than any horse and attract less notice, too. His keen avian eyes saw everything below, from the wolves slogging through the marshes to the poor wretches that tried to live in the blighted lands.

Eventually, even wizards grew weary. Merlin began to search for a dry place to spend the night, safe from the unsavory creatures that prowled the marshes once the sun set. He selected a towering pine tree and circled as he descended, searching for any sign of predators. After choosing a sturdy branch, he landed. As a falcon, his powerful talons could hold fast to the bough through the night, which was lucky for him: the sun was setting, and Merlin was tired. He raised one darkly feathered wing, tucked his head beneath it, and soon fell asleep.

The smoke woke him, the smell making his stomach rumble angrily. Food had not been a priority on this journey, and while he could hunt and kill as a falcon, he did not savor the taste of raw meat the way other birds did. The smell of smoked fish, on the other hand, did spark a craving in the wizard. With a leap, he was in the air again, spreading powerful wings and circling the small hill where the tree stood. The ground there was less wet, but nor was it completely dry. A tiny fire had been kindled, and two hooded figures huddled near the golden light.

Merlin dropped toward the ground and reverted to his human form just as his feet met the earth. He stood straight, stretching the muscles in his back without making a sound. In the darkness beyond the tiny fire's light, he was completely shrouded in darkness.

"Hello at the camp," Merlin said calmly.

"Who's there?" one of the hooded figures demanded. It was a man, skinny and covered in filthy rags, but holding a knife in one hand.

"A friend; I mean you no harm," Merlin said. "I smelled the fish you're smoking and hoped there might be enough for me."

He stepped closer, into the light. His long robe hung to the top of his boots and was cinched at the waist with a golden sash. The soft whiskers that covered his jawline and chin were streaked with gray, and his long hair was tied together at the back of his neck. From inside the sleeve of his robe, Merlin produced a silver coin, polished bright and reflecting the firelight as he held it out.

"Umvar, take the coin," the other traveler demanded.

Merlin held out the coin to the man, who took it and

slipped it into his belt.

"We've only enough for two," Umvar insisted.

"You can go hungry one night for a silver coin," his companion insisted.

Merlin didn't necessarily like taking the man's meal, but he had done without on his long journey. A belly full of smoked fish would give him strength to return to his estates in Butan.

"May I?" Merlin asked, pointing to the tiny fire.

"Please, join us," the second traveler said.

It was a woman who sat leaned against the tree, her arms and legs pulled up around her distended belly. Merlin could feel the child she carried: it was almost to term and had not yet been named. Looking up, Merlin could see the moon was nearly full. The silvery light seemed swallowed up in the darkness of the salt marshes, which were black as pitch. She would have the baby soon, maybe in only a few days.

"My name is Cryslov," she said, taking a spit from above the fire where the two headless fish had been smoked. Each body was split down the middle, leaving the two sides hanging on either side of the stick. The skin was blackened, the flesh white. Merlin took the stick and began to pull the flaky white meat from the bones of one of the fish. It was rich with the flavor of the smoke, and salty, too. The man, Umvar, handed Merlin a water skin.

"You'll have to drink water—we have nothing better," he said.

Merlin took the skin and held it in one hand. With the other, he waved an intricate pattern while whispering a spell. Cryslov looked up, her eyes bright. She clearly wanted to speak, but she waited—it wasn't wise to interrupt a wizard in the middle of a spell. When he was finished, Merlin lifted the water skin and took a long pull. The water had become a sharp, full-bodied wine.

"It is more than water now," Merlin said, handing the skin back to Umvar.

"You're a wizard?" Cryslov said. "I didn't know there were any of the gifted south of Atal."

"There are a few," Merlin said. "I'm Errol ap'Tunnar Foyl, but most people call me Merlin."

"Like the bird," Umvar said, as if it were an insult.

"The falcon, yes," Merlin said without affect, quietly closing to topic and moving on. "Cryslov, the fish is excellent."

"Thank you," Cryslov said.

"Where are you headed?" Merlin asked.

"Wrydan's Ferry," Cryslov said. "Hopefully we make it before the baby comes."

"It will come with the full moon," Merlin said.

"How can you know that?" Umvar asked.

He was standing and still had the knife in one hand. It was wise not to trust strangers, especially those who wandered alone in the dark, but Merlin had paid for his meal and pledged not to harm them. The knife was more tool than weapon and wouldn't be much use against a wizard. Merlin was tempted to turn the blade into an eel, or maybe a snake, but it was plain to see that the couple had precious little in the world. Ruining the knife wouldn't help them, and Merlin realized that he was intrigued by the child Cryslov was carrying.

"Your wife is near term," Merlin said. "Many babies are born when the moon is full. It is simple observation."

Cryslov rubbed her ample stomach, smiling. "Umvar is my brother. The baby isn't his."

"And that is why you haven't named the child?" Merlin asked, referring to the powerful blessing a child received from its father and mother.

"I'm waiting on the father," Cryslov said. "He will come."

"Why isn't he here now?" Merlin asked.

"There is rumor of war," Umvar said. "The Farkian outcasts are massing near the border. Their dark magic is a threat to all living kind."

Abruptly, he took a swig from the water skin, as if talking had suddenly dried his throat. He wiped his mouth and nodded to Merlin before settling back down in front of the fire. In the distance, wolves howled and an owl screeched. Night in the salt marshes was not for the faint of heart.

"He is a Bright One, your mate?" Merlin asked, referring to the powerful Atals, who were more than human and served as the guardians of magic.

Cryslov nodded. "He is. When it is safe, he will come and take us home."

"She's been living in Atland," Umvar said. "She's beginning to think she's highborn."

"We are all precious creations," Merlin said.

"Easy for you to say," Umvar continued. "Wizards and princes and all the Bright Ones who have no fear of death speak of equality—but they don't know poverty or hunger. They don't know what it's like to scratch and claw for your next meal, never knowing when some monster is going to come for you in the dark."

Merlin knew more than most about magical creatures, or 'monsters,' as Umvar had called them: his closest companion was a water spirit that lived in the Black Lake near Butan. And hadn't he just parted with good silver for a few smoked fish? Merlin had lived off field mice, weasels, and other small birds in his falcon form many times. He had sacrificed decades of his life to learn the magic that the Bright Ones of Atal were loath to share. But most common folk didn't want to hear of his own hardships, not when he could do things with magic that they could scarcely imagine.

Still, it was very unusual for any of the Bright Ones to bond with a mortal being. All the magic in the world couldn't make a human live forever, no matter what people like Umvar believed. Such a romance would eventually end in heartbreak. Their child would certainly be gifted, but unless the immortal genes of the father were dominant, it would be considered lowborn. The Atals wouldn't accept him, nor would most humans. He would be an outsider everywhere he went. Yet Merlin could feel a sense of destiny from within the baby, the way that gold felt heavy in the hand, or a well-made sword seemed to lend strength when you held it. He made his decision quickly. Agonizing was not his way; he could be impulsive, but he rarely gave his doubts any heed once his mind was made up.

Reaching out, he put his hand on Cryslov's stomach. She tensed, but he looked into her eyes, his own glowing golden against the gloom of the night.

"Never fear," he said quietly, letting magic flow from his body. It was like breathing out, simple yet profound. The bonding spell was a matter of will, not magical strength. "All is well."

Cryslov didn't pull away, and Umvar was oblivious that anything was taking place other than a man feeling the baby. It was not an unusual thing for people to do, although more women than men seemed to care about feeling a child still in its mother's womb. When Merlin finished his spell a moment later, he sat back and reached into his robe for the bag of coins he had hidden there.

He handed the pouch of gold and silver to Cryslov. "For the boy."

"It's a boy?" she asked, taking the coins.

"He is. And I will watch over him, as often as I can."

Umvar grunted but didn't say anything. He had been drinking the magically crafted wine since Merlin had handed it back to him and was starting to move past tipsiness to true drunkenness. Magical spirits were often more potent than natural beverages. Cryslov smiled and put her hand on her belly. It was obvious that she loved her baby and was lost in her own thoughts of motherhood. Neither of the two distracted common folk heard the serpent slither up the far side of the small hill, but Merlin sensed it well before it appeared. He rose slowly to his feet just as the snake loomed up behind the tree. It was a huge creature, big enough to swallow any of them whole—and probably two of them before its appetite was sated.

"Make no sudden movements," Merlin said.

"Eh?" Umvar asked.

There was no time to explain. Merlin reached one hand toward the fire and stretched the other toward the towering serpent already preparing to strike. Flames from the tiny campfire leaped toward the wizard, swirled around his body for a moment, and then shot out toward the snake.

CHAPTER TWO

Most animals fear fire, but there are times when hunger overcomes fear. The huge serpent dodged the fire, dropping low and striking at Merlin's feet. But despite his well-worn robes and graying beard, Merlin was not frail. He leaped back, avoiding the serpent's strike.

Umvar was quick to react too, despite being drunk. He lunged forward with his knife and drove it into the snake's side. The knife wasn't big—the blade was about as long a man's hand from palm to fingertips—and the snake's hide was tough, as were the thick muscles beneath. Umvar only managed to stab the knife halfway into the serpent before it swung around, jerking the weapon from his hand and slamming into him. The drunken man flew from the little hill they had been camping on and fell into a swampy pool of water.

Merlin took advantage of Umvar's foolish attack to

give a powerful, magical nudge that drove the knife to its hilt into the serpent's side. It reared again, hissing in pain, but Merlin wasn't done. The knife was their best chance for victory: while he had the ability to conjure something from nothing, it took time. It was much easier to manipulate what was already at hand, and in the salt marshes, there weren't many other options able to stop such a beast. Merlin latched onto the knife with his magical power and gave it a twist. The snake dove to the side, driving its head into the ground hard enough to shake the limbs of the tree that crowned the little knoll. The animal was reacting to the pain, expecting an enemy combatant to be at its side, but Merlin was eight or nine paces from it.

"Get behind me," he ordered Cryslov.

It took her an agonizingly long moment to rise to her feet. The baby in her womb was heavy, and her protruding stomach wrought havoc on her balance. She had to lean against the trunk of the tree to pull herself up to a standing position. Once she was on her feet, she moved only a little faster to waddle her way behind the wizard.

Merlin gave the knife another jerk, ripping it through the snake's flesh but being careful not to pull it out. He could lift and move objects in the air, but controlling the knife while it was lodged in the serpent's side was easier than holding it aloft. The huge creature flipped over onto its uninjured side and thrashed wildly.

"Watch out," Merlin warned, backing Cryslov down the hill toward the swampy water where Umvar was struggling through the mud to reach them. "It can still hurt us if we aren't careful."

"It would have killed us if not for you," Cryslov said, her hand on the wizard's shoulder.

"The salt marshes are not a safe place, especially at night," Merlin replied. "I thought the fire would keep threats at bay, but even wizards are wrong sometimes."

The snake continued to thrash as blood flowed from the wound in its side. Several times it hit the tree; as large and sturdy as it was, some of the tree branches broke and fell from the impact. Merlin had to levitate one of the heavy boughs away to keep it from dropping on top of the trio. He also continued to drive the knife through the snake's flesh, ripping it closer and closer to the beast's head. It convulsed, shaking hard as if it were freezing. Through the large gash left by the knife, the wizard took hold of the muscle just beneath the scaly skin with his magic and ripped out a large chunk.

This was the last straw for the serpent, which was wounded but far from dead. It dove off the hill, slithering quickly toward the water.

"It's getting away with my knife!" Umvar shouted.

"Let it go," Merlin said, putting a hand on the man's arm. "I've given you more than enough to get a new blade."

"I was partial to that one," Umvar whined.

"Then go and get it," Merlin said, as he walked back up the little hill toward the tree.

The stringy grass was crushed and smeared with the snake's blood, although everything in the salt marshes was already damp and tainted with salt. The waters flowed inland each day with the tide, spreading across the swamp. It was barely land at all, much like the fault land at the southern edge of Atlandia that was slowly being eroded by the tides. Finding a spot to spend the night that was only damp, as opposed to soaked, was sheer luck.

He picked up the chunk of snake muscle. It wasn't the best of meat, but it was edible. He broke some branches from the newly fallen tree limbs. Some were laid across the embers of their campfire, while others he quickly stripped of bark using a simple magical spell. Soon, happy, bright flames were burning, and the snake meat was sizzling over the flames.

"Are we really going to eat that?" Cryslov said, wrinkling her nose.

"It's food," Merlin said, taking a small pouch from his belt and sprinkling a mixture of herbs on the meat. "Not the best, but more filling than the fish. It will keep you warm and give you energy."

"As long as it isn't venomous," Umvar declared, looking at his water skin, which had spilled during the fight with the snake. He was clearly disappointed by the loss.

"You mean poisonous," Merlin corrected him. "And this meat is perfectly edible. What we don't eat this evening you can finish in the morning."

"Why should we believe you?" Umvar said.

"Umvar!" Cryslov chided.

"He's a wizard. How do we know he isn't enchanting us right now?" the man insisted. "Da always said, never trust a man who uses magic."

"You don't have to trust me," Merlin said. "I'm not asking you to."

"He's just shaken up," Cryslov said. "He's a good man."

"I never doubted it," Merlin declared, but in truth, he thought Umvar was shortsighted and foolish. Marching through the salt marshes was dangerous, and Umvar should have been on his guard. Instead, he had spent the evening drinking the wine that Merlin had conjured. Even if Merlin and his wine hadn't come along, the likelihood that Umvar could have protected his sister and her unborn child from the snake was very low. He would have died, and Cryslov, if she escaped the serpent, most likely would have perished in the swamps. Perhaps there was a reason they had camped under the same tree wherein Merlin had roosted. He looked at Cryslov's belly. It was possible there were divine forces at work, orchestrating protection for the child.

Merlin produced a small knife. It was a thin blade, barely as long as his pinkie finger, but sharp. He sliced off a sliver of the meat. It was hot, and he waved it around to cool before popping the morsel into his mouth. It was stringy and required chewing.

"Well?" Umvar asked.

"Passable," Merlin said after he swallowed. "A bit tough and gamey, but it's food."

Umvar had gotten over his objections. When Merlin cut off a larger portion, Umvar took it and ripped it apart with his teeth. The wizard watched the famished man eat. There wasn't much fat in the snake meat, but what little there was ran down into Umvar's beard and greased his fingers.

"Thank you," Cryslov said.

Merlin turned to face her. She was looking down at her stomach, her hands on either side, holding her baby already. Merlin could feel the love radiating from the young mother-to-be. The baby was a physical manifestation of her love for the father. People thought wizards were powerful, but nothing

Merlin could do was as grand as the creation of another human being; and in his experience, nothing was as strong as a mother's love. He felt the absence of his own mother's affection keenly. As a child of only eleven years, he had made the decision to devote himself to magic and was taken far away from the land of his birth. When he returned many years later, his mother and father were both dead. The child Cryslov carried would not have that gaping wound in his psyche.

"For what?" Merlin asked.

"Saving us," she said, without looking up.

"Just protecting my investment," Merlin said.

"Investment?" Cryslov asked. "You mean the coins?"

"No, the child," Merlin said. "The shadow of the Most High has fallen on him."

Merlin wasn't sure why he said it; prophecy wasn't his gifting. He could heal, but it was a laborious task. Likewise, alchemy was within his skillset, but not his strong suit. Merlin was what the Atals called an enchanter: he had great power over objects—including people, in the right situations. All magic flowed from the higher plane of the divine, and their creator was active in the lives of his creation, although his purposes were his own. Still, Merlin could tell that the baby Cryslov carried had the attention of the Most High—that much was obvious.

"He will be special?" Cryslov asked.

"Undoubtedly," Merlin confirmed.

He pulled out a tiny roll of vellum and used his finger to direct a tiny flow of magic onto the surface. Then he rolled it back up and sealed it with a small bead of wax.

"Take this," Merlin said. "Do not look at it. If the boy's

father does come to name him, throw it into the fire. But if he doesn't—"

"He will," Cryslov insisted.

Merlin nodded. "If he doesn't, you may open it on his eleventh birthday."

He handed the tiny bit of parchment to Cryslov. It was smaller than his finger from the middle joint to the tip and rolled tight. She took it and tucked it into the pouch with the coins he had given to her.

"Now I must continue my journey," Merlin said.

"You can't stay the night?" Cryslov asked, fear creeping into her voice.

"That isn't necessary," Merlin said. "The snake has marked this ground with its blood. Between the scent of the serpent and the campfire, you'll be safe here through the night."

"But don't you need rest?" Cryslov asked.

"Don't hold him," Umvar said, his mouth full of meat.

Cryslov looked upset, but Merlin put a hand on her shoulder. "You will see me again," he assured her. "Never fear."

Before she could continue the argument, he walked away from them, away from the light of the campfire. Once he was sure that he was lost in the darkness, he summoned the changing magic that brought on a wizard's animal form, his falcon counterpart. He had slept, and he had eaten. His strength was restored. It was time to fly.

CHAPTER THREE

"I don't understand," the young boy complained.

"It's what your mother wanted," the old woman snapped. "Now move your feet, Arthur, we haven't got all day."

Tears filled his eyes, which had happened too often of late—the tears came unbidden and without warning. They did nothing useful, his tears. They didn't douse the grief that raged inside him over his mother's death. They did not give him the strength he needed to exact some form of revenge on the wizard Merlin, who could have come to heal her but hadn't. They rolled down Arthur's young cheeks, marking him as a weakling to the people around him.

The old woman, Myrta, dragged him along by the arm. Arthur had no idea where he was going, only that he was leaving everything he knew behind. Lontown had been his home for his entire short life. His abode wasn't a castle, just a tiny cottage that he shared with his mother, but it was all he knew. Once his mother had died from a nagging sickness that had dragged on for months, men had laid claim to their small home. Myrta, the nosy neighbor and self-proclaimed healer of their section of the city, had taken him away.

They stopped beside a wagon that was loaded with supplies. Two men sat on the driver's bench, decked in priestly robes. Arthur looked up at them, unable to keep the fear from his face or the tears from his eyes.

"Here he is," Myrta announced.

She pulled a pouch from her belt. There were only a few coins left inside. Arthur recognized it as his mother's, although what had happened to the coins that had once filled it he could only guess. Myrta's own coin pouch looked fat enough, and even though he was just a child, Arthur knew that the spiteful old woman had stolen from him. She handed the pouch up to one of the priests.

"It's all they had," she said.

The priest nodded. "Climb onto the back, my son."

Arthur was about to protest and point out that he wasn't the priest's son, but before he could, Myrta jerked him toward the rear of the wagon. Another man sat there already, a great, hulking brute in a hooded gray cloak. He slid over, but there wasn't much room.

"Get on the wagon," Myrta told him. "You're going to live with the priests now. Don't make trouble, or you'll be handed over to the devil."

"Don't tell him that," the man said in a deep, rumbling voice.

Myrta pushed Arthur toward the man and sneered. "He's your problem now."

She didn't wait to see what Arthur did. He had no doubt

that she couldn't have cared less if he lived or died. Myrta's supposed healing of his mother's illness had done nothing to save her. At first, the stinking concoctions she brewed helped ease his mother's pain, but it didn't slow the sickness. By the end, nothing could stop the pain. It raged in her like a wildfire and cost her the final shreds of strength and sanity she had. The last time Arthur had spoken to his mother, she hadn't even known who he was.

The temptation to run was strong, but there was nowhere to go. Arthur was alone in the world. He had never known his father, and his uncle had died in a tavern brawl when he was six. The only other person of note in their lives was Merlin, but the mysterious, gray-bearded wizard was completely unreliable, and Arthur didn't want anything to do with him. That left him in a difficult position now. The priests were willing to take him in, and if nothing else, it would be a start. Not that he even considered following in their professional footsteps—Arthur had much bigger plans. He had already begun learning sword craft, the one thing the young orphan didn't resent Merlin for. The wizard had suggested it, though his mother hadn't liked the idea. But in time, Arthur knew he would grow strong enough to wield a real sword expertly. Perhaps he would be a war hero, or a dragon slayer. His imagination knew no bounds; at the same time, he knew he needed a place to eat and sleep to make these dreams happen. The monastery wasn't his first choice, but it was better than starving in the street.

Arthur turned his back to the wagon and heaved himself up beside the man in gray. "We are ready," the stranger called out.

The priests didn't reply, but they flicked the reins and

clucked their tongues to get the mules started. Against his will, the tears flooded Arthur's eyes again as he watched Lontown recede from the back of the wagon. He had no love for the village, yet he felt unmoored and vulnerable. With the back of his hand, he swiped the tears away. When he set his hand back down between the stranger and himself, he accidentally bumped the man in gray and felt the hard edge of a sheath under the man's cloak. Arthur looked up. He could see the man's chin sticking out of the hood; the rest of his face was hidden. The chin was covered with brown and gray whiskers that formed a point.

"Are you a warrior?" Arthur asked.

"No," the man grumbled. "Just a poor fool, waiting to die."

His words made Arthur feel weak and shaky. He knew death, and it was not a kind thing, nor was it anything he would joke about. There was, however, no levity in the man's voice.

"You're sick?"

"After a fashion," the man said. "Heart-sick, mostly."

He turned and looked down at Arthur, allowing the young boy to see the older man's face clearly for the first time. The stranger had a white scar that cut across the bridge of his nose and the cheek under his left eye.

"Heart-sick?" Arthur repeated, confused.

"Sadness," the man explained.

Arthur nodded. Sadness he'd experienced in spades; his own heart felt shattered.

"Me too," Arthur said.

"Not you—you're just a nip," the man said.

"My mother died," Arthur said without looking up, as the tears dripped from his eyes.

"What about your father?"

"I never knew him."

"Well," the man in gray said, with a note of sadness in his voice, "then I'd say you're right where you belong. I'm Jon."

"I'm Arthur," the boy replied, still keeping his eyes down. "You're not a priest?"

"No," Jon replied. "More like a lost soul the brothers had pity on."

Arthur nodded, and they rode for a long time in silence. The wagon jostled and creaked as they made their way north, into the hill country. The beauty of the grassy hills and rocky bluffs was lost on Arthur. He could only think of his dead mother and his fear about what his life would be like in a monastery. The only thing he knew about priests was that they spent hours and hours praying and reading their sacred scrolls. Arthur couldn't read, and he said his prayers sparingly. He couldn't imagine staying quiet and still for hours...it would be torture.

"What's it like?" he asked Jon.

"What is what like?"

"The monastery."

"Peaceful," Jon replied.

Arthur felt his hopes dwindling. Peaceful, he knew, was another word for boring.

As the afternoon waned, the priests stopped the wagon to make camp. "Boy, go and gather firewood," the taller of the two priests said.

Arthur was happy for an excuse to get out of the wagon. He was stiff from the ride, and it felt good to stretch his legs. There were trees scattered nearby, and a small stream meandered through the hills. It didn't take long to gather as much dead wood as he could carry. When he got back to the camp, the priests had driven two tall stakes into the ground and tied a canvas cover from the wagon to the stakes. One was starting a small fire, while the other was gathering food from their supplies in the bed of the wagon. Jon was seeing to the mules. When Arthur delivered his wood, the tall priest handed him a pot.

"Fill this with water," the priest commanded.

Arthur returned to the stream. He was about to bend down and scoop up some water when a crow called out from a nearby tree. Arthur looked at the bird for a moment before deciding that it wasn't Merlin—the wizard turned into a falcon, not a crow. Still, Arthur picked up a rock and hurled it at the bird, which flew away with an angry screech. He filled the water pot and carried it back to the camp, only to be sent back again for more firewood.

When he returned with his second load of wood, the priests were tending to their supper. Bacon sizzled in a pan that was sitting on rocks at the edge of the campfire. The pot of water was heating over the flames.

"What's your name, lad?" the shorter priest asked.

"Arthur."

"Your full name, boy," the tall priest demanded.

"That *is* my full name," Arthur said.

"A bastard, then," the tall priest said. "Why am I not surprised?"

"My father will come one day," Arthur said, repeating the phrase he'd heard his mother say many times in his short life.

"How old are you?" the shorter man asked.

"Ten years, nearly eleven," Arthur said.

"If your father hasn't come to name you by now," the taller priest said with a slight sneer, "he won't ever come."

"That's not true," Arthur argued in a loud but quavering voice.

"Stop tormenting the boy," Jon said quietly. "He's been through enough."

"We didn't ask your opinion," the taller priest snapped. "The boy is our ward. We shall do what we like with him."

"See to that bacon, Brother Bryun," the shorter man said. "Let's not have our dinner burned. Jon, would you care to open the keg of ale? We could all do with a sup."

"Aye," the tall priest named Bryun agreed. "My throat is clogged with dust from the road."

Arthur didn't think the road was dusty, but he didn't point that out. The tall priest didn't like him, and that was perfectly fine with him—Arthur didn't like him either, so they were even. Rice and beans went into the pot of boiling water, and cornmeal was mixed with an egg and a bit of sugar before being fried in the bacon grease. The priests each drank several mugs of ale while they saw to the dinner they were preparing. Arthur wandered around the camp, spending most of his time with the mules. He liked animals, and the mules looked wise, when they bothered to look up at him. They spent most of their time chewing the lush grass at their hooves, but they seemed content to listen when Arthur spoke.

When the sun set, Arthur returned to the camp, drawn to the light of the fire. He didn't mind sleeping outdoors— he had done that often enough—but the darkness still made him uneasy. Jon had laid a blanket out for him. Arthur lay upon it and looked up at the stars, ignoring the priests, who were eating their fill first. Bryun, who was as skinny as he was tall, didn't eat much, but he drank as if he were dying of thirst. The shorter priest, Percy, had a round belly and ate twice as much as Bryun. They were both on the verge of drunkenness when Jon ladled out a bowl of the rice and beans for Arthur. The priests had eaten all the bacon and corn bread, but the bacon grease was littered with the corn-meal. A spoonful mixed in with the rice and beans gave the meal some flavor.

Arthur had just finished his supper when Bryun pulled out the little pouch Myrta had given him, upending it into his palm. Several silver coins fell out. Arthur had no real understanding of money, but he knew that the silver was worth more than the bronze coins. He also realized that all the golden coins his mother had were gone. There was also a roll of parchment, little more than a scrap, mixed among the coins.

"Your life isn't worth much," Bryun said with a chuckle as he looked at the coins.

Arthur ignored him. Bryun picked through the silver and held up the roll of vellum to examine it by the light of the fire.

"What's that?" Percy asked.

"I dunno," Bryun said. "Looks like a bit of leather."

"It's vellum," Arthur said, although he didn't really know what vellum was; he'd only heard his mother speak of it. She'd held it up with reverence and talked of his future. Arthur hadn't known what the tiny paper was, only that his mother had considered it precious. "I'm supposed to open it when I turn eleven."

"Well, why wait?" Bryun said. "I doubt it's anything of use to us."

"No, I'm supposed to wait," Arthur said.

"Well then, it won't hurt if I open it and take a look," Bryun said. "I'm well past eleven years now."

He chuckled and hiccupped. Arthur sat up, feeling helpless and angry. Bryun was already fumbling with the roll of parchment, but the ale had made his fingers clumsy.

"You shouldn't do that," Jon said softly. "It's not yours to open."

"Shut your bleeding mouth," Bryun screeched belligerently at the older man. "You're nothing, just a damned nuisance trying save yourself from the eternal fires. I won't be talked down to by the likes of you."

"Then maybe you'll listen to me," a familiar voice said.

Jon leaped to his feet faster than Arthur thought possible. Beside Bryun, his back propped against a sack of grain, Percy sat up, his eyes bugging out in fear. The taller priest threw up his hands and called out for divine protection, but no lightning came from the sky as Merlin the wizard strolled into the camp.

"Be at ease," Merlin told Jon, ignoring the priests. "I've come to see the boy."

CHAPTER FOUR

"No!" Arthur shouted.

"Arthur, what's wrong?" Merlin asked.

Tears flooded his eyes again. Arthur hated crying, but he couldn't stop it. The tears came again, as did the pain of his mother's loss. It hit like a physical blow so strong he thought he might simply crumple to the ground, crushed by his grief.

"Where were you?" Arthur yelled. "Why didn't you come?"

"I couldn't," Merlin said. "I'm sorry."

"You're sorry? My mother's dead because of you! It's all your fault!"

"What's he talking about?" Jon asked, his hand on the hilt of his sword. Arthur couldn't see the weapon, only the outline beneath Jon's gray cloak.

"I am Errol ap'Tunnar Foyl, called Merlin by those who

know me. I knew his mother, Cryslov. She was a good friend."

"You're here for the boy?" Bryun said. "Take him and be on your way."

"I am here to see Arthur," Merlin said as he approached the fire. "But he will remain in your care."

"Isn't that grand?" Bryun said.

"You're drunk," Merlin said, his eyes flashing. "You should sleep it off."

Bryun sighed, then slumped over on his side. Merlin turned his golden eyes on Percy. In the flickering light from the fire, he looked like his namesake: his nose was hooked slightly, like a falcon's beak, and those golden eyes brimmed with magic.

"Take care of that parchment," Merlin said, as the small vellum roll floated up into the air in front of the short priest. "It's not to be opened until Arthur turns eleven."

"Ye-yes," Percy stammered. "Eleven years old."

"His birthday is one month from today," Merlin declared.

"One month," the priest repeated.

"Arthur, I don't have much time," Merlin said, turning away from the campfire. "Walk with me."

Arthur didn't want to. If anything, he wanted to snatch Jon's sword and run it through the wizard's guts. But with Jon on the far side of the campfire, it was impossible. Both he and Arthur were on the edges of the canopy made by the canvas awning. Percy and Bryun had taken the best spots between the wagon and the fire.

Not that it would do any good, either, Arthur knew. He had seen fools try to fight Merlin. They underestimated his abilities and always paid a heavy toll for their mistakes. Arthur got to his feet and started walking into the darkness, moving faster than the wizard.

"You're angry, and I understand that," Merlin said. "Believe me: I wanted to come."

"Then why didn't you?" Arthur asked.

"Because, just like you, I am a human. I do not even have the highborn blood that runs through your veins."

"What?" Arthur was distracted by that statement, completely confused by the wizard.

"I have masters," Merlin said. "Obligations. I didn't know your mother was ill. When I found out, I came as fast as I could. But the Most High has reasons for everything."

"What reason could there be for her to die?" Arthur could contain himself no longer and burst into tears. Merlin was the only person left that he had known his entire life. Against his will, he threw himself against the wizard, who wrapped his arms around the young boy.

"I know," Merlin said softly. "I'm sorry."

"I'm...I'm all...alone."

"That isn't true," Merlin said. "We are bonded, you and I."

"What?"

"We are connected," Merlin said. "Never forget that. We are like the metal in a smith's forge, heated to the melting point and blended together to make a stronger material. It is right for you to grieve your mother, but do not fret about your future, Arthur. Your life's journey has barely begun, and I will be with you to guide you along."

"Do you promise?" Arthur begged.

"Yes," Merlin said. "But for now, you must go with the priests."

"They're mean," Arthur said.

"Of course they are," Merlin said. "They have taken on many burdens and vows to the Most High, and that can wear on even the strongest of men. But they will see that you are fed, clothed, and, most importantly, educated."

"Educated?" Arthur repeated, trying out the unfamiliar word.

"They will teach you to read," Merlin said. "This will serve you well. You will learn other skills besides reading, too. Perhaps Jon Longarm will continue your lessons with the sword. You could do worse than a teacher like him."

Arthur sniffed and looked back at the camp. Jon was still standing and staring in their direction, a worried expression creasing his face.

"Don't hold their harsh ways against them, Arthur," Merlin said. "The priests prize discipline dearly. It is the cornerstone of their order, a harsh, unbendable lifestyle. It will not be pleasant, but it will strengthen you."

"When will you come back?" Arthur said.

Even if Merlin hadn't said that his time there was short, Arthur would have known that the wizard was about to leave again. It was the way of a wizard to appear and disappear suddenly. Arthur didn't like it, but he was used to it. In fact, he could usually tell when Merlin would arrive and depart without being told.

They turned back toward the camp. "To celebrate your birthday," Merlin answered. "Don't open the vellum until I arrive."

Arthur nodded. They moved up the hill; despite wanting

to hate the wizard, Arthur felt better having Merlin by his side. It didn't hurt to know that Merlin would return for his birthday, either. In the midst of the darkest season of his life, there was something to look forward to.

"Jon," Merlin said as they entered the ring of light from the campfire, "would you do me the great favor of teaching Arthur sword craft? He's an apt pupil, and I would be in your debt."

"I can do that, with the abbot's approval, of course," the man in gray said.

"I have no doubt he will approve," Merlin said. "Make him strong. He will need it."

Jon nodded. Bryun was still passed out and snoring slightly, while Percy watched the wizard with wide, frightened eyes. Merlin got down on one knee and looked up at Arthur. The boy was only ten years of age, yet he was already tall and growing stronger by the day.

"Look for me in one month, Arthur," Merlin said. "I will not let you down."

Arthur nodded, meeting Merlin's eyes and seeing them flash the golden color that made him both mysterious and a little frightening. Then Merlin stood up and reached out a hand to Jon, who slowly took it. Arthur saw the respect that passed between the two men. His work done, Merlin walked away from the camp. It was too dark to see him, but Arthur heard the familiar flutter of wings and knew that Merlin the wizard was gone.

"We should get some rest," Jon suggested after a brief pause.

Arthur lay back down on his blanket and looked up at the stars, which swam in his vision as his eyes filled with tears again. He told himself that everything would be fine and that he wasn't alone. Still, the hot tears ran down the sides of his face as he took hold of one side of the blanket and pulled it over his body. Nearby, the fire crackled, and the priest snored. Arthur didn't have to look to know that Jon Longarm was watching over the camp. He couldn't ignore the gaping wound in his soul that resulted from his mother's death, but indeed he wasn't alone, and for the time being, that was good enough.

CHAPTER FIVE

I t took four days to reach the Byth El monastery. The
journey could have taken less time, but the priests
weren't exactly in a hurry. Bryun woke up sick on the
first morning after Merlin had appeared and complained for
the next two days. It seemed that he and Percy were loath
to return to their duties and dawdled accordingly. Along the
way, Jon found a suitable piece of wood and spent most time
when he wasn't doing chores carving it into a practice sword
for Arthur.

The monastery was built at the terminus of an inlet that
was part of the North Sea, the body of water separating
Atlandia from the mainland. It marked the boundary
between Byrtan and Bernia. Arthur couldn't help but marvel
at the towering line of fir trees that grew along the
boundary of the two eastern kingdoms. To the south were
the green rolling hills they had just traveled through, and to

the north, the sea. Arthur could smell the salt air long before he saw the shimmering blue waters.

"Your new home," Jon said as the monastery came into view.

They were walking beside the wagon, easily keeping pace with the mules. The priests rarely spoke to them, but Arthur didn't care, freshly grieving as he was. He hadn't healed from the loss of his mother and didn't think he ever would, but there were moments when he forgot about his sorrow. Seeing the monastery was one of them. It was made of stone and timber, with a short rock wall around the temple, work buildings, and dormitories. It wasn't just the size or number of buildings that impressed Arthur. He had seen buildings even bigger than the temple before, but nothing as ornate— all of the woodwork in the monastery was carved with designs and flourishes. The stonework was sturdy and straight. There were no shanties or huts, and everything was immaculately maintained, with the paths swept clean and lined with flagstones. Ringing the monastery were hedges, all neatly trimmed, and flowers were blooming everywhere. To top it all off, the temple had a brightly polished brass bell that reflected the late afternoon light.

"It's incredible," Arthur said.

"Don't expect a warm welcome," Bryun warned from his perch at the front of the wagon. "Orphans are a burden, not a blessing."

"Don't listen to him," Jon whispered.

They were met just inside the wide gate of the monastery by monks and priests in flowing robes. Most had closely cropped hair and wide smiles. Unlike Bryun and

Percy, they seemed happy to help unload the wagon, which was full of supplies. Jon was also quick to help, always picking the heaviest items from the wagon. Arthur did his best, but there were many eager hands for the task, and he didn't know where anything went.

"Brothers, you have returned at last," a tall man in bright white robes said as he approached the wagon. "I was beginning to think that bandits had robbed you and left you for dead."

"We were burdened with more than we expected," Bryun said, jerking a thumb at Arthur.

"And who is this?" the tall man asked.

Arthur felt a tremble of fear. Even swathed in robes, it was clear that underneath them the man in white was powerfully built. Normally, Arthur did his best to avoid such men. In Lontown, children, seen as endlessly greedy mouths to feed, were not welcomed by most adults. While Arthur felt that he was leaving his childhood behind—he was almost eleven years old, after all—he still knew better than to draw the attention of men who might just as soon backhand him as look at him.

"This is Arthur," Percy said. "His mother died and sent him to us."

Arthur felt the sting in his eyes that heralded the tears. Just the mention of his mother was enough to make them appear. He desperately fought them back; he didn't want to cry in front of the tall, impressive stranger.

"She sent this with him," Bryun said, holding out the coin pouch. "It isn't much."

"Every gift is precious," the tall man said, taking the bag.

"Merlin, the wizard, has a bond with the boy," Percy said. "He came to us the first night of our journey back."

"Merlin appeared?" the tall man said, speaking directly to Arthur. "You know him?"

"Yes, he knew my mother," Arthur managed to say in a trembling voice.

"That is impressive indeed," the tall man said with a beaming smile. "Most wizards don't care for children."

"He said he will be here when the brat turns eleven," Bryun said.

"Don't call him that," the tall man reproved the priest. "Words are powerful, Brother Bryun. We mustn't throw them about carelessly. Every soul is precious to the Most High."

"It is so," the clergy chanted in unison, even though Arthur didn't think they had actually heard the conversation.

"My name is Abbot Gryald ap'Conor," the tall man said. "Welcome to Byth El."

Arthur nodded, trying not to let the tears welling in his eyes run down his cheeks.

"Any friend of Merlin is welcome here," the abbot said. "We shall find a place for you. But the spiritual life is not one of ease—oh, no. Discipline and study are the hallmarks of our order."

"The wizard asked me to teach him the sword," Jon said quietly.

Arthur hadn't even noticed that the wagon was unloaded and that the older man had joined him. The monks had finished the chore in no time and were gathered around, now listening intently to the exchange.

"Then I will leave that to you," Abbot Gryald said to Jon. "Physical training is good. You shall work with the boy for two hours before we break fast and for an hour after evening prayers. That should help him sleep well. Brother Yancy shall see to the training of his mind, every day but the holy days, from the end of morning prayers until we break bread at midday."

"It would be my pleasure," a young monk with bushy eyebrows and crooked teeth said.

"And Brother Orval can see to his spiritual training for two hours after lunch," the abbot continued. "In the afternoon, he can work in the stables with Brother Haymore. There, that's settled, Arthur. Why don't you help Brother Haymore with the mules now, then wash up before supper? Friend Jon will see that you have a bunk in the common house."

"Yes, sir," Arthur said without much enthusiasm.

"Don't be sad," Abbot Gryald said kindly. "I can see that you are grieving for your dearly departed mother. What you feel in your heart, my young friend, is love. Have no fear; the Most High is looking after her. Trust me when I say you will see her again."

Arthur had to swipe at a few tears that escaped his eyes. Everything was changing. He was in what seemed like a wonderful new place, but he didn't know if he could please the abbot. If he failed, what then? If he couldn't learn fast enough to satisfy his new instructors, would he be expelled from the monastery? His mother had prayed to the Most High, but the creator seemed like an abstract concept to Arthur—not to mention that he'd heard stories of other gods, some that threw bolts of lighting and others that rode rainbows. Beyond the borders of Atlandia, he'd heard, people worshiped entire pantheons of supernatural beings. Arthur didn't know much about it, and he feared that he might never learn. No one had ever tried to teach him before.

"Very good, brothers. Let us return to our duties," the abbot said.

The group slowly broke apart. A hunched man with a pockmarked face and one lazy eye waved to Arthur. He was holding the bridle of one of the mules, and it didn't take much to guess who he was. Brother Haymore would be his master when he worked in the stables.

"Come on," Haymore said. "We'll take these beauties to the barn and get them rubbed down. They've had a long, difficult week, I'd say."

Arthur thought it was strange that the monk spoke so affectionately to the beasts of burden, but then, he had often seen people being cruel to animals, and he also didn't like that at all. Perhaps they did deserve the solicitude—after all, the mules had pulled the wagon and its heavy load all the way from Lontown. Arthur fell in beside the hunchback.

"I'm Brother Haymore," the monk introduced himself.

"I'm Arthur."

"It's nice to make your acquaintance. Do you like animals?"

"Well enough," Arthur said.

"Oh, that's good. We have the great privilege of caring for these. It is commanded by the Most High."

Arthur nodded, not sure what to say. He had never owned a horse or a mule, nor even a milk cow or a goat. Just the same, he liked animals and often felt more comfortable around them than people, especially grown-ups. They crossed the open courtyard, which was a beautifully maintained space covered with thick, well-trimmed grass. Arthur didn't see a single weed in the large square. At the far side, directly across from the gate, was the temple. It was made at the gables with several of the biggest logs that Arthur had ever seen. The two-storied barn was no meager structure, either. The bottom contained a fleet of stalls for the animals; above was a hay loft. The floor was hard-packed earth, but there were no piles of manure littering the barn. The building smelled of animals, fresh hay, and leather, all merging together into one unique but welcome smell.

"We have horses and mules, four milk cows, one lucky bull, and several flocks of sheep that are kept on the hills until it's time to shear them or harvest one. We even have a herd of goats." Haymore was clearly proud of their livestock.

It was more wealth than Arthur could imagine. In Lontown, a single animal was a luxury. The monks had more than Arthur had ever considered one person, or one group, could have. In fact, this monastery held more animals than the entire village of Lontown combined.

"You keep them all?" Arthur asked.

"Not by myself," Haymore said. "But I have a connection with livestock. It's my gift."

"Your gift?"

"We all have gifts from the Most High. Some people call them talents, but we like to think of them as gifts. They point us to our purpose."

Arthur didn't know what to say—these ideas were all so

new to him. They unhitched the mules, and Haymore taught Arthur how to rub the animals down with soft brushes. They gave the mules oats and cool water before pushing the wagon into a shed at the side of the barn. Haymore seemed happy to teach Arthur about caring for the animals, and while the boy still felt friendless in the world, it felt good to groom and watch after the mules. He could focus his mind on the mule he was brushing and banish the sad memories of his mother. It took a force of will to remember her before the illness struck her low, back to a time when she was all smiles and laughter. His mother had always been tinged with sadness for his father and sometimes spent hours staring out the tiny window of their cottage, as if he might suddenly appear. When she wasn't lost in her own memories, though, she made life fun for him. The illness had not only wrecked Arthur's world, but it had also forever tainted his memory of his mother. When he thought of her, it was usually the withered, frail shadow of her former self that filled his mind. Thinking of her that way only made him sadder.

After seeing to the animals, Haymore heated a tub of water. Baths were never something Arthur enjoyed, but he didn't have much of a choice, and the process was as pain-less as possible. The warm water was put into a container and hoisted over his head. It was a quick, efficient way to get clean. His old, tattered clothes were taken away, and he was given a set of robes much like those the monks wore, a simple rope cinching the billowing garment around his narrow waist.

Once they were clean, they went into a building with two long tables. The monks and priests sat on the benches at one table; the other was reserved for those outside the order. Jon Longarm wasn't the only "friend," as he was called. There were several others, mostly elderly men but also a few older boys. A monk served the meal in large containers, from which the diners took to fill their plates. A platter with roast mutton surrounded by potatoes, carrots, onions, and garlic was set on the table. The entire platter was drizzled with a thick, brown gravy and sprinkled with herbs. Jon Longarm sipped at goblets of dark wine, while Arthur drank water. Now wearing a green jerkin over a brown wool shirt, the older man looked strange without his familiar gray cloak. His pants were brown as well, and his sword was missing.

"So," he started, after scooping food onto their plates, "what do you think?"

Arthur stared down at the hunk of meat on his plate. It looked rich and delicious, but for some reason, he wasn't hungry. His eyes burned, and he couldn't find the words to respond. He didn't want to think that the swordsman was the reason he was unhappy, but he felt that if he tried to speak, he would burst into sobs. As wonderful as the monastery appeared to be, all Arthur could think of was the fact that it wasn't home.

"Don't worry, you'll get used it," Jon murmured kindly. "I did. We all do, in time."

Arthur struggled to control his emotions. The other people at the table were talking and eating, seemingly without a care in the world. Arthur envied them.

"Keep in mind, this isn't permanent," Jon said, halfway through his meal. "You aren't here to become a monk."

"I don't know what I'll become," Arthur said.

40

"You don't have to know now," Jon said. "When the time is right, you'll know."

Arthur looked at the big man. He had a square jaw and rugged features, but there was an unmistakable depth of painful emotion in his eyes. In some ways, looking into Jon's eyes was like looking into a mirror.

"Eat up, lad," Jon encouraged him. "Tonight we begin your training in earnest. You'll need your strength."

Arthur thought about that. The one thing he wanted in all the world was to be strong. He didn't want anything to ever be taken from him again. Jon would teach him the way of the sword, and Arthur was determined to be a good student. He picked up his knife and fork and began to eat.

CHAPTER SIX

"No!" Jon said in a commanding voice that was completely different from the character Arthur had come to know on the road. The Jon Longarm Arthur knew had proven to be a kind, gentle man, always looking out for Arthur's interests. During the sword instruction, however, he had become forceful and authoritarian. It seemed that Arthur could do nothing right. He felt frustrated, but there was no time to feel sorry for himself. Jon's keen eyes were on him, and he had to move.

"That's it," Jon said as Arthur reset his stance. "Sword fighting isn't like you think. You don't stand there swinging swords at one another. If that were the case, the strongest fighter would always win, and swords would break all the time. Metal is strong, but it's not unstoppable, and it can break when you least expect it. Never take the full force of an opponent's strike on your blade if you can avoid it."

He was talking and moving, using a broom handle to

swing at Arthur, who was holding the wooden sword Jon
had carved for him. It was heavy, making his forearms ache,
and whenever he tried to block with it, the vibrations
through the wood burned like fire in his hands. Sweat was
running down his face as he gasped for breath. Jon looked at
ease and moved with the grace of a cat, while Arthur stumbled about like a drunkard.

A small group of spectators was watching. He heard
them chuckle when he made especially awkward blunders.
It was embarrassing, yet he didn't want to quit. Jon swung
the broomstick at Arthur's head, and the young boy
managed to duck. He was too tired to even think of striking
a counterblow—he just wanted to survive his first lesson. It
was nothing like what the swordsman in Lontown had
taught. There, Arthur had learned how to stand, how to
hold a sword, and how to execute a simple series of strikes.
Faced with a sparring partner like Jon, he was starting to
think such instruction was worthless. Arthur knew how to
swing a sword, but he didn't know how to connect with the
practiced older man, who always managed to step out of the
path of the wooden weapon, and whose counterstrikes were
painful.

"You're slow," Jon said, forcing Arthur back. "And
clumsy."

He made the pronouncement just before Arthur stumbled backward and fell hard.

"Don't get up," Jon said. "Breathe deep, in through your
nose, and out in a solid huff from your gut. Get the bad air
out—you'll feel better soon."

Arthur was so exhausted that his muscles quivered. The
closest he had ever come to being so tired was playing chase

with the other children in Lontown, but it was not the same. He breathed as instructed and listened as Jon paced.

"Sword fighting is a nasty business, Arthur. Never think otherwise. And if you draw your weapon against another man, you must understand that it is a life-and-death struggle. One wrong move, and you could die. Do you hear me? This is important."

"I hear...you," Arthur wheezed.

"Good," Jon shot back. "This isn't a game. Fighting isn't fun. You may come to enjoy the training, but never the fighting. People die, Arthur. You and I, we understand that better than most. We've felt the sting of it. We know the shadow of death that hangs over us, and we must never rush to take life. Are you sure you understand?"

"Yes," Arthur said. And it was true—he did understand. He hadn't before that moment, perhaps, but it was clear to him now as he lay exhausted on the ground outside the kitchens of the monastery. Sword craft wasn't a game, and it wasn't all parries and thrusts and glory. Yet there was something about it that stirred a force deep inside of Arthur. He wanted to be good, like Jon—to move with grace and efficiency in every step.

"Get up, then," Jon said, reaching out a hand. "We have a lot to learn, and you may not enjoy it at first. We have to build you up to make you strong, but more importantly, fast. Speed is the key in any fight. Once you've gotten strong and fast, we'll learn the dance of death with a sword. You can know all the steps, Arthur, and still die within seconds of your first fight. The sword cuts both ways."

"I will remember," Arthur said earnestly.

"Good," Jon said. "Let me show you where you'll be sleeping."

The monks had their own dormitory. Those who had taken vows were given tiny cells in which to sleep and keep their personal belongs. Those in training and the friends of the monastery, like Jon, slept in an open room lined with narrow beds. The dorm was a low-roofed building, with a fireplace and a few wooden chairs. Arthur was given a thick wool blanket and a pillow stuffed with goose feathers. He had thought his bed would be near Jon's, but he was shown to a bunk at the far end of the room, near the privy in the back of the building. He could smell the odor but was too tired to care, instead dropping straight onto his bunk, lying down, and immediately falling asleep.

The next thing he knew, Jon was shaking him awake. The bell began to ring, and a rooster crowed in the distance. The dorm was still very dark, but everyone was getting up.

"Time to train," Jon said gruffly. "Come with me."

Arthur obeyed, still half asleep. He was accustomed to being told what to do by adults and wordlessly followed Jon outside. It was still dark, but the sky was shifting to a light shade of gray. Arthur had to hurry to keep up with Jon Longarm, who had an even longer stride.

As his mind began to clear from sleep, he felt an intense pang of wanting to see his mother. It was immediately followed by the gut-wrenching realization that she wasn't there and would never be there for him again. The tears didn't just fill his eyes—the drops sprang from them, and he couldn't hold back a sob.

"Mornings are hard," Jon said. "We'll attack them together."

He handed Arthur the wooden sword. The boy took it, but in that moment, he didn't want to train, nor did he want to learn to fight. All he wanted was his mother.

"Keep that with you whenever we train," Jon said. "Carrying it will make you strong."

"I don't feel strong," Arthur said.

"You will," Jon replied. "But first you're going to feel tired and weak. It's the way of the world. You can have whatever you want, Arthur, but you have to work to get it, and sometimes you have to work even harder to hold on to it."

He also handed Arthur a bucket and led him to a well, nothing more than a deep pit lined with stones. An older man, one of the friends of the monastery, was lowering a bucket into the well and drawing up water. He poured it into a wooden trough, which was already half full of water. Jon dipped two buckets into the water trough, filling them, and started for the kitchens.

"Come on, Arthur, fill your bucket," Jon ordered. "The monks need water."

Arthur dropped his bucket into the trough and filled it. He struggled to follow Jon while holding both the heavy bucket and the wooden sword. Jon moved with strength and confidence and didn't spill a single drop. By the time they reached the kitchens, Arthur on the other hand was wet, his bucket was half empty from sloshing the water with each clumsy step, and he was already breathing hard.

They made three trips to the kitchens, then moved to the wood pile. Arthur soon forgot about his grief as he carried rough chunks of firewood into the kitchen. His arms burned from the effort, and his legs and feet ached. It wasn't the type of sword training he'd been expecting. When they finished with the firewood, they moved outside the short wall of the monastery.

"Every day," Jon said, "you will run around the wall."

"Why?" Arthur asked. "I don't intend to run from a fight."

"No one ever expects to run from a fight," Jon said with a grin. "But I've seen plenty of men do it. That's not why you're running, Arthur. We have to strengthen your body and build your stamina. Start moving. If you get tired, you can walk—but if I catch up to you, there will be a price to pay."

Arthur was about to ask about the price when Jon pulled a short whip from the folds of his gray robe. It unfurled, and Arthur understood. He didn't bother asking the question; instead, he turned and ran. Running had never been a chore for Arthur since, like most young boys, he loved to play and chase. This morning, he was tired before he started, and his run soon became a slow jog. By the time he reached the seaward side of the monastery, he had to stop and catch his breath. In the distance, there was a ship at sea that was neither coming or going. Arthur thought it was strange, but soon Jon came into sight, and Arthur decided he could ask questions later.

He barely made it around the monastery before Jon caught up to him. Arthur was trudging at the end, his bare feet barely rising off the ground and the tip of the wooden sword dragging through the dirt behind him. He leaned against the gate, fearful that his trembling stomach might revolt on him.

"Now you know," Jon said, coming up behind him, the whip nowhere in sight.

"I know...what?" Arthur asked.

"Now you know what it's like to fight in a battle," the big man said. "Raise your sword. Face me."

Arthur tried to obey. He held the wooden sword with both hands, but he could barely lift it. He knew fighting would be impossible, but he didn't think he could run away, either. He felt stuck—trapped, desperate, and depressed.

"Every day, we will work this hard," Jon said, his voice softer than before. "But it won't always *be* this hard. Day by day, you will get stronger." The big man took the wooden sword.

And, just as he'd promised on that first morning, he woke Arthur every day for training. They carried water, chopped and carried wood, and ran. In the evenings, they sparred with swords. It was difficult, grueling work, and the boy fell asleep exhausted and bruised, his mind swimming with the lessons he had been taught each day. More than once, he drifted off during the morning or evening prayers. Taxed in his training as he was, Arthur felt that perhaps the best feature of the monastery was the food. It was more food, served with more frequency, than Arthur had ever enjoyed before. He ate everything and never seemed to get full.

The days blurred together. Before he knew it, a month had passed, and it was his birthday.

CHAPTER SEVEN

Merlin flew over the monastery and landed on the temple's bell tower to watch the yards with his keen eyes, which could spot a field mouse creeping through the grass from the top of one of the mighty fir trees. It was late in the afternoon, and while the activities of the monastery didn't interest him, he was very interested in how Arthur was getting along in his new home. The difference in the young boy was unmistakable. He was only eleven years old, and yet he had grown in the last month since Merlin had seen the boy in the hills outside of Lontown. His shoulders seemed larger, and the robes worn by the friends of the monastery showed the new bulk of his muscles. Merlin was amazed and had to remind himself that the boy had the blood of the Bright Ones running through his veins. He wasn't exactly human, nor was he completely Atal, either. But he was growing faster than expected, and he carried himself differently, too. The shadow of heartbreak was gone; the death of his mother hadn't left him completely unfazed, but he was recovering.

As Merlin watched, the young boy hurried from the scriptorium toward the large barn. Merlin hopped from the bell tower, extending his wings and gliding toward the barn. He landed at the window of the hay loft. The interior was stuffed with dry straw, and his falcon senses picked up the scent of mice sneaking through the piles of hay. Falcon instincts were strong, but as tempting as they were in his present state, his human mind remained, and he abstained from the raw flesh.

Below him and just outside the barn, Arthur met with one of the monks, a hunchbacked, kindly old man who clearly held a surprise behind him for the boy.

"It's your birthday," the monk said. "I bet you thought I'd forgotten."

"Actually," Arthur said, "*I* forgot."

"I remember when I first arrived," the monk said. "It took a while to adjust. Here, I got you something."

He held out an old set of farrier's tools that had been polished up and rolled inside a leather kit.

"What is it?" Arthur asked.

"Tools," the monk said. "You've done everything I've asked of you, and it hasn't gone unnoticed. Perhaps it's time you learned to care for the horses. These tools are for cleaning and caring for their hooves."

"And they're mine?" Arthur looked at the monk with surprise.

"That's right. Just a little birthday presen—"

He didn't get to finish before Arthur threw his arms around the man. The sudden show of affection caught the monk by surprise. Merlin heard the emotion in his voice when he continued.

"Take care of them, and those tools will last you a lifetime."

Arthur released him, and the monk staggered back a little, swiping furtively at his eyes.

"Thank you," Arthur said. "I will take care of them. You'll see."

"Aye, that I will. Now, let's get busy."

They went into the barn, and Merlin felt sense of relief. Leaving the boy with the monks had been his idea long before Arthur had lost his mother. Merlin could not think of Cryslov without a pang of guilt. Perhaps healing the woman would have been possible, as there were many things that Merlin could resolve in the human body. Over the years, however, Cryslov had begun to lose sight of reality in a much deeper and more dangerous way. Arthur's father wasn't coming, despite her protestations. The Atals were too deeply entangled with the Farkians. In the west, the land was ravaged by dark magic, and eventually, it would spill over into the east. The humans living in Byrtan and Bernia would be caught up in the conflict, and Cryslov hadn't been ensuring that Arthur would be prepared. When Merlin had sensed that something was wrong with the boy's mother, even before she herself knew that she wasn't well, he had planted the idea in her mind. Then he had stayed away, waiting for the inevitable. It was a decision that haunted him, but he could sense what was coming and what sacrifices had to be made. Merlin couldn't see what role the boy might play, but he could feel the hand of the Most High resting on him. Arthur was

TOBY NEIGHBORS

special, and it was time he understood just how special
he was.

Another leap and a flap of his wings took Merlin from
the barn and down into a shadow between the buildings.
There, he morphed back to his human form and adjusted
his robes. He ran his fingers though his hair and smoothed
down his beard as best he could. It seemed he was growing
wilder in appearance every day, likely because he was
spending too much time as a falcon, but it couldn't be
helped. There was no other way to traverse the wide realm
at speed, and Merlin was one of the few people who had a
grasp on what was truly taking place in Atlandia.

He left the shadows and went straight to the kitchens.
There were several monks at work tending a large pot of
stew. The smells of freshly baked bread, savory broth, and
roasting hare filled him with an intense hunger. One of the
monks was brushing butter over a row of butchered hares
that were turning on a spit over the fire. Abbot Gyrald was
mixing up the ingredients for honey cakes at a nearby
table.

"Praise the Most High," the abbot declared, as Merlin
stood taking in the smells of cooking food. "You made it."

"I told the boy I would," Merlin replied.

"Brother Farrel, get our friend a mug of ale," Abbot
Gyrald said. "What news do you bring, Merlin?"

"More of the same," Merlin replied, moving to a stool
near a side table. "Darkness gathers in the west."

"The darkness can never extinguish the light," Abbot
Gryald said.

"And yet there are fewer and fewer Bright Ones to carry
that light and hold it back," Merlin said. "More and more

52

frequently are there raids into Avon. The Farkians are growing bolder."

"It is so," the abbot said, completely unconcerned. "The more powerful they become, the greater will be the victory of the Most High."

Merlin didn't bother to point out that the monastery's own sacred writings foretold an eventual cataclysmic event that would usher in a new era of the world. Perhaps the Most High planned to use the greed of the Farkians to carry out his divine plans.

A tall mug of frothy ale was set on the table beside Merlin. The monk also settled a plate with sliced fruit and cheese. Merlin took a long drink of the cool ale. It went down easily and spread a welcome warmth through his body. The wizard was more tired and hungry than he'd realized. He picked up a slice of apple and popped it into his mouth. The juice was sweet and made his jaws tingle as he chewed the perfectly ripe fruit. He added a bit of cheese. It was soft and creamy, and had just a touch of salt.

"You look thin," Gryald said. "And tired. Perhaps you should sleep before you see the boy."

"There's no time," Merlin said. "I need to speak with Jon Longarm."

"He is carrying out your wishes," the abbot said. "But the clash of swords is not a welcome sound. Many of our friends have been scarred by violence, and the sound of swords reminds them of their pasts. How long do you wish the boy to stay?"

"As long as possible," Merlin replied. "He's still only a child."

"Tonight, you will give him his name," Gryald said, his

hands covered in batter as he poured it into pans for the oven. "We shall see who he will become. Perhaps his future is here, in service to the Most High."

Merlin didn't comment. He knew that priests and monks had their place, but he felt that Arthur's destiny was bigger, almost as if the boy might be the linchpin that would hold their entire way of life together. Still, he wasn't a sooth-sayer: he couldn't read the stars, and he had never been given the gift of prophecy by the Most High. Instead, he felt his way through the world via a sensitivity to magic—and there was a strong aura of magic around the boy, even if Merlin couldn't say what it actually meant.

Merlin finished the platter of fruit, saving the plumpest fig for last, and stood up. He wasn't quite eye-to-eye with the abbot—few men were—but he didn't break the taller man's intense gaze.

"I would not deny him a life here for as long as that is possible," Merlin said.

"But you do not think he is destined for service?"

The truth was that Merlin felt a great magical shift was approaching. It was like an old wound that ached before a storm hit. Merlin could sense the darkness approaching, and when it arrived, he didn't want the boy anywhere near it.

"I think we must be prepared for anything," Merlin said.

"You must do what you think is best," the abbot said. "We all serve the Most High in one fashion or another, even enchanters."

Merlin bowed slightly, conceding the abbot's point. He worshipped the creator in his own way, but it was just as real and potent as the priests and monks of the monastery.

"I must find Jon Longarm," Merlin repeated.

"He no longer wishes to be known by that name," the abbot shared. "His skill with the sword did not spare his family."

"It might have, if he had been there when they were killed," Merlin said. "His skill at arms may serve us all yet again."

"It is so," Gryald said. "He is in the temple. His custom is to intercede for his family at this hour. He is quite devoted."

"Good men usually are," Merlin replied.

His hunger sated for the moment, Merlin went in search of his old acquaintance. The temple was the largest structure in the monastery compound, so the wizard had no trouble finding it or locating Jon inside, where he was stooped in prayer near a small cluster of candles. Merlin approached his friend without speaking but let his feet drag on the floor so that the warrior would hear him. Jon didn't move at first, and Merlin sat on a nearby bench to wait. Minutes passed. Then—

"Has it been a month already?" Jon said without looking up.

"Indeed," Merlin replied. "The boy has grown."

"As they are wont to do at that age," Jon replied. "He has an aptitude for hard labor."

"And the sword?"

"He is learning." Jon was sparing with praise. "He has a child's youthful eagerness when it comes to fighting."

"But is there an aptitude for it? Is he a warrior, Jon?"

"How should I know?"

"It takes one to see one," Merlin pointed out.

"Then you will be disappointed," Jon said, getting up from having knelt for hours in one smooth motion.

Merlin could tell at a glance that Arthur wasn't the only one benefiting from their combat lessons. Jon turned, his face a mask that hid most of his emotions, although the grief over the loss of his family was still evident.

"It isn't your fault," Merlin said. "It never was."

"You didn't come here to lecture me on my failings as a man, I hope." Jon moved to the bench and sat down beside the wizard. "If so, you can save us both the time and effort. I know what I am and what burdens I carry. Not even you can take them from me."

Merlin glanced up at the far end of the temple to the altar, where three loaves of bread sat next to a crystal decanter of wine. Above it, a golden circle represented the Most High, and around it burned beeswax candles. Light from the late afternoon sun filtered in from high windows on the western wall. Merlin hoped that, in time, such tranquility would help Jon find his own peace; the wizard had a different task to follow.

"I'm here for the boy," Merlin said. "Tonight I will give him his true name."

"That is for a father to do," Jon said. "Are you his father?"

"The closest thing he has ever known to one," Merlin said. "His father was from Atal."

"From Atal? You mean, he was a Bright One?"

"Yes," Merlin replied. "He has Celestial blood in his veins. And he will need your help now more than ever."

"I should have known," Jon said.

"How could you? He looks no different than any other

boy—bigger, perhaps, but not unnaturally so. He should be treated no differently."

"He will be," Jon said. "The brothers may be kept in check, but there are some here who are not as enlightened."

"So you will look after him," Merlin said casually, although he knew that there were people who resented anyone who had associations to Atal. It was partly fear and partly envy, but those two feelings together often resulted in hate.

"You should take him from here. Spare him the pain of being exposed and alone, surrounded by people who will despise him for no reason."

"Are you offering to take him and train him? He must learn the way of the sword—surely you see that."

"What I see is a child who is about to be ostracized for something he has no say in or control over."

"We don't choose our parents," Merlin pointed out.

"That doesn't make it any better," Jon snapped. "Have you no heart?"

"I have a bond with the boy," Merlin said calmly. "To shelter him from the truth will not help him. He must see it, deal with it, and master it. He will not be spared from the painful truth of it, nor from the glorious reality of it. Can't you see that? Jon, he can bridge two worlds. He might bring us together in a way no human king ever could."

"So that is what this is about," Jon said, leaning forward, his hands clasped together so tightly his knuckles were white. "You're a king-maker now."

"I'm a practical person," Merlin said. "My knowledge of and bond to the boy was providence—I'm convinced of that. My task is to help him and to stand beside him as he embraces his destiny. I will not decide it for him."

"What if he meets a young maid and decides that all he wants is a quiet life in the country?" Jon asked. "Would you deny him that?"

"No," Merlin said. "But I think that is naïve. I've never met a man who wanted so little."

"I would give up everything for one day of that life with my love," Jon said, his voice shaking.

"That was not your purpose, Jon. You were meant for more."

"I should have died with them," he said, the tears rolling down his face.

His shoulders shook with silent sobs, and Merlin felt sorry for him, but comfort was not his gift. The wizard could not accomplish what the priests and monks of the Byth El monastery had failed to do.

"Wake up, old friend. You still have a purpose to accomplish. Perhaps it is to instruct Arthur."

Jon didn't respond, so Merlin left him to his anguish. The wizard still had much to attend to, and the day was waning. It was almost time for the naming.

CHAPTER EIGHT

Arthur had just cleaned up after working with the horses. There was something soothing about helping the animals. He liked rubbing them down and being close to the affectionate creatures. For their part, they sensed his kind nature and responded with playful fondness. Haymore was teaching Arthur to care for their hooves, and he enjoyed the added responsibility. It made him feel as if he were progressing in his efforts, just as being able to run the entire circumference of the monastery did. His studies were progressing more slowly, but he was learning. At times, he felt like a sponge that soaked up what he was taught with eagerness. At other times, sitting in the scriptorium or chapel was difficult to manage. He preferred being outside and active, even as the weather began to turn cooler.

After washing, he took his set of tools back to the dormitory. Other than them, he had no real possessions other than a second set of robes and the wooden sword. Stashing his new tools and putting on clean robes, he paused and sat on the end of his bed for a moment. It was his eleventh birthday, and he had completely forgotten, a realization that made him sad. His mother had never forgotten and always made him feel special on his birthdays. The pain of losing her was still hard to bear, but with each passing day, he accepted it a little more. He had been at the monastery a month, although sometimes it felt like longer. His past life was fading, but so was the horror of watching his mother wither away and die. What remained were the feelings of love and safety she had given to him. Thinking back on his past life was still painful, but it didn't immediately bring tears to his eyes anymore.

"Hey, Arthur," said Cassyus, one of the older boys who was friendly to him. "Jon is waiting for you."

"Thanks," Arthur said.

He got up from his bunk and walked through the dormitory. Night had fallen, and Arthur could see the flickering lights of fires burning outside. When he reached the door, he stopped. A group of men were waiting for him. Arthur recognized the abbot Gryald and his tutors, Brother Yancy and Brother Orval. The hunched form of Brother Haymore was there too, along with Jon Longarm and, somewhat to Arthur's surprise, Merlin. Compared to the wizard, the monks looked drab. Merlin wore tall boots that were polished to a shine that reflected the light of a bonfire that was leaping into the night air, sending sparks up like fireflies. His purple robes were hemmed in silver, and he wore a broad belt around his waist.

"Welcome, Arthur," Abbot Gryald said. "And happy

birthday. We can't do this for everyone, every year, but this is a special day."

"Special? Me?" Arthur was confused.

Merlin stepped forward, carrying in his hand a little roll of vellum—the same one that the wizard had given to Arthur's mother before he was born. He held it up in the firelight so that Arthur could see that the seal wasn't broken.

"Most children are named by their father shortly after they are born," Merlin said. "My name is Errol ap'Tunnar Foyl. It means 'one who flies by night fiercely.' You never knew your father. What did your mother tell you about him?"

"Only that he was kind and loving," Arthur said softly. He felt strangely out of place, as if he wasn't ready for what the others were doing. "And that he would come for us one day."

"Your father," Merlin said, and Arthur saw Jon grimace, "was from Atal."

"Atal?"

"That's right," Merlin said. "Your father was one of the Bright Ones. I cannot speak for him. Even though I have been to the western lands many times, I have never discovered who he was. But there was a time when the Celestial folk took human mates. Their children were people of two worlds. You have more of your mother in you than your father, but his blood is there, running through your veins. I felt it before you were born and bonded with you because of it, Arthur. Our futures are intertwined.

"Throughout a man's life, he may be known by many names. Most folk call me Merlin, but I answer to other names. Often, a person is called by a name that reflects a behavior or ability. Our friend Jon is called 'Longarm' because of his prowess in combat. Today, on your eleventh birthday, as you pass from boyhood into manhood, I am giving you this name," he said, dropping the tiny scroll of vellum into Arthur's hand. "It is your Atal name."

The tiny scrap of parchment was rough in Arthur's hand. Time had dried the animal skin it was made of. The drop of wax felt out of place. Arthur's hand trembled as he looked down at the tiny scroll.

"Go to the fire and open it," Jon told him.

Arthur looked at the faces of the people he respected. The abbot was tall and strong, but his face, as always, was friendly and encouraging. His tutors all looked expectant. Jon's face, by contrast, was set with grim determination. The look made Arthur nervous; was something bad going to come from opening the little scroll? He wondered briefly what would happen if he just tossed the scrap into the fire. Would he remain the orphan boy? Would everything just return to normal?"

His stomach growled, reminding him that time hadn't stopped, and he felt the weight of gazes on him as he approached the bonfire. The heat on his face was nothing compared to the stares from the others behind him. He looked down at the roll of parchment. With a flick of his fingernail, the drop of hardened wax broke free and dropped to the ground. The parchment slowly unrolled in his hand. Arthur had learned his letters in the month he had been at the monastery and could read, although it was slow and he had to sound out the words. The writing on the dark fragment was silver and glistened in the firelight. Arthur unrolled the scrap and looked at the words.

Artici ap'Alal Os

"Can you read it?" Merlin asked.

Arthur nodded. He was working out the strange words in his head. As he did, an unfamiliar sensation came over him. His blood grew hot inside him—he could feel it rush from his heart through his body and out into every limb—and awoke a tingling sensation in his mind. His vision became preternaturally sharp, so much so that he could see the minute cracks in the vellum. The words seemed to dance with a liquidity that reminded Arthur of quicksilver he had seen once as a child.

He also felt a strengthening in his body: his bones hardened and the fibers in his muscles thickened as if he was becoming something new, or as if something already inside him was waking up. He could hear the group behind him breathing, even over the crackle of the bonfire. The most surprising thing was a brand new sense, different from sight or smell yet just as potent: he could sense the magic inside of Merlin. Arthur could feel the living, organic eagerness of it. It was unique, like the sound of a person's voice, or smell of a particular room. He had never noticed it before, and yet the sense of magic coming from Merlin was as familiar as the robes that Arthur wore.

The Bright Ones, sometimes called the Ancients or Celestials by the common folk, were the inhabitants of the western lands. Arthur didn't know a lot about them except that they had their own language and their own customs, and that magic came from the Atals; the entire realm was named in their honor. There was no reason for Arthur to know what his name meant—Artici ap'Alal Os, or 'Arthur, son of Atlandia's hope—yet the knowledge sprang to his mind unbidden. As soon as it had arrived, doubt followed it. Maybe he was going crazy; maybe this was some sort of dark spell. A shiver passed through his body, and Arthur turned around, the scrap of parchment clutched safely in his hand.

"You have seen it," Merlin said. "Understanding will come with time."

"You named me?" Arthur asked.

"I was the tool, but the name came from magic," Merlin replied.

"From magic?"

"You still have a lot to learn," the wizard said. "Fortunately, we have time for that, too. Tonight, you should bask in the journey you are making into manhood."

"I'm a man now?"

"Not yet," Jon said. "But you are no longer a boy."

"Just as you are no longer simply a human," Merlin added.

"Life is about growth, young Arthur," the abbot said in his melodious voice. "This is merely a replanting so that you may grow as the Most High intended. Sink your roots down deep into him, and you will have the strength to face whatever comes in this life."

"It is so," the monks said in union.

"Tomorrow, you will return to your studies," Merlin said. "Tonight, we will feast, and I will answer your questions as best I can. If the Atal blood is strong enough, you may even dream of your future this night."

"Come," Abbot Gryald said. "The feast awaits."

They left the bonfire and moved to a smaller building

that Arthur had never before entered. It was different from the other dwellings, but it was obviously made to be a home of sorts. A large stone fireplace filled one wall, just past a round table laden with rich dishes in the center of the main room. A staircase at the back led to a loft above, where Arthur guessed there were sleeping quarters. Open windows let the cool night air into the room, wafting the smells of slow-roasted hare and grouse, bowls of vegetables, and a platter stacked with loaves of crusty bread. A wheel of soft cheese sat on a cutting board, and there was a crock of freshly churned butter. The yeasty aroma of bread and beer filled the small building. On the floor were plushy tufted rugs. Golden candle stands cast yellow light all around the room. The walls were hung with tapestries, and the seats around the table were lined with thick cushions.

Arthur stood in the doorway, taking it all in. He had never seen such wealth or luxury. Nowhere else in the monastery were the quarters so lavishly appointed. His own bunk near the privy reeked most days and held just a narrow cot with a straw mattress. Its only luxury was the goose-down pillow he had been given.

"What is this place?" Arthur asked.

"It is our guest house," Abbot Gryald said, "reserved for our most favored visitors. Kings have stayed here, young Arthur, as have noblemen and visitors from distant lands."

"Tonight, it is for you," Merlin said. "Come—sit and eat!"

They sat down. Merlin poured equal parts wine and water into a goblet for Arthur.

"Do you really think that's a good idea?" Jon said.

"He is becoming a man," Merlin said. "It is time to put

away childish things. Besides, he must learn, as we all do, to control his impulses. Wine, Arthur, is like most things: best in moderation."

Arthur lifted the goblet and gave the watered wine a sniff, wrinkling his nose a bit at the pungent aroma. He could smell the fruit laced with alcohol from the fermentation of the grape's sugars. A single sip told him what he wanted to know: wine was not something he craved.

"Sip it," Brother Yancy said. "The wine sharpens your palate."

"My what?" Arthur asked.

"The way things taste," Jon explained.

The warrior sat to one side of Arthur, and the wizard took the other seat. Soon, the adults were talking and laughing. The food was rich and delicious, and Arthur ate his fill joyfully. Although he never wanted for food at the monastery, it was the first time he could remember being truly good and full. He consumed an entire hare and a whole grouse, a plateful of vegetables, and two small loaves of bread slathered in butter. He drank mostly water but sipped from the goblet of wine from time to time. The taste wasn't really appealing, but the heat from the wine that spread through his body felt good. By the end of the meal, he felt loose and relaxed.

"The guest house is yours for the night," Abbot Gryald said. "My brothers and I are off to evening prayers. Jon, Arthur, you are both excused from prayers this evening. Know that you are both in mine."

"Thank you, Abbot," Jon said.

The monks left the guest house, and Merlin began packing a long pipe he had hidden in his robes. There was still plenty of food, including the honey cakes made by the abbot himself. Arthur nibbled at his as he joined his two companions in stretching their feet out toward the fireplace. Merlin waved his hand, and a thin tongue of fire leapt from the fireplace and encircled his index finger.

"Does that burn?" Arthur asked, as the wizard lit his pipe.

"No," Merlin said. "The magic holds the fire in check, like a thick rag around the handle of a hot cookpot." After a pause, he changed the course of the conversation. "Will you tell us the name you were given, Arthur?"

"He doesn't have to," Jon said.

"No, he doesn't," Merlin agreed. "In fact, you should be wary about sharing it with others. There's power in a name —knowing a person's true name gives a measure of control over them."

"You shared your real name," Arthur pointed out.

"That is right, I did," Merlin agreed. "But I trust the abbot and his monks."

"Trust is something else you should be careful of," Jon said. "Not everyone deserves your trust."

"I shouldn't trust people?" Arthur didn't like the sound of that.

"You should be careful who you trust," Merlin clarified. "Only the Most High can measure the fathoms of a man's heart."

"I don't understand what's happening," Arthur said. "I feel different, and yet everything is the same. I'm still here. I'm still just a boy."

"No, not just a boy," Merlin said. "You are on the road to

becoming a man. A journey is rarely completed in a single day, Arthur. This will take time."

Arthur thought about this. "I hope it doesn't take too long. I'd hate to be behind. After all, doesn't every boy become a man?"

"Children grow up," Jon said. "But not every adult is a man."

"Becoming a man is about taking responsibility for yourself and for the people you care about," Merlin explained. "Someday, things will be asked of you, Arthur—perhaps incredibly important things. Now is the time to prepare. Set your mind to learning all that Jon and the monks here have to teach. The next time you see me, it will be time to leave this place."

The idea of leaving both frightened and excited Arthur. As much as he liked the home he'd found in the monastery, in some ways, he felt like a prisoner. The monks kept to a rigid schedule, and Arthur had no say in what he did. Even on the one day of the week when he wasn't busy from sun up until bedtime, his time was not his own.

"When?" Arthur asked.

"I cannot say," the wizard replied. "When you are needed, I will come."

"When I'm needed?" Arthur repeated. "Can't you just answer me plainly?"

Jon laughed out loud, the first mirth he had shown all night. He threw his head back in a deep guffaw.

Merlin ignored this. "I would if I could, Arthur. I don't know what the future holds; but I can feel the unseen forces of the world at work around us. What they are shaping, I cannot say—only that we will know when we know. And when I know, I'll come for you."

Arthur thought about this and what the men had said about adulthood for a while. The pipe smoke was pleasant and the guest house warm. Full as he was, it felt good to relax. Yet his mind was busy trying to untangle the ideas and concepts Merlin was sharing with him. Arthur knew from his studies with Brother Orval that the Most High was a spirit being. He didn't know exactly what that meant, so he thought of it sort of like a ghost. The monk taught that there were other spirit beings: some that served the Most High, and others that fought against him. These were invisible beings, but they still had influence on the world of men. Arthur couldn't see them or hear them, and he certainly couldn't feel them the way Merlin suggested that he could. All the young man could do was trust the wizard. In that moment, he decided that he would trust Merlin, and Jon, too.

"Artici," he said, pronouncing the name R-T-C. "That was what was written on the parchment.

"It is a fine name," Jon said.

"Indeed," Merlin agreed. "Thank you for sharing it with us."

The name was Arthur's, something private that belonged only to him, but it felt good to share it with the two men he admired and looked up to. It also felt good to keep part of the name to himself. His hand went to the pocket of his robe and felt the roll of parchment there. It was his secret, a tiny treasure of his very own.

"It is getting late," Merlin said, standing up. "I have a few more gifts to share before the evening ends."

He moved over to a chest against the wall, one that Arthur had seen upon entering and assumed was part of the furnishings of the guest house. Merlin threw back the lid and pulled out a pair of soft boots made of well-tanned deer hide. The leather upper flopped down to the side.

"You still have a lot of growing to do," Merlin said. "These should last a while, but they are soft enough to stretch if needed."

He turned back and brought out a matching dagger and smaller utility knife. "Tools," he said. "Not weapons. Jon will show you how to use them."

"Aye," the big man said.

Finally, Merlin pulled out a pouch of coins. The wizard pulled the bindings and spilled the coins out on the table. They were silver, bright and shining in the golden light from the candles.

"And you should have some coin," Merlin said. "It is yours to do with as you choose, but I would suggest that you let Jon hold it for you. There's no need for it here in the monastery, and some others might be jealous. Even in a place committed to knowledge and worship of the Most High, there are some who might steal if the opportunity arises. You'll want the coin when you travel."

Arthur couldn't believe his eyes. As a child, he'd had some toys, but nothing of real value. When his mother died, he was left with nothing, since the dishonest adults around him had stolen all that Cryslov had owned. To be in possession of such treasures suddenly made his head spin.

"All this," Arthur queried incredulously, "for me?"

"It's for you," Merlin said. "Now let us retire. I am anxious to know what you will see in your dreams tonight."

Arthur picked up the dagger, still in its sheath of stiff leather. It was heavier than he expected, with a brass finger guard and a dark stained wooden handle. Arthur pulled it free and looked at the blade, which had a blue cast to it. In the center of the blade were forge marks, but the edges were keen.

"We'll find a good whetstone soon," Jon said. "You can learn to care for it after that."

Merlin scooped up the coins and put them back in the pouch, pulling the drawstrings tightly closed. He led the way up the stairs. Arthur tucked the dagger and matching knife, both in their sheaths, between his belt and robe. He felt like a king as he picked up the boots. They were even softer than he expected, except for the soles, which were thicker and tougher than the deer hide uppers. He followed the wizard up to the loft, where three beds were arranged in a row. Arthur sat on the middle bed and immediately realized that the mattress was stuffed with goose down, just like his pillow. It was cushier than any bed he had ever slept on.

"Tonight, we are rich men," Merlin said, setting his pipe on a table between the beds.

"And tomorrow, we return to the real world," Jon said.

"All the more reason to enjoy this moment," Merlin said to Arthur with a wink.

Arthur knew he would never forget his eleventh birthday. It had snuck up on him, and he hadn't expected it to be any different from any other day, but it had turned out to be a monument in his life. While his existence might go back to the rigid schedule and long days he had become used to, he would never be the same.

CHAPTER NINE

Arthur was standing on the tower of a huge castle built high up on a hill. Below him, a city spread out partly on the hillsides, partly around the bottom. The city was hemmed in by a strong wall, and beyond the wall was a sparking lake that stretched out as far as he could see.

On either side of the city were massive trees, towering evergreens that stood hundreds of feet tall. Behind him, a wide road ran through the trees to the east. To either side of the long lake were gentle hills of the greenest grass Arthur had ever seen. The air was cold and bracing on his face. He reached up to his cold cheeks and felt a soft beard. Looking down at himself, Arthur saw armor and finery. A mighty sword hung from his belt—not a bejeweled weapon for show, but a perfectly crafted blade built for war.

Turning his attention back to the city, Arthur saw people

moving in the broad, cobblestone lined streets. But there was something unusual about the citizens. He leaned against the parapet and looked closer. A swirl of magic coursed through him. It was a giddy feeling, the way it felt to run and leap out of a second-story hayloft before landing in the mounds of straw below. His vision raced down, and if he hadn't been holding onto the thick stone wall of the tower, he would have thought he was falling. The breath caught in his throat as the villagers sharpened and became clear. There were average common people moving from place to place, but among them were taller beings who seemed to glow. Their skin tones ran the gamut, from pale white to dark black and all shades in between. They were exceptionally thin and moved with a fluid grace that Arthur had only seen in fish.

Above all, the people seemed happy. They were smiling and waving, talking and sharing news. It seemed like an idyllic place. Arthur couldn't say how long he stood there, staring down at this city that seemed to glisten with a pristine air of joy. Perhaps that didn't make sense—a person couldn't see joy—but Arthur could feel it, and he never wanted to leave. He felt at home, even though he was far removed from the people below.

"Artici," a soft voice said from behind him.

He stood up, feeling a swirl of magic as his vision returned to normal, and turned around. Standing just behind him was a woman with golden eyes, alabaster skin, and full red lips.

"What are you doing?" she asked.

"Just watching them," Arthur said. "Just taking it all in.

This entire place, it's so majestic. I've never felt more at home."

She took his arm, leaning her head on his shoulder as they looked across the sparkling lake. Her hair was like spun gold, and Arthur felt a thrill of magic coursing through him from her touch. It was different from Merlin's: sweeter, more tantalizing.

"It should," she said softly, with an amused tone. "You built it."

Arthur's breath caught in his throat, and he felt a lump in his stomach. He was speechless. The city below him was breathtaking, its people so happy. He was on top of the castle, but he felt as if he were on top of the world. Tears stung his eyes.

"My love, what is that?" the woman asked.

In the distance, too far to see clearly, a dark smog was growing—not storm clouds, yet it had the same feeling. Something dangerous lay on the horizon. As they watched, the threat grew and grew.

"No," Arthur said. "No, it can't."

He jerked awake, the bitter regret so tangible inside him that the tears came unbidden. Sitting up on the soft bed, he saw Merlin watching him. There was regret mirrored in the wizard's eyes. A single candle burned between them on a small beside table.

"You saw something," Merlin said quietly.

Arthur nodded, looking over his shoulder at where Jon lay sleeping.

"Come," Merlin said. "See me off. The best thing you can do after a magical dream is to feel yourself in the waking world. The exercise of your body will drive the dream away, as will the sharing of it."

Normally, Arthur valued his sleep. It was still dark out, and soon it would be time for Arthur to return to the long days of constant training. The guest house with its luxuries would be off limits, and he would have to return to the dorm and his lonely bunk by the smelly latrine. Yet the thought of going back to sleep after his vivid dream was frightening. He didn't want to see what the darkness was— he didn't want to face it.

Instead, he pulled on the new boots, slipping his feet into the pliant leather. It felt strange to have anything on his feet, but most men wore boots. Arthur had even looked at Merlin's tall boots with envy not long ago. He stood up, slid the dagger and knife into his wide leather belt, and followed the wizard downstairs. Merlin carried the candle in one hand, holding his other in front of the flame to keep it from fluttering out.

When they reached the bottom of the stairs, Merlin took one of the honey cakes and moved over to the fireplace, where he stirred the embers with a metal poker. Two of the pieces of wood had only partially burned, and fresh flames soon danced up around them. Merlin turned to face Arthur, his back to the fire.

"Tell me about the dream," he said.

Arthur told him every detail he could remember. The intensity of it was starting to fade, but the fearful emotion was just as strong as ever.

"Dreams are often symbolic," Merline mused. "Perhaps the castle, the village, even the woman were all symbols of something we can't even guess at. Or perhaps it's a literal place and person. We shall have to wait and see."

"*You* weren't there," Arthur said.

"That means nothing, Artici," Merlin replied, using the name that Arthur had only just received the night before. "I will always be with you. We are bonded."

"Unless you can't be," Arthur said. "People die—good people, too. No matter what anyone does, they die."

"You're right," Merlin said. "But I'm not going to die any time soon."

"But you don't know that," Arthur argued, his voice getting a little too loud. "No one knows when they will die. Abbot Gryald is always saying so. He says our souls will be required of us...whatever that means."

Merlin smiled. "When I was your age, I had my first magical dream, and I have had it many times since. It is always the same for me. In it, I am an old man, with a long gray beard."

"You've got gray in your beard now," Arthur said.

"But it's short," Merlin teased.

Arthur smiled briefly, but it faded as he remembered his strange dream once again. Merlin caught sight of this and added, "Never fear—I will be here when you need me. Do not worry too much about the dream. Threats always loom on the horizon. We can't avoid them, but we can face them. Many are nothing more than shadows."

Outside, a rooster crowed. Through the open windows, Arthur could see the monastery waking up. He wished that he could hold on to the night a little longer. It was so good to have friends and to be surrounded by people he knew and cared about. His birthday had been grand in a way he hadn't expected; he didn't want it to end.

"There are good things in our future," Merlin said when he finished the last bite of the honey cake. "Never stop looking for them, my young friend. Our time will arise before you know it."

"I hope so," Arthur said. "I'll miss you."

"And I will miss you," Merlin said. "But try to enjoy your time here. One day, you will look back and realize how special it was. Even if it was born out of tragedy, Artici. Loss often makes room for something new in our lives. Listen to Jon."

With a flourish of his robes, the wizard transformed in a falcon. Arthur was nearly knocked over by the wave of potent magic; it was shocking that something so powerful could come from a creature only a fraction of his size. The bird turned its golden eyes on him, and Arthur could feel the magic he had recognized as Merlin's signature. In a smooth movement, the bird hopped from the table to the windowsill, turning its head back toward Arthur.

"Goodbye," the boy said.

The falcon chirped in reply, then flew off, just as the first bell of the day began to ring.

"Time to go to work," Jon said as he came down the stairs.

"Do we have to?" Arthur complained.

"We don't have to. We get to," Jon said. "Meet me at the well...just as soon as you stash the rest of those honey cakes."

"I can keep them?" Arthur was delighted.

"Absolutely—just don't let the others find them, or you'll have to share," Jon said with a wink.

Arthur picked up a sack and quickly stuffed in the honey cakes, the rest of the soft cheese, and the remaining loaves of bread. Then he hurried out of the guest house behind Jon, his magical dream nearly forgotten.

CHAPTER TEN

The broom handle whistled through the air, but Arthur wasn't there to meet it. He stepped back nimbly, more than a little amazed at how clearly he could see the strikes coming. All day, he, and even the monks around him, had noticed little differences in him. No longer did the water spill when Arthur carried it, nor did his morning run wind him: he ran the entire perimeter of the monastery in a steady, even jog that kept him well ahead of Jon and was barely winded when he returned to the main gate. His mind absorbed his lessons, and even the animals in the stables responded to him as if he were different, straining their necks from their stalls in an effort to get near him.

After dinner and their evening prayers, Arthur and Jon took up their sword lessons, only Arthur felt like a new person. The heavy wooden sword was light in his hands. He moved with efficiency, stepping just out of reach of Jon's wicked broomstick. Perhaps Jon always moved in the same, predictable pattern when they sparred and Arthur had simply never noticed it before, but he found now that he could tell exactly what the big man was going to do. For his part, Arthur stayed just within reach, letting the attacks come. He was finding it so easy to avoid them that he couldn't stop smiling.

"What's so funny?" Jon said, swinging the broom handle at his head.

Arthur ducked, pivoted on his back foot, and raised his front leg to avoid Jon's sweeping backstroke.

"I'm having fun," Arthur said.

"What did I tell you about battle?" Jon snarled as he sped up his attack. "It's not a game."

He thrust the broomstick at Arthur's stomach, but the younger man spun away. He brought the tip of his wooden sword up and took hold of the end of the blade. Jon was already arcing his broomstick in an overhead chop, but Arthur held up his weapon to block it. The broomstick rebounded off the wooden sword with a snap. Arthur expected the vibration to shock his hands as it had early on in his training, but holding the sword on either end somehow diminished the power of the blow. Jon leveled another swing at Arthur's side, but he blocked that one as well.

"When are you going to teach me to strike back?" Arthur asked.

"When you stop yapping and concentrate," Jon shouted, rushing forward with a flurry of blows.

Arthur couldn't block them all and backpedaled. He could see the attacks coming but was only barely able to avoid them. Jon was puffing when he pulled back, a strange look in his eyes.

"How did you do that?" Jon asked.

Arthur let the sword tip drop to the ground and used it as a crutch to lean against while he caught his breath. There were times when Jon's ferocity in combat frightened Arthur. He had seen the attacks coming but still felt helpless to stop the big man, which he hated.

"I was doing what you taught me," Arthur said.

"You've improved," Jon said, his eyes narrowing. "What did Merlin do?"

"What?"

"He enchanted you somehow," Jon said.

"I've seen you make that attack before," Arthur said. "I recognized the pattern."

"You recognized the pattern?" Jon asked.

Arthur nodded.

"You were taught this sword pattern?" Jon asked.

"No," Arthur said.

"Remarkable. Come with me."

Jon led Arthur to a wooden pole where robes were hung from a line to dry after washing. The warrior tapped the wooden pole with his broomstick. "Show me."

"Show you what?" Arthur asked.

"You said I attacked with a pattern," Jon said. "Show me the pattern."

Arthur felt frustrated. Jon hadn't taught him the series of sword strikes. Just because Arthur had recognized them didn't mean he could replicate them, but he didn't seem to have a choice. He lifted his wooden sword, holding it with the blade straight up, the way that Jon often did with the broomstick.

Without knowing how, he could visualize the first strike: a level slash across the midsection on his strong side. He swung the sword and hit the post. The vibration stung his hand and the sword bounced away from the target, but that played perfectly into his next stroke. He let the sword's momentum spin him around as he dipped his weapon low; as he turned, Arthur brought the weapon up in a glancing slash against the side of the pole. Stepping to the side, he reversed the sword's direction and chopped down into a diagonal cut that struck the pole high, only he let the practice sword slash across the pole so that it didn't sting his hands or bounce away. Arthur stepped back, leveling the sword and thrusting it straight into the pole as he stepped forward again. He paused for a moment, his arm taut, the sword suspended between him and the pole.

"That's all I remember," Arthur said.

The truth was, he hadn't really remembered anything. The entire exercise had been like a dance: each strike flowed to the next. He let the weapon dictate his movements and followed it's lead. There was a grace and simplicity that appealed to him. His first blow had been a lesson, he wasn't chopping firewood, and he couldn't bang away against the post. Instead, he let the sword do the work and found an economy of motion, effort, and skill.

"That's all you remember," Jon repeated, shaking his head. "It's your damn Atal blood."

"What?" Arthur asked, shocked by his mentor's sudden hateful attitude.

"That is all for tonight," Jon said. "But know this: people

are watching you. Don't give them a reason to hate or fear you."

The big man walked away. Arthur felt a sting he had never experienced before. Wasn't he supposed to learn? Wasn't he training to become a good fighter? Why, he wondered, was Jon angry that he was starting to understand combat?

After getting a drink of water from the well, Arthur went to the dorm. Most of the older men were already sleeping, their gentle snores a familiar sound. But the younger men, boys older than Arthur, often stayed awake for a while at night. Arthur knew them by name, but there had been no time to bond with the boys. Some of them shared in the lessons he was being taught by Brother Yancy and Brother Orval.

Arthur sat on the edge of his narrow bunk and began pulling off his boots when two of the older boys approached. Arthur knew their names but wasn't sure of their ages—he thought them to be around fourteen or fifteen years old. Arthur was tall for his age and growing stronger every day, but the older boys were still bigger.

"Nice boots," Cephas said.

"Where'd a mite like you get new boots?" Mattao asked.

"A friend gave them to me," Arthur said. "Yesterday was my birthday."

"Is that a fact?" Mattao continued. "That friend of yours wouldn't happen to be a warlock named Raven or something, would it?"

"Merlin," Arthur corrected him.

"That's right, Merlin the Mad," Cephas said with a chuckle.

"What else did the old fool give you?" Mattao asked.

Arthur thought of the knife and dagger he had stashed under the straw mattress of his bed. He looked up at the older boys and saw their taunting expressions. Somehow, he knew they were up to something. Arthur started to stand up, but Mattao pushed him back onto his bunk.

"Anything he's got will stink of the privy," Cephas said. "Just like he does."

"You should learn your place, boy," Mattao said. "The first rule around here is that we get first dibs on anything we find."

He pulled back a fold of his robe to reveal the dagger that Merlin had given to Arthur. It was tucked into his belt, but hidden by the baggy material. Arthur felt a spark of anger that quickly grew into a blazing rage as Cephas casually flaunted the matching short knife.

"You can keep the tools," Mattao said. "We don't have a use for them. But I'm taking those boots."

"No," Arthur said.

"It's not a request," Cephas said.

"A little snot like you doesn't need boots anyway," Mattao sneered.

Arthur started up again. Cephas moved to push him back down, but Arthur was quick. He turned as he stood and shoved Cephas's clumsy attack away. Instinctively, he ducked, knowing that Mattao would strike at him. The older boy's punch missed, and Arthur threw his shoulder into Mattao, who fell backward.

"Hey!" Cephas yelled as he grabbed the back of Arthur's robe.

"Give me my knife!" Arthur demanded as he turned back to Cephas.

This time, the older boy was ready. Stepping close, he rammed his knee into Arthur's groin. Pain flooded Arthur with shocking severity. He started to fall, but Cephas caught him and turned him around. The older boy twisted Arthur's left arm behind his back with one hand and wrapped his other around the younger boy's throat.

Arthur felt paralyzed by pain and fear. He could hardly breathe with Cephas' arm around his throat. When he reached up to pull the older boy's chokehold away, Cephas twisted Arthur's left arm. More pain shot like bolts of lightning from his shoulder down into his body.

Mattao was getting up. "Hold him," he snarled as he drew the dagger that Merlin had given to Arthur for his birthday.

He swung the dagger in a wicked slash. Arthur pushed back with both feet, trying to avoid the blade. It was razor sharp and cut through the front of Arthur's robes. Fire erupted across his stomach.

"I said hold him!" Mattao shouted.

"Hey, what's going on over there?" one of the older men demanded.

It was dark in the dormitory. The boys were just shadows, and no one moved to intervene. It slipped through Arthur's mind that Jon should have been there—his mentor should have rescued him—but there was no time left. Mattao had drawn his arm back, preparing to thrust the dagger straight into Arthur's chest.

Arthur stomped down onto Cephas's toes with the heel of his foot, causing the older boy's grip on him ease just slightly. As Mattao rushed forward with the dagger, Arthur lunged for his bunk. He fell, taking Cephas with him. Arthur had just enough leverage to drive his elbow back into Cephas; the older boy released him with a grunt. Arthur threw his body across the bed and fell off the other side, but he had managed to snatch up his wooden sword.

"Grab him!" Mattao shouted.

Arthur rose with the sword just as Mattao tried to stab him. Arthur swayed to the side to avoid the thrust, and before the older boy could pull his arm back, Arthur chopped down with the wooden sword. It had no cutting edge, but it was heavy. Arthur let the full weight of the practice weapon smash Mattao's forearm. There was a snapping sound like someone stepping on a dry twig, and the older boy howled in pain as he dropped the dagger. The weapon clattered on the floor.

Cephas dove across the bed, but Arthur quickly stepped out of reach and kicked upward, driving the top of his foot into the older boy's face. There was a sickening crunch, and Cephas moaned as he collapsed to the floor.

Light from a lantern suddenly lit the surroundings. Arthur looked up and saw Jon holding the light high, his face furious. "What's going on here?" Jon demanded.

"They stole my dagger and knife," Arthur said. "They were going to take my boots."

"So you beat them?" Jon said.

"He broke my arm," Mattao cried.

Cephas was spitting blood, which was gushing into his mouth from his nose. Arthur felt a sudden, terrible revulsion at the hurt he had caused. The boys were older and they were thieves, but Arthur had inflicted pain and injury on them. It was frightening to realize what he had done.

"Arthur, what did you do?" Jon asked.

The question was laced with disappointment. Arthur turned, planning to explain himself: he hadn't meant to hurt the older boys—he didn't want to fight them at all. But they...they...

He staggered. Jon caught him by the arm, and the pain across Arthur's stomach flared to life.

"Arthur?" Jon said. "Have mercy! You're bleeding. Someone get a healer! Now!"

Arthur sank to one knee. He leaned onto his wooden sword to try to stay upright, but the pain across his stomach was getting worse, and warm liquid was running down his hips and onto his thighs, soaking his robes and weighting them down. Jon pulled him onto his back. There was a ripping sound, and the man cursed.

"I need help!" he shouted.

Arthur felt pressure suddenly pushing down on his stomach, making it hard to breathe. He looked up at Jon. There was fear on the big man's face that made Arthur's own fear even worse. He blinked as tears filled his eyes. The pain was so intense, a burning, searing ache that he would have done anything to stop, but there was no way to escape it.

"You'll be all right," Jon told him, but his voice was shaking.

Arthur didn't believe him. Someone was covering the lantern; or maybe not, but, at any rate, the room was growing dark. He felt the sweet relief of oblivion whisking him away from the pain—and he let it take him.

CHAPTER ELEVEN

"We've sewn the wound closed," a monk said. "It's clean. He should recover."

The words had a strange, dreamlike quality to them. Arthur was conscious, but he wasn't quite awake. He couldn't feel anything, but that was somewhat of a relief—he didn't want the pain to come back, and some part of his foggy brain knew it was still there, waiting just underneath the surface of this haze.

"I want to know what happened!" Abbot Gryald said.

Arthur had never heard the big abbot angry. The next voice to speak was Jon's. He sounded more like himself, which made Arthur feel better.

"Mattao and Cephas stole from Arthur. They had taken his dagger and knife and were trying to get his boots."

"You gave him weapons?" the abbot said. "Why on earth would you give him weapons?"

"I didn't," Jon replied. "Merlin gave them to him."

"I should have known better," Gryald said.

"It's not the boy's fault," Jon said.

"That may be so, but it looks like his fault," Gryald said. "Everyone knows you've been training him to fight, and now he's broken one boy's arm, and another's nose."

"They tried to kill him," Jon said. "The other boys all told the same story. And look at him."

"The cut wasn't deep," the healer said. "It barely lacerated the muscles."

"But it did do so," Jon argued. "They would have done worse, too."

"Yes, yes, I understand that," Gryald said. "The boys who did it will be dealt with. There is no place for thieves in the monastery. But that brings up another problem: we can't show favoritism to Arthur."

"What does that mean?" Jon asked.

"He'll have to be disciplined," Gryald said. "And no more fighting lessons—I must insist on that. We are an order of peace. There can be no more fighting within these walls."

"You don't want me to train him?"

"Not with the sword," the abbot insisted. "You can teach the boys archery. Not just Arthur, but all of the young friends of the monastery. That should settle things."

"You can't punish him for defending himself," Jon said.

"Order must be maintained," the abbot said. "Violence is never a solution to our problems, Jon. You of all people must recognize this."

"What was he supposed to do?"

"He should have come to us," Gryald said. "And you should have never let him keep a dagger in the first place."

"Maybe you are right," Jon said. "I will take the blame. Punish me."

"It does my heart good to see that our teachings on the virtue of selflessness have taken root in you, my friend, but people must see Arthur atoning for his poor judgment. When he is well, he will scrub chamber pots and dig new latrines for a month. That is my decision, and it is final. In that time, there will be no combat training of any kind. When his month of service is complete, you can begin archery lessons. That will satisfy the wizard's desire that Arthur learn martial skills."

A moment later, Arthur heard the door close, and his eyes fluttered open. He was in a small, unfamiliar room suffused with unpleasant, mingling smells of herbs and incense. Jon moved into view above Arthur and smiled.

"You're awake," he said.

"Am I?" Arthur asked. "This feels like a dream."

"That's the poppy talking," the monk who served as the healer for the monastery said. "How's your pain?"

"Pain?" Arthur asked, still struggling through the fog in his mind.

"You're going to be all right," Jon said. "Everything will be fine."

Arthur closed his eyes again, feeling sleep wash over him. He was safe; Jon had said so.

"You rest," Jon said. "When you wake up, I'll be here."

The next time Arthur woke up, it was dark, and the first thing he understood was pain, although it wasn't as intense as before. The fire had been quenched, but there was an ache in his middle that only became more intense when he tried to move in search of a more comfortable position.

"Easy," Jon said as Arthur groaned. "Try not to move too much."

"Hurts," Arthur gasped.

"I know," Jon replied. "I've been where you are. The good news is, you'll heal. Just give it time. You don't want to move too much, or you'll reopen that wound."

Arthur stopped his fidgeting and looked around. There were other beds filled with patients. Jon seemed to be the only visitor.

"Where are they?" Arthur asked.

Jon instantly knew who Arthur meant. "Their injuries were treated, but Mattao and Cephas have both been removed from the monastery. I'll be taking them as far as Luz in a few days when I make a trip with the priests."

"You're leaving?" Arthur asked.

"I serve as protection when the priests travel," Jon said. "It is part of my commitment to the monastery. I had planned to take you with me."

"I'll go," Arthur said. He foolishly tried to sit up, which sent waves of pain radiating through his body.

"No," Jon said. "You couldn't go now, even if you were well. The abbot is restricting your privileges."

"Why?"

"Because although you were defending yourself, he feels that violence inside the monastery walls must be punished."

"I'm in trouble?"

"No," Jon said. "You did nothing wrong, and no one blames you."

Arthur's lip quivered. "I didn't mean to hurt them."

"I know. We have witnesses who told us everything. For now, let's take things slow. You need time to heal and regain your strength. When you're better, I'll teach you to shoot a bow."

"But no more sword lessons," Arthur said, just barely remembering the argument between the abbot and his mentor.

"For now," Jon confirmed. "But you need not worry about any of that. All you need to focus on is healing. Rest and food—those are the building blocks of recovery."

"I'm sorry," Arthur said.

"Don't be," Jon said. "I admit, I was angry when I saw you fighting, but I am not angry now. In fact, I'm proud of you. What you did took courage, and, like it or not, this is a lesson every warrior needs to learn."

"What pain feels like?"

"No, I would never wish that on you," Jon said. "But now you know the consequences that come from fighting. It should always be a last resort."

Arthur nodded. The lesson learned in his dormitory scuffle would not soon be forgotten. Though his eyelids were growing heavy, the thought of the scuffle brought one last question to his lips.

"My dagger," he said softly.

"I have it," Jon said. "The knife and your boots, too—it's all safe. Now rest, Arthur. All is well."

"All is well," Arthur repeated, already halfway to sleep.

CHAPTER TWELVE

T he gradual accumulation of hostilities was in some
ways worse than sudden violence. For five years,
Merlin had been watching the growing unrest
between Farkia and the rest of Atlandia. The Atals, the
Celestial protectors, had no king, no central leadership; they
followed the laws of the Most High, seeking his wisdom for
every decision. Yet that did not stop the Farkians from
growing stronger and more threatening by the day.

Merlin had known for a long time that this day would
come. It was inevitable, the way that two strong men in
close proximity would, sooner or later, have to know who
was the strongest. As Merlin glided on a thermal draft high
in the sky over the western realm of Farkia, the dark ships
from Ran sailed down the Ra'An river toward the sea. The
slowly building tension between Alal, home of the Bright
Ones, and Farkia, the lovers of the dark, was finally spilling
over into action, and there could be only one outcome: true

war. He, Merlin, would fulfill his obligation to the Atals, who had shared the secrets of magic with him, by warning them of the danger from Farkia. Then he could return to the Byth El monastery.

He wondered how much Arthur had changed since they'd seen each other last. The dream Arthur had shared with Merlin at that time was never far from the wizard's mind. Perhaps it was a prophetic dream. He hoped it was, but dreams often left much to the interpretation. Arthur also had astutely pointed out one thing that gave the wizard pause: why hadn't Merlin been part of Arthur's dream? It was a mystery—one that might have meant nothing at all, or possibly more than Merlin could fathom. Only time would tell.

The ships, great hulking vessels painted black and sporting dark gray sails and long oars, left the estuary and moved out into the sea. It wasn't surprising to see them turning north, but Merlin had to be sure and waited until the sails unfurled. A strong southern breeze filled them, and the dark ships leapt north over the choppy waves. Likewise, Merlin turned north and flapped the long, powerful wings he controlled in his animal form. The ships were faster than horses—perhaps even faster than a falcon—but Merlin could make directly for Ava, situated deep in the mountains. The country between the coast south of Newspan and the Ra'An river was rugged, so it would take an army significant time to reach the mountain stronghold. If he could beat the Farkians there and warn the Atals at Ava, they could use their magical abilities to warn the rest of their celestial countrymen.

It didn't take long for the first outcroppings of arid,

rocky hills to come into sight. Merlin flew over them without stopping, even as the sun dipped toward the sea. In the distance, Merlin could see the taller mountains, towering, craggy peaks perpetually covered in snow. The golden light of the setting sun glistened from the mountain tops, among which nestled his destination.

It took several hours to reach Ava, and it was completely dark when he descended from the cloudy sky toward the torches that burned through the night from the powerful fortress, built of heavy stone mined from the mountains on every side. It was also a stunning city: clean, symmetrical, and perfectly maintained. It blended into the mountains, since parts of the city were carved straight into towering cliffs with stunning detail. Nothing about Ava was plain—it all spoke of a majesty that no human settlement had ever even dreamed of matching. The greatest castles of the wealthiest human kings paled in comparison to the cities of the Atals.

Merlin had no time to marvel or contemplate how the Bright Ones planned their grand structures or moved the massive stones into place. He had a message to deliver, and quickly. The fear that he had been gone from his ward for too long hung over him. Five years was a long time. There was no doubt that Arthur would still remember him, but would he trust the wizard? That was a different matter completely.

He dove for a portico, flaring his wings at the last minute and transforming back into his true form before dropping lightly onto his feet. Standing where he had landed, Merlin took a moment to straighten his robes and make sure that everything was in place. His knife was tucked into his belt, as was his coin purse; in the inner pockets of his robes were a variety of herbs and magical trinkets. He was pleased to find that everything was as it should be after a long time spent in his bird form.

"Merlin the Enchanter," a tall Atal said as he walked from a side room onto the portico.

"La'Rish," Merlin replied. "I have news."

"Always so hasty, humans are. Always in a rush. Would you care for refreshment?"

"Please," Merlin said, his stomach growling at the very thought of food. He hadn't eaten since before dawn.

La'Rish stopped at a fountain that gurgled in the center of the portico and looked up at the stars, hardly seeming to remember that Merlin was there. The wizard knew that it was useless to rush the Celestial. La'Rish would hear Merlin's news only when he was ready for it.

"So many stars," La'Rish said. "One could spend a thousand years studying them and still not know them all."

"A thousand years is a long time," Merlin said.

"Yes, I suppose it is," La'Rish replied agreeably.

Merlin couldn't tell if La'Rish was taunting him with his immortality or if he'd simply forgotten how short a human's life span was. Even Merlin, whose magic slowed his own aging process, would not live a thousand years.

"Looking up always reminds me," La'Rish went on, "that our problems down here are minor, temporary ills. Do you agree?"

"Most of the time," Merlin said. "But things are changing."

"The more they change, the more they stay the same," La'Rish said. "I remember when this world was young."

"Your wisdom is immense, I have no doubt," Merlin said.

"Do the humans enjoy your wisdom, Merlin? Your abilities?"

"Some," Merlin said. "Most do not."

"I have often wondered why you would devote yourself so fully to our ways. You can neither be one of us, nor fully one of your own now. You are tainted. Isn't that what the humans think—that we have infected you with our...*magic*?"

He said the last word with contempt. The Atals used magic with an effortless ability that Merlin couldn't help but admire—so effortless, in fact, that they didn't think of it as magic. Instead of a skill to be mastered, they considered their abilities to be something more akin to the supernatural powers of the Most High.

"Some people do fear magic," Merlin said, "but there are much worse things to fear...such as the warships that are sailing into Atal waters as we speak."

"You cannot help yourself," La'Rish said with a smile. "You must tell me your news right away, as if someone else might rush in and reveal the secret before you have the chance."

"I only wish to fulfill my oath. The Farkians are mobilizing against your people. I swore to watch them until it was obvious what their intent was, and I have done that."

"You can tell from a single ship that our dark cousins wish to bathe the world in blood?"

"It wasn't a single ship," Merlin insisted. "It was six ships, the rails lined with war shields. It was more than a raiding party, my lord. What I saw leaving the Ra'An and sailing north was an invasion fleet."

A female Atal joined them. She had dark red skin and glossy black hair. La'Rish, on the other hand, was pale, his hair the color of snow; even the irises of his eyes were white. As different as the colors of their features were, it was easy to tell that they were both Atals by their dress alone. The Atals didn't wear robes and instead traditionally donned breeches and tight-fitting shirts that accented their thin bodies. They looked frail, a superficial delicacy that Merlin knew hid untold powers.

"Ah, our refreshments," La'Rish said, as his companion set down a tray with a tall container filled with wine.

There were fruits, breads, cheeses, and nuts arranged neatly on the tray. The Atals rarely ate meat. It wasn't forbidden— they simply preferred to cultivate growth rather than death. The female Atal, Mos'Ash, smiled at Merlin as she sat on a stone bench. Even after years of living among them, Merlin still marveled at the way the Atals moved. They were almost languorous, but their grace and ease of movement belied great energy and strength. Atals were beautiful as well, in a way that was completely different from humans. Merlin had never felt romantic desire for any of them, but he appreciated the Atals the way one admired the work of a master craftsman.

"You have come to tell us what is going on in the world beyond our mountains," Mos'Ash said. "I so enjoy the stories you tell us."

Merlin was tempted to tell her that his news wasn't a story. The massing of Farkian ships wasn't a tall tale or a ballad of a forgotten hero. It was the happenings of the world that would, sooner or later, affect even the Atals in their mountain fortress.

"I have come to warn you," Merlin said. "The Farkians are coming to wage war on your people."

"How dire," Mos'Ash said idly.

"Come, eat, Merlin—it will improve your outlook on the world," La'Rish said.

Arguing would do no good. Merlin couldn't make La'Rish or Mos'Ash believe him or take the news seriously. His only duty was to convey it. If they failed to heed the warning, then that was their choice. In the end, they would pass it on, he knew; whether or not they did so in a timely fashion was not clear. Merlin could only hope they would share the news before the ships full of warriors, empowered by the dark magic of the Farkians, fell on the inhabitants of Newspan. Atals were powerful beings, but they were few in number, and the Farkians were magical beings too. Moreover, unlike the Atals, they had no qualms about using their powers to hurt and harm. As a people, the Bright Ones were builders. Killing was not in their nature, which made them poor warriors.

Merlin picked up a handful of nuts and began to eat as La'Rish poured three goblets of wine. He handed one to Merlin, and the wizard took a drink. Atal wines were the finest in all the world, a perfect balance between the sweet fruit and the ardent spirit. The wine flowed over his tongue and down his parched throat like a cool breeze. At the same time, the wine warmed him and did, in fact, take the edge off his worry.

"Better," La'Rish said with a smile. "Now tell us your news. You say that the Farkians are coming."

"I do not think they will come here," Merlin said. "Not

at first. They will attack the coastal cities. Newspan will be the hardest hit."

"Why just the coastal cities?" Mos'Ash asked.

"If they are successful against the villages," Merlin said, swallowing a bite of bread, "they will want to take Atland."

"The Celestial City?" La'Rish said. "That cannot be."

"What would they hope to gain?" Mos'Ash asked.

"They hope to break your hold on the land," Merlin said. "Once you are no longer around to keep them in check, they will turn on the humans."

"Why do you suppose they hate you so?" La'Rish said. "Humans are the Most High's greatest creation."

"Perhaps it is simply as you have said," Merlin replied. "They hate us because the Most High loves us."

"Fascinating," Mos'Ash said.

"Utterly," La'Rish agreed. "Merlin, finish your repast. Then you shall rest here a full night and day."

"My oath is fulfilled," Merlin said, thinking of Arthur.

"I will pass on your news," La'Rish continued, as if Merlin hadn't spoken at all. "The elders may wish to speak with you."

Merlin could have refused, but he wouldn't turn his back on the Atals. They had given him much that they didn't have to share. His feelings of loyalty for them were strong, and while he longed to be free of his obligation, he respected their wishes. Arthur could wait a little longer.

"As you wish," he said with a slight bow.

CHAPTER THIRTEEN

Arthur moved through the woods alone, careful not to make a sound. At sixteen years old, he was as tall as the abbot, with broad shoulders and long, sinewy limbs. His sandy blond hair was long and tied at the back of his neck to keep it from his smooth face, which still betrayed his youth.

In the distance at the edge of a clearing, a stag was contemplating the sweet wildflowers that grew there. Arthur had lain in wait for a few hours, watching, listening, even smelling the air that came toward him in light breezes. He had no supernatural powers, but being alone in the forest, on the hunt with his bow, had its own magic and was one of the things he enjoyed most in life. There was a freedom in the wilderness that was unmatched.

It was a welcome respite from the monastery as well. While his mind was more than capable in its studies, his body had continued growing exponentially, and he strove to be kind to everyone, most of the friends of the monastery viewed him with either outright jealousy or fear. The monks initially had lauded his strides in the arts of reading, mathematics, and theology, but when he began to see the flaws in their doctrines, he'd quickly lost their favor, too. Only the cooks treated him with respect, and that was due to his talent for bringing fresh meat to their kitchens.

The abbot had been struck by a debilitating illness that kept him bedridden. Jon Longarm remained Arthur's only friend in the monastery. Unfortunately, the older man's duties kept him busy most of the time, and that left Arthur on his own. He didn't mind: in the woods, he could while away the hours stalking animals or lounging by the many streams that flowed between the massive fir trees. He knew the animals by sight and by the tracks they made. A tuft of hair snagged on the bark of a tree was as plain to Arthur as a painted sign. And in the isolation of the forest, he was free to practice his other passions: archery and sword craft.

Arthur was not a violent person. He didn't like hurting people, or even hunting animals, truth be told. Still, there was a feeling of self-assurance that was only available to a person who knew they could fend for themselves. In the forests, Arthur could tell which plants were edible versus those that weren't, so he often found berries and greens that he would eat on his outings. He was adept with a spear as well and could catch fish with a line and hook.

Over the previous five years, he had traveled with Jon and the priests on their regular trips to the villages that surrounded the monastery. In Arthur's mind, civilizations were just as savage as the forest, oftentimes more so. Whatever wilds he found himself in, Arthur felt that he could survive and even thrive. He was young, but smart and strong. If he had to fight, just as he had all those years ago in the dormitory at the monastery, he could.

There had been other scuffles, but none with the monks or within their walls. A few of the older boys had tried to fight Arthur early on, before his size matched or exceeded theirs, and always outside the monastery. No one wanted to be banished, the way that Cephas and Mattao had been. In those instances, Arthur used the knowledge that Jon had taught him to avoid the clumsy blows of the bullies. He would let them wear themselves out before a well-timed shove—and no more—put them on the ground. They hated him for his mercy almost as much as his strength.

Eventually, Arthur spent more and more time outside the monastery. His tutors didn't seem to mind his absence. In the mornings he trained with Jon, and in the evenings he worked beside Brother Haymore in the stables. But there were many days, and more than a few nights, when he stayed in the forest, far away from the constant striving of the more ambitious monks and the friends of the monastery, many of whom were constantly looking for a way to curry favor and get ahead.

The stag finally decided it was safe in the clearing. He moved out slowly, the big head turning from side to side, searching for any sign of danger. The wind was blowing away from the animal, toward Arthur, and it couldn't smell him. Arthur wasn't really hidden, but his dull brown clothing blended into the trees, and his face was obscured inside a baggy hood. As long as Arthur didn't make any sudden movements, the deer wouldn't notice him.

When it reached the wildflowers, the stag's heavy head

dropped toward the ground. It pulled a mouthful of the sweet flora, then looked straight at Arthur, although he hadn't moved. His left hand held his bow with an arrow nocked, while his right hand held the feathered fletching of the arrow, the tips of his fingers carefully placed on the string. Waiting was important, and timing the deer's movements was key. When the stag's head dropped to pull another bite, Arthur raised his arms a little, moving slowly. As soon as the deer looked up again, he stopped. The process of raising his arms and hands into the firing position took a few minutes, but it allowed Arthur the time to calm his heart rate and steady his breathing.

Once he had the bow high enough, he drew the arrow back. It was the fastest he had moved since the deer appeared: one steady pull bent the bowstring. The deer looked up, now aware that something was wrong. Perhaps it had heard the fibers of the wood creaking, even though Arthur couldn't hear them. Maybe it picked up the faint sound of the arrow scraping along the polished wood of the bow. It was impossible to know for sure, but whatever it was, the deer's sense of danger didn't send it dashing away.

It was too late for the stag to gain its senses. Arthur didn't hold the bow at full draw for more than a second. The bottom of his thumb, where the wide joint met the fleshy palm, touched his cheekbone. He aimed instinctively, with no thought to the actual mechanics. Mere moments later, his fingers released the bowstring with a quick flick to reduce their drag across the pads of his fingertips. The arrow shot forward and flew true, slamming into the deer before it even realized something was coming. The metal point pierced the deer's hide, stabbed through the muscle below its shoulder, and tore into the animal's heart. It jumped once, an automatic reflex to the danger, crumpling to the ground as it landed. The stag had died instantly, probably before the pain of its mortal wound even registered in the animal's mind.

Arthur breathed a long sigh. His nerves felt like they were humming. Succeeding in the hunt was a thrill, and yet it was bittersweet. He walked from his hiding place toward the clearing. Like the deer, he looked around as he moved slowly and silently through the forest. There were only a few other predators that might challenge a human to a kill —wolves roamed the forest, and bears, too—but Arthur saw no sign of any other creatures. He moved to the deer and retrieved his arrow. It was undamaged, which was a boon. Had he missed, he might have bent the shaft; worse still, had he missed the deer altogether, he would have lost the arrow in the forest. He set the arrow aside to clean later and drew his knife, the same small blade that Merlin had given him.

Arthur's jaw tightened slightly at the thought of the wizard. He had long ago stopped expecting the mysterious man to come back. If he returned—and there was certainly no guarantee that he would—wishing for it wouldn't make it happen any faster. Hunting had taught Arthur a great deal about the world. Many of the same virtues, like patience, were useful in both.

He took his time removing the organs from the deer. The liver and heart he saved, but the rest he left for scavengers. There were times when he cleaned the intestines, which he could cut, dry, and use for a variety of uses, including making arrows and bowstring. Sinew had fewer uses, so he left it behind. The rest of the animal would be used at the monastery, even its hooves. They couldn't do a lot with the bones, but the cooks would boil some of them to make broth for the abbot. The hide would be tanned, the meat would be eaten, and even the antlers would be used to make trinkets that could be sold to support the monastery. Bringing in the animals was Arthur's offering to his home.

He hoisted the deer onto his shoulder and started the long walk back to the monastery. Alone in the woods, he had the luxury of uninterrupted rumination. Much of it was taken up with a thought that had been nagging at his mind for several months. He had begun to feel a need for change, which led him to wonder how much longer he should stay at the monastery. Money wasn't an issue that was holding him there, luckily. He certainly wasn't rich, but he had enough coin to get started somewhere. More importantly, he was willing to work; the only question was what type of work would he do. Blacksmithing was possible—Arthur was certain he could get an apprenticeship somewhere and learn the trade. He didn't relish the idea of spending all day long pounding metal, but he thought he would be a good weapons maker. Time alone in the woods had given him the chance to carve several types of practice swords for himself over the years. He preferred a double-edged longsword, but the balance was tricky, and hacking and slashing wasn't really his style. Jon had taught him to move, to use an opponent's weaknesses against him, and to strike with precision. A heavy blade made fighting more difficult, as did a sword that was too heavy at the pommel.

One of the things Arthur looked forward to most was purchasing his own weapons. The abbot had allowed him to keep the knife that Merlin had given to him, but the dagger had been put away. Nor was he allowed to carry a sword, even when on trips with Jon to guard the priests as they traveled. If he took up smithing, he could forge his own weapons. The problem, on the other hand, was that most smiths spent the majority of their time making tools and utensils, not weapons. He also wanted the ability to continue to hunt on a regular basis. Perhaps instead he could be a hunter, selling the meat and hides he harvested, not to mention the other bounty that grew in the forest. Mushrooms, berries, roots—there were enough secret treasures in the wild places to provide for a man. If he was willing to work hard—and he was—there were any number of ways to earn a living.

Arthur adjusted the deer carcass across his shoulder. He didn't mind hard work, but there was something about the future that made him hesitate. Leaving would mean being truly alone. He might not be a full-fledged part of the monastery, but he had a bed and could eat his meals with the other friends, including Jon, who was the closest thing to family he had. Morning and evening prayers were times of private contemplation, and yet they were carried out within the community of people living together in the monastery. It wasn't quite home, but it did feel safe.

When he thought of home, he remembered the dream he'd had on his eleventh birthday. How that dream had stuck in his memory, he couldn't explain. Most dreams fled his mind the moment he woke up; others he shook off in just a few hours. But the high castle, the beautiful city, and the woman he had dreamed of lingered in his memory. While Arthur now struggled to remember what his mother had looked like, he could see the face of the woman in his dream any time he closed his eyes.

Just cutting wood or hammering iron wouldn't be enough to build the city of his dreams. It would be like settling for a few leaves of watercress when he was famished. Somehow, Arthur knew that learning a trade alone wouldn't fulfill him. It might satisfy him for a while, and it might even help to build the foundation of knowledge he required to do something bigger in life, but he couldn't commit to an ordinary life. It scared him to think that he was dreaming of greater things. Who was he to want anything more than an honest living, and perhaps a wife and children? At the end of the day, he was an orphan with no connections and even fewer prospects.

He came out of the forest and into view of the monastery. It was still early—midmorning, he thought. There was plenty of time for the monks to butcher the deer and roast its haunches for the evening meal. Beyond the monastery, a ship had come ashore. He was less than a dozen paces from the tree line when he noticed it. Most ships stayed out in the deeper waters when they came to the monastery, which commanded the terminus of the inlet.

When the temple bell began to clang, it wasn't the stately, rhythmic tolling that called the monastery to prayers, but a frantic, fearful clashing. Arthur knew that something was wrong. He tossed the deer from his shoulder with a single heave and slung his quiver of arrows onto his back. Part of him wanted to run to the monastery, but there were over a hundred paces of open ground between the property's short wall and the trees. He forced himself back into the cover of the forest and began to move toward the water. Soon he could see the invaders, a group of ferocious-looking warriors in thick furs carrying war axes and spears. They had square shields that were painted blue. Some were climbing the rock walls of the monastery, which offered some protection but were not true battlements, being only as tall as Arthur's shoulder and made of local stones and mortar. They would slow an enemy, but not stop them.

From within the walls, Arthur could hear the faint sounds of shouting. Someone on the inside of the wall was fighting; Arthur had no doubt it was Jon Longarm. A spear thrust sent one of the raiders toppling backward over the wall. Most of the invaders were running around the wall toward the gate. Only a few were trying to climb it, and Arthur could see that they were merely working to distract the monastery inhabitants so that the gate wouldn't be heavily defended.

With steady hands, Arthur nocked an arrow. He drew and let the arrow fly, not bothering to watch where it landed. He had already nocked a second arrow when the first took in the back a raider who was trying to get over the wall. Arthur turned, taking aim with his second shot at the man leading the charge around the wall. It was obvious to Arthur at a glance that this man wasn't in charge of the raid: he was a thin young man, not much older than Arthur, and he wore less armor than the others. The arrow that Arthur loosed arced up, then raced down, slamming into the runner just above his hip. The man fell to the ground, his momentum carrying him forward in a roll that drove the arrow deeper into his own guts. His screams made the hair on Arthur's arms stand on end.

Several of the raiders carried bows. They stopped

running and prepared to fire on Arthur. He knew in that second he had a decision to make. He could escape into the trees, perhaps picking off a few more raiders as he went, but he wouldn't stop them. This was the smart thing to do, since victory seemed unlikely at best. He guessed there were over thirty warriors in the band, whereas, other than a few older men, there were no warriors in the monastery to stop them. In all likelihood, the people Arthur had known for the last five years would be slaughtered. His other option was to charge ahead. If he was going to fight, he would need one of the raider's weapons, which meant picking off a straggler and taking his weapon. First, though, he would have to kill the archers before they killed or wounded him.

Arrows from the raiding party launched upward some-what haphazardly—the raiders clearly weren't used to firing at a distance. Arthur, with nothing better to do, had trained with his own bow until he was proficient even at maximum distance. He didn't bother moving out of the way, since he could tell the arrows would miss. Their first volley would land behind him, mostly in the trees. Arthur nocked an arrow, drew, and fired. As soon it had flown, he pulled another arrow, moving forward before he even had it posi-tioned. The first shot was aimed at one of the archers, who saw it coming and dove to the ground. Fortunately for Arthur, the arrow caught one of the raiders passing behind the archer in the thigh. The man fell, dropping his spear. That was a weapon Arthur could use.

He kept moving, stopping only to fire back at the raiders. The archers realized quickly that they were outclassed. Two hurried along with the rest of their party toward the gate, seeking the protection of the monastery wall. Another was taken in the shoulder by one of Arthur's arrows, and the fourth broke his bow. The rest of the raiders had slowed, using their shields to fend off Arthur's shots as best they could.

Using the last of his arrows, Arthur managed to hit another of the raiders. He was wounding, not killing, although that wasn't his decision: the raiders were smart enough to protect their vital organs. However, their legs were left exposed. Out of ammo, Arthur sprinted toward the fallen warriors. The spearman he had shot was sitting up, holding his leg. Arthur dashed to the fallen man's spear and snatched it up. He slung his bow over his head and shoulder so that he wouldn't lose it, then turned on the raider, who held up both hands, pleading for mercy. Arthur knew he didn't deserve it—the man had attacked priests, monks, and the unfortunates who had come into the care of the monastery. While there were stores of gold, silver, and other valuables in the monastery, these riches were devoted to the Most High. Likewise, the men who lived there engaged in service to their creator. How any man could steal from a monastery and expect to profit was beyond Arthur. The monks might not be frightening, but the deity they served was. Fighting the temptation to run the raider through, Arthur instead ran past the wounded man. It was less mercy and more the need to stop the rest of the raiders that spurred him on.

The second man he had shot was working to get the arrow out of the back of his leg as Arthur approached. It was a flesh wound, and certainly not debilitating. He heard Arthur running toward him and turned, displaying a crude but long-bladed knife that he held out threateningly. Arthur had the advantage of reach with his newfound spear, which had a long shaft, almost as tall as the sixteen-year-old. The spearhead was shaped like a leaf and spanned the length of Arthur's hand from palm to fingertips. He held the spear across his body in a defensive posture as he neared the raider. The man was screaming at him, although Arthur hardly heard the raider's curses. He slashed the spear wildly, a lame first move in their deadly dance, and the raider swayed back, easily avoiding the spear's reach. Arthur's goal was less to land the blow and more to see what he was up against in the raider, disguising his own intentions by giving the false impression that he was unskilled with the spear.

If the arrow was affecting the raider's mobility, Arthur couldn't tell. The man danced away nimbly, then lunged forward. Arthur slid to the side, avoiding the raider's dagger thrust, and kicked toward the man. The blow missed the raider, but Arthur wasn't aiming for him. Instead, his booted foot hit the arrow lodged in his enemy's leg. The raider cried out in pain and stumbled. Arthur spun the spear around and gave a quick thrust that took the man low in his ribs and dropped him. With a jerk, Arthur pulled the spear free, only stopping long enough to snatch up the dagger. It was an artless weapon: heavy, only sharpened on one side, and even slightly warped. Still, it was a weapon, and Arthur needed everything he could get.

Again pausing quickly, just long enough to slip the naked blade between his belt and hip, Arthur continued his charge. He could hear the monks inside the monastery walls, many of them yelling or screaming in panic. Suddenly, one commanding voice rang out above the frightened voices. It was Jon Longarm.

"To the gate!" he was shouting. "Defend the gate!"

Arthur spared a glance over the wall and saw several spearheads bobbing toward the gate. Jon was rallying a defense, but it wouldn't be enough. He charged forward, adding his own war cry to that of the raiders. A trio of men bringing up the rear of the raiding party heard him and stopped to raise their shields and brandish their axes. Positioned abreast as they were, they effectively blocked his way, but Arthur couldn't afford to let that stop him: he needed to cause enough damage to divert the raiders from the gate.

He leveled his spear at the man on his far right, who braced himself behind his shield, just as Arthur anticipated. At the last second, he brought the weapon up high and jumped. His boot hit the shield with enough force to knock the raider backward. As he landed, Arthur brought the spear down into the middle man's shoulder. It cut deep before the blade wedged into the man's shoulder blade and stuck fast. Arthur had felt his hunting spear vibrate in the same fashion when driving into a wild boar and knew that holding on to the weapon was a mistake, so he let it go. The middle raider dropped to his knees, howling a death cry as blood fountained upward.

The third raider, trying to take advantage of Arthur's distraction, threw his war axe through the spraying blood. Had Arthur not already been ducking so low to snatch the middle man's fallen weapon, it would have killed him. He felt the rush of air as the axe flew over his head. Perhaps it was luck, or some sort of intuition, that had led him to move when he had, but Arthur didn't stop to consider it. Warm blood sprayed the side of his face as his fingers plucked the axe from the ground where it had fallen.

He was just rising back up when the third raider crashed into him with a blue shield. Arthur felt the rough-hewn planks scraping against him as the pair dropped to the ground. It was a jarring blow, but Arthur had a good grip on the war axe, a short-handled weapon no longer than his forearm and sporting a simple blade. Arthur swung the axe around the shield, felt it strike flesh, and jerked it free. The warrior with the shield was wounded, albeit not mortally, and stumbled back. Arthur rose to his knees, but the first raider had regained his feet and was rushing forward. Arthur threw the axe at him and drew the stolen dagger. The axe hit a glancing blow on the first raider's boot, cutting a small gash in his leg, but didn't stop the man. Arthur had no choice left. He started to rise and then dove toward his attacker's feet.

The warrior had just raised his own war axe, clearly planning to batter Arthur with a charge and hack into him. He raised his shield and lowered his head just before Arthur dove to the ground. Arthur's shoulder caught the raider's legs, and he toppled face first over the younger man's back.

In the woods, Arthur had learned how to strike a killing blow; he knew how to use his knife to cut a wounded animal's throat. He didn't hesitate to follow his attacker to the ground and landed on the man's back, close enough to smell the animal stench from the dirty furs the raider wore around his shoulders. Jamming the curved knife into the man's back wasn't easy. The point on the blade was sharp, but the warp in the metal made the angle of attack awkward, and the thick fur softened the blow. Instead of ramming the blade in deep enough to kill, he only managed a painful cut. The man screamed and bucked Arthur off his back. They both rolled apart in a rush to get up, but Arthur was faster. He gained his feet and moved in with a simple, backhanded slash. The blade glanced off the man's shoulder and sliced through his neck just below the jawbone. His long beard fell as blood splashed down the front of his filthy clothes. The man was finished, but he assayed one last weak attempt to take Arthur down with him, swinging his axe forward in a chopping, overhanded strike. Arthur caught the handle of the weapon as it came down and stopped the attack before it could inflict any harm.

For a moment, the man stared at Arthur with hatred in his eyes. Then Arthur jerked the axe away, and the man fell to the ground. Arthur stuck the dagger in one side of his belt and the war axe in the other. Planting his foot on the raider's corpse, he wrenched the long spear free. Arthur was covered in blood and dirt, all the more determined to make a difference in the battle. With a cry of anger and resolution, he turned toward the gate and started running.

CHAPTER FOURTEEN

There were more than twenty raiders at the gate. Most were trying to push the wooden barricade down, but a few were climbing the short walls on either side. Inside the gate, Arthur saw a cluster of spears that took out the climbers on either side, to the sounds of screams. The battle was chaos and terror, yet Arthur felt himself coming alive in the madness.

Above the shouting, he heard the wooden gate pop as the hinges started to break loose. The raiders were nearly through. One man in a thick cloak of white fur stood behind the others, shouting at them, "Push harder! Tear the wall down!"

Running at full speed, Arthur brought the spear to his shoulder. It wasn't balanced correctly for throwing and wouldn't fly true for very far, but he hurled it anyway with all the strength and momentum he had. Somehow, the spear found its mark, hitting the man in white just under his left arm. The blade bit deep, and he staggered to the side. Arthur had just enough time to draw the war axe into his right hand and the crooked dagger in his left before he rushed behind the men at the gate.

Despite the injury to the man in white, the raiders were still focused on the gate. A group of monks were struggling to hold the wooden barricade in place. Leaning down, Arthur slashed the back of one man's leg and came up to chop down with the axe on the back of another's neck. His activity caught the attention of the group's seeming leader. The man in white fur was huge, and, notwithstanding the spear lodged in his side, he charged at Arthur with his enormous double-edged sword. With a shout of fury, the man swung it down at Arthur, who spun away. The blade hit one of his own men in the back, opening a gash down the unsuspecting warrior's flank.

Arthur chopped at the man in white with his axe, but the huge warrior brought his sword around to stop the blow. Arthur felt the sword's blade bite into the wooden axe handle before the weapon was jerked from his grasp by the raider. Fortunately for Arthur, the axe hung onto the blade, making the sword unwieldy. As Arthur moved the dagger from his left hand to his right, the man, moving faster than a person with a spear in their side should have been able to move, tried to slash at him. The tip of the blade dropped too low, and Arthur was able to jump out of reach.

The robed raider screamed, spitting blood, his eyes bulging as he charged forward to drive the sword tip straight at Arthur. The young man spun to the side in such a way that he moved closer to his assailant and grabbed the spear. With a jerk, he pulled it free in a cascade of blood and viscera. The man in white, his thick furs stained with his life's blood, roared in agony. When he turned to face Arthur again, it was clear that his wounds had caught up with him. Arthur stepped forward and drove the spear straight into his throat. The man dropped to his knees, his sword falling from his hand as Arthur pulled the spear out once more. Lifting both hands to his throat, the raider tried to save his own life, but the blood couldn't be held back. The man in white fell face first into the dirt and died there.

Arthur turned back to the gate, which was crumbling before the raiders. One was on the wall, raising his axe to throw it down into the crowd of monks below. Arthur threw the spear again. It hit the man in the back and knocked him off the wall. Glancing down, Arthur saw the sword that the man in white had dropped, a brutish, one-handed weapon. He picked it up, wrenching the axe free from the blade and hurling it toward another raider.

A few of the warriors had noticed Arthur. They turned to face their attacker, and he rushed to meet them. Perhaps it was his terrible appearance, covered in blood as well as dirt from spending the morning in the woods, that fright-ened the men, or maybe it was seeing their leader struck down; but something shook the raiders. One stepped forward, raising his axe, but Arthur anticipated such a move. He feinted to his right, then dashed to his left, sweeping the sword across the man's belly as he moved. Arthur stepped beside the warrior, whose axe had met nothing but air and whose entrails were at that moment spilling from the gaping wound in his stomach. He stood still for a few seconds while his companions stared in horror, then dropped to the ground without a sound.

The others broke and ran. Even those battling inside the broken gate heard the call for retreat and ran away. Arthur, however, wasn't content to let them regroup. He stabbed one fleeing raider so that the sword's angled tip bit deep into the man's side. With a horrible wail, the man dropped to his knees. Arthur spun around and hit the raider with all his strength in a savage chop that severed the head. The grisly trophy flew through the air and landed in the dirt. It rolled across the ground and came to a rest beside the monastery wall.

Arthur had no time to admire his handiwork: he was too busy chasing the fleeing raiders. The disparity in numbers was no longer a concern with the crude sword in his hand. For it was not well made—even in the heat of battle, Arthur could see the nicks in the edge of the blade. Its design, however, allowed it to cut deep and to avoid getting stuck in the sucking flesh of wounds, making it a proficient killing tool. Arthur, unencumbered by heavy furs and fit from running every day around the perimeter of the monastery, easily kept pace with the raiders. Most didn't try to fight. They were panicked, their only thought escape.

Aiming for their legs, Arthur severed several hamstrings, leaving the raiders helpless on the ground with gaping wounds in the backs of their thighs. One tripped, and Arthur slowed down long enough to stab the man in his back as he ran past. Only a handful made it to their ship. They threw themselves into the beached vessel, heaving it off the sand and climbing in like frightened children. Arthur wanted to follow them—to kill every last one who had dared attack the monastery—but he stopped at the water's edge.

"Don't come back," Arthur shouted. "Don't *ever* come back!"

He watched them for a few minutes, somewhat bitter that they were able to get four oars working. When he turned back to Byth El, there were several monks watching him with fear on their faces—fear of the raiders and also fear of him. Arthur ignored them and started back around the stone wall. He was tired now, the ebb of the seemingly boundless energy he'd funneled into the fight leaving him weak and shaky. Around the wall of the monastery's western side lay a trail of bodies. Most were still alive but too hurt to get away; a few were attempting to crawl. The sight was gruesome, and the sounds of their dying moans was enough to make Arthur want to finish them off. He had heard wounded animals in the forest yelping their final calls, but the raiders sounded worse than any animal. Some were even crying for their mothers. When Arthur looked at the sword still clutched in his hand, covered with blood and gore, he thought he might be sick.

"Arthur!" a young boy shouted. He had climbed the wall and was waving one arm at him. "Arthur, come quick! Jon's been hurt. He's asking for you."

Fear squeezed Arthur's chest. It was like he had been bound in rope, and he couldn't seem to draw a breath. He started running, but his legs felt heavy. As he passed the wounded bodies of the raiders, those that saw him cowered and covered their heads, expecting him to strike a killing blow, the fight gone from their hearts. Arthur, however, was no longer interested in the raiders. Already, he was regretting the entire battle and felt a deep sense of guilt about killing people. Now, his attention was entirely focused on reaching his mentor's side.

When Arthur finally made it back to the front gates, he was met with the sight of more carnage. The huge raider in white fur lay face down in a puddle of his own blood, already beset by buzzing flies. The gate was in pieces, and even some of the stone wall had been broken down. There were several bodies lying just inside the gate. Most were raiders, but one was familiar.

A group of monks was gathered around Jon Longarm. They moved back as Arthur approached. He ignored the looks of fear and loathing on many of their faces, knowing that if not for him and the grisly work he'd done, they would all be dead. He had killed over ten men and wounded more, in exchange for the safety of dozens of monks, priests, and innocent friends of the monastery. Their home would have been in shambles, most likely burned; the survivors would have been destitute. Arthur was certain of that, especially when he saw his best friend and mentor on the ground. Arthur's eyes flooded with tears when he saw the bloody gash in Jon's side. The older man's skin, where it wasn't smeared with blood, was deadly pale.

Arthur bent down, scrambling for something he might do to save Jon, but he was helpless. There was nothing he hated more than this feeling of being unable to stop the terrible inevitable. And yet, when he looked into Jon's eyes, he knew that his friend was going to die.

"Arthur," Jon said, his voice so weak it was nearly a whisper.

"I'm here," Arthur replied, his own voice croaking in his throat.

"Did you stop them?"

"I did. They won't be back."

"Good, good," Jon said, a spasm of pain twisting his features. "The monastery is safe, praise the Most High. You did...well...my son."

The words felt like burning coals on Arthur's heart, searing their way into him. He bent his head and wept.

"Are you...hurt?" Jon was struggling to talk.

Arthur shook his head. "I'm fine, Jon."

"Good. Don't be...sad...for me."

"Oh, Jon, please don't die," Arthur begged, feeling like the little boy on the cart being carried away from Lontown all over again, with no control over his own life.

"I'm getting...what I...want," Jon rasped. "I've waited...a long time...to see...my family...again."

Arthur nodded. He didn't know what to say. Jon had never spoken of his life before coming to the monastery. Arthur knew something terrible had happened, but never the details.

"I had...two little...girls, Arthur. Did...you know...that?"

"No, Jon, I didn't."

"Always wanted...a son...though..." he added, lifting a trembling hand that was stained with blood.

Arthur took Jon's hand and gripped it hard in both of his. Tears were running down his face, leaving tracks in the blood and dirt on his cheeks. He could feel his friend slipping away, and Arthur tried desperately to hold on to him.

"You...have been...a son to me," Jon said. "And I am... proud...of you."

"I love you, Jon," Arthur whispered.

He couldn't tell if his mentor heard him. Jon's eyes lost focus and he breathed out a gurgling wheeze. And with barely more than a sound, Jon Longarm died.

CHAPTER FIFTEEN

A rthur rose slowly to his feet. He felt hollow inside; and despite the group of monks, priests, and friends of the monastery gathered in a solemn crowd just beyond the carnage at the gate, he felt completely alone in the world.

"Let's move him," Brother Haymore said. "I'll see to the body."

"We'll dig his grave." A trio of old men stepped forward.

"I'll help," Arthur volunteered, moving toward them.

He was immediately blocked by a priest with a fringe of gray hair ringing his bald head around his ears. There was a familiar look of disgust on his face. Arthur recognized him, since their paths had crossed occasionally since their first meeting many years ago on the cart: it was Brother Bryun, the same drunken priest who had taken Cryslov's silver and made himself sick on ale during the journey from Lontown when Arthur was just a boy.

"No, you'll not enter this holy place looking like that," Bryun said.

Despite his weakness for ale and his natural tendency toward laziness, Bryun was a charismatic preacher and had risen in prominence within the monastery as Abbot Gryald's health declined. Arthur expected him to be named the new head of the Byth El monastery one day and was just as certain that his first decision after becoming abbot would be to expel Arthur.

"I just saved this monastery," Arthur said, his anger sending the hot acid from his stomach up the back of his throat. "Jon died defending it. I won't let you keep me from seeing that he is buried properly."

A shadow of fear crossed Bryun's eyes. The tense moment was saved by one of the old men.

"We'll get the tools, Arthur."

"And meet you in the graveyard," another added.

"If you want to come back in here, you will clean yourself up properly," Bryun ordered. "Show some respect for the Most High, or your time here will be short."

Arthur knew his time at the monastery was not just short—it was over. He couldn't stay without Jon. In fact, he didn't want to stay. After he saw that his friend was buried, he could move on. There was nothing holding him back anymore.

"I understand," Arthur said.

"All right, let's move these bodies," Bryun said to the rest of the crowd, obviously emboldened by Arthur's acceptance of his demands. There was no doubt that he loved being able to give orders like the lord of a manor. "Send for the healers. Tell them to bring something for the wounded.

I don't want to listen to their groaning and weeping all night."

Arthur left the gate and walked slowly back toward the woods. He found the stag he had killed earlier in the day where he had dropped it. The day had been cool, and there was still time to get the meat harvested from the animal, his parting gift to the Byth El community. He carried it back to the monastery and handed it off to a group of young boys. One, a young lad with dark hair and big eyes, looked at Arthur, who had the raider's sword in his belt, with big, shining eyes that were full of admiration. It was not what the young man expected, as most of the people in the monastery either feared or resented him. With some regret, Arthur realized he didn't even know the boy's name.

The old men returned to the gate with shovels and picks. Arthur took the heavier tools and followed them to the graveyard. The oldest among them marked out the grave, using a shovel to outline where they should dig.

"Jon was tall," he said. "Let's give him plenty of room."

Arthur used the pick and churned up the soil, then stood back while the others shoveled it out. They went back and forth until the grave was finished. Once the ground was ready for Jon, they moved out of the graveyard and into a space between the monastery and the sea. In the distance, Arthur could still see the ship. It had a square sail and was moving slowly away. He hoped the survivors would tell about the horrors of attacking the monastery; it might keep the place safe for a few years.

They dug a mass grave in the loamy soil. Even at high tide, the water didn't reach the monastery, but the ground between the stone wall and the beach was soft. It made digging the grave easy enough, although Arthur knew the bodies wouldn't last long in the damp earth.

When they finished digging, Arthur stripped off his filthy clothes and bathed in the sea. With the help of the salty seawater, he scrubbed the thick wool pants and shirt with sand until the bloodstains came out. By the time he finished, the monks were carrying the dead raiders to the mass grave and dumping the bodies. Arthur rammed the sword he had taken from their leader into the ground to mark the grave. He didn't want the poorly made weapon— he didn't want anything to remind him of the men he had killed or the day his closest friend had died.

At the monastery, he donned the only other set of civilian clothes he had. He had never liked the baggy garb of the monks: the robes were too easily tangled when moving quickly, and Arthur was not the type to take things slowly. He went to the stables, where he had long ago learned he could keep his meager possessions without worry that someone would try to take them. In preparation to depart, Arthur tucked his knife into his belt and slung a satchel with his farrier's tools and extra arrowheads, bowstring, and feathers for fletching over one shoulder.

"I had a feeling you'd be here," a sad and quiet voice said.

Arthur turned and found Brother Haymore helping Abbot Gryald into the barn.

"I'll be leaving once Jon's buried," Arthur said.

"You don't have to," Gryald said. "Without Jon, we need you more than ever."

Arthur looked down, smiling tightly. "I don't think many others feel the way you do. It's best if I go now."

The abbot leaned against a post and waved Haymore

forward. "These things belonged to Jon. He told me once that if anything ever happened to him, he wanted you to have them."

Haymore held out a fine-looking cloak of wool that was lined with fox fur and held a pouch of coins. Arthur took the cloak, but not the money.

"He would want the monastery to have his coin," Arthur said.

"He already gave to us, in both his money and his time. He earned his keep and more," Abbot Gryald said. "You both have. I've been told that if you hadn't intervened, we would have been overrun."

"I did what anyone would have done," Arthur said, pulling the cloak around his shoulders.

"That's not true, Arthur. You were able to do more than anyone else here," Gryald said. "I couldn't have stopped them. Jon died trying to hold the gate closed. The Most High gave you the strength and the courage to fend off the attackers."

"It is so," Haymore said.

"I will not ask you to stay again," Gryald said. "This is not a life for everyone, and no man should take the vows unless they do so with a free heart. But I give you the opportunity, Arthur. Or should I say, Artici?"

Arthur hadn't thought much about the name he had been given by Merlin or the story that the wizard had told of his real father. He had shared it once with the Abbot not long after Merlin had given it to him as he struggled to understand what it really meant. Since then, it had become like a fairy tale to him, or perhaps a dream. Nothing had changed with the telling, and Merlin was long gone.

"I thank you, Abbot," Arthur said. "But it is time for me to leave."

"I understand. It is always my hope that those unfortunate souls who come here will find the strength to stand on their own again. I implore you to remember what you have learned here when you depart. You see, this life is fleeting. It is like the dew on the grass: it will pass away with the rising of the sun. One moment we are here, and the next we are gone. Only our deeds will remain. You are a man of integrity, Arthur—never lose that. Live justly, embrace mercy, and walk humbly with the Most High."

"I will do my best," Arthur said.

"That is all any of us can do," the abbot said. "Now, when Merlin returns, where can I tell him you have gone?"

"I don't know." Arthur doubted that this would ever come to pass. "For now, I'm going west."

"West it is," the abbot repeated, his strength clearly starting to fade. "I have said my farewell to Jon Longarm, and I bid you the same, Arthur. May the blessing and favor of the Most High rest on you. Brother Haymore, help me back to my chambers. This has been a trying day indeed."

Arthur watched them go before taking a deep breath. It was time; but there was another farewell to be made. He stopped by a white horse with a black star on its forehead on his way out of the barn, his very favorite steed.

"So long, my friend," Arthur told the horse. "I shall miss you."

The horse nickered and bobbed its head. Arthur rubbed its nose and then left the barn forever.

CHAPTER SIXTEEN

Arthur collected his other belongings from the shelf in the kitchen where Jon had thought it best to keep them. The fine dagger would have been handy when Arthur was defending the monastery, he thought glumly. He checked inside the small coin pouch and found the small scrap of vellum that had his name written on it. The cloak that Jon had bequeathed to Arthur had a hidden pocket on the inside, and Arthur slipped the pouch into it. He tucked the dagger into his belt at the small of his back, where no one would see it. There was also a traveler's pack on the shelf. Inside was a small map of Atlandia and a weatherproof cloak that Arthur had only used when escorting the priests with Jon.

He took it all with him, the meager belongings of a poor young man about to start his life. Outside, the monks, priests, and friends of the monastery were gathering around a wooden litter, where Jon's body had been wrapped in a burial cloth, leaving only his face visible. When Arthur approached his mentor, tears stung his eyes.

"His cloak looks good on you," Brother Haymore said.

"He was generous, even in death," answered Arthur.

They carried the litter out of the monastery to the graveyard and settled the body, still on the litter, into the grave. One of the monks gave a eulogy, but Arthur didn't really listen, instead remembering the kindness of the man who had helped him onto the back of a wagon when Arthur was just a boy who had lost his mother. Never having known his own father, Arthur let himself grieve for the father he'd found in Jon. The man had been kind and imparted his wisdom freely; Arthur also had to admit that he was bitter and never happy. Even when he was deep into his cups, he didn't laugh or sing. Instead, Jon was a brooder. Whatever had happened to his family long before had left an open wound that never healed, not even in the peaceful setting of the monastery.

When the funeral was over, Arthur stayed to watch the old men throw dirt down on Jon's body. His face had been covered before they lowered him down into the dark hole in the ground. It all gave Arthur a feeling of bleak fear. He believed in the Most High and the promised life for the faithful that passed on, yet he felt a sickly gnawing deep in the pit of his stomach. He couldn't shake the knowledge that one day he too would be entombed in the dirt with only worms and mold for company, crushed by the weight of the earth on top of him.

He also couldn't shake the horror of what had transpired that day, and by his own hand. Even though the wounded raiders had been tended to by the merciful monks, Arthur could still see in his mind's eye the blood gushing from their bodies and hear their wails of agony. He knew the memories would haunt his dreams, but in the pain of losing Jon, suffering seemed appropriate. Always in the past, when he imagined leaving the monastery, he had thought it would be a joyful, exciting time. Instead, it was turning out to be wretched, miserable experience that he knew he would never be able to forget.

Arthur walked back to the gate, where he had left his bow, quiver, and a few arrows that had been recovered after the battle. He would need to make more, but the few he had would keep him supplied for a while. Once he gathered his few possessions, he gave the monastery one last look, considering his options. Where to now? It was tempting to return to Lontown and see the place where his mother was buried. But he knew someone else lived in their cottage, and he didn't want to see that, nor think about the people who had rushed to take advantage of her death. Instead, he would go west, into the wilderness. He would explore at his leisure and see what life brought him.

Across the open yard of well-trimmed grass, bushes, flowers, and paths made from pebbles rounded by the rolling waves on the beach, Arthur caught sight of Brother Haymore leading the white-faced horse named Thunder toward him, lifting a hand as he did so. It was his way of asking Arthur to wait: the gentle, hunchbacked monk didn't like raising his voice. Pausing just beside the gate, which had been moved outside the short wall that surrounded the monastery grounds, Arthur eyed the monks repairing the walls around the wooden posts that had held the gate in place. Some of the stones had been knocked loose, both from the general melee of the battle and from the raiders climbing over the wall. To mend it, the monks had mixed a mortar of clay, sand, water, and ash and were spackling the pasty substance on thickly before stacking up the fallen stones. Others were bringing out more wood and tools to repair the gate itself. The monks were nothing if not productive.

"Arthur," Brother Haymore greeted him as he approached with the horse. It was saddled and had a leather bag hanging behind it. "Abbot Gryald told me to gift you this horse."

"The abbot wants me to have him?" Arthur asked incredulously, noticing Brother Bryun across the yard, staring balefully at him.

"In truth, he may have done it to spite Brother Bryun. But it makes no difference: the horse and saddle are yours now. Do you still have the tools to care for him?"

"I do," Arthur said. "I'll look after him just as you taught me."

"Good," Brother Haymore said. "Do not forget us."

"Never," Arthur promised, although, in truth, he now felt that there was little he would remember about the monastery with fondness.

Brother Haymore nodded, then lumbered away. There was nothing else holding Arthur to the monastery. It had been a place to eat and sleep, to study and work—but despite the abundance of prayer and the monks' devotion to the Most High, there was very little love there. Even Haymore seemed to care more for the animals than for the humans that worked in the barn with him.

Arthur climbed up into the saddle in one smooth,

graceful motion without bothering to look back again. Instead, he nudged the horse with his heels and clucked his tongue. Thunder obediently headed toward the forest.

He only rode for a short way into the forest before getting down and leading the horse. On the ground, most of the trees branches cleared his head, but astride Thunder, Arthur kept having to duck to avoid the limbs. It was easier to walk. He made his way to a little glen near a stream where he often camped. Little preparation was required: already, he had built a simple shelter and kept a ring of rocks for a fire. With these out of the way, Arthur settled in quickly.

That night, Arthur built the fire up, hobbled Thunder, and spread his blanket on a bed of evergreen boughs. The pouches behind the saddle proved to be full of bread and cheese. Arthur ate a little but didn't have much of an appetite. Jon wouldn't have believed it; he had always teased Arthur about how much food the younger man ate. Given the events of the day, it felt wrong to think of enjoying anything that night.

Eventually, Arthur slept in fitful bouts, his dreams haunted by the men he had wounded and killed. The memory of how the spear felt as he drove it hard into a man's body kept coming back to him, and the solid impact of the raider's sword against human legs made him squirm. The bed of branches wasn't very soft, and whenever a particularly stiff limb poked him, he imagined it was an arrow or dagger. When the morning came, he was exhausted but thankful. After saddling Thunder and checking his hooves, Arthur packed his supplies, leaving the small shelter. He wouldn't need the little lean-to anymore, but someone else might.

The pair pushed on, going farther into the woods than he had ever been before. Before long, he found a cluster of mushrooms that he picked for an evening meal, and as he wandered through the forest, he gathered different edible greens. In the afternoon, he spotted a porcupine and took it down with his bow and arrow. After a lean meal the previous day, Arthur found that he was famished, and he decided it was time to stop and make camp.

Although a bit prickly to dress, he soon had the porcupine cooking in a little pot over the fire he built. He rendered some of the fat, stirring first the mushrooms into it and then the greens. With the bread and cheese from the monastery, it made a pleasant little feast that he ate with enjoyment. Thunder grazed nearby as Arthur prepared for another long night by the fire. He was gazing blankly into the flames, thinking of Jon, when a flutter of wings shook him from his reverie.

"Well, isn't this nice," Merlin said. "You've a nice warm fire going. Any food left?"

"Where did you come from?" Arthur yelped, unable to hide the shock in his voice.

"Most recently, I was in Ava. It's a long, long flight, and I'm hungry. Do you have food?"

Arthur had cut some of the lean parts of the porcupine meat into strips and hung them over the fire, letting the smoke penetrate the muscle fibers to preserve the food. He had planned to eat it the following day, but he pulled it off for Merlin, along with some of the bread and cheese from the monastery. The wizard ate ravenously. He looked tired, his face drawn; his beard was longer and mostly gray.

"Jon Longarm is dead," Arthur said, leaving out the *"Do you even care?"* that he felt like tagging on at the end.

"Yes, I saw his grave," Merlin said. "It's a shame. He was a good man."

"'A good man?' That's it?" Arthur growled. "He was my friend, and the only person who stood by me no matter what."

Merlin leaned back. He was nestled between the fire and a fallen log, his dirty robes gathered around him like a nest. He looked at Arthur with penetrating eyes.

"Do you think I had something to do with his death?"

"I think you had very little to do with his life," Arthur shot back. "Jon was killed because the monastery was attacked—and of course you show up acting like nothing happened."

"I saw the abbot," Merlin said. "He is dying; is that my fault as well? I can't save the whole world, Arthur, and neither can you. We can't foster childish thinking if we're going to work together."

"Work together?" Arthur repeated angrily. "What are you talking about? I'm not working with you or anyone. Just leave me alone."

He got up and walked away from the fire, although not far. He had already cut branches for a bed and laid out his blanket. The saddle made an excellent pillow, and he didn't want the wizard to make use of it.

"That's a fine horse," Merlin said, as if nothing cross had happened.

"Thunder," Arthur said. "His name is Thunder."

"Fitting," Merlin replied, his mouth full of food. "May I ask you a question, Arthur?"

The young man gave no reply. He didn't want to engage with the wizard. Merlin was tricky: it seemed that he was never around when he could really be of use, and while he had been generous with Arthur on his eleventh birthday, he had left the young boy with more questions than answers. In the five years since, Arthur had become more independent and less trusting.

He returned to the fire. "Are you staying?" Arthur asked.

"Staying here?" Merlin asked, looking around.

"Staying with me."

"I should think so," Merlin said.

Arthur huffed impatiently. "What do you want from me?"

"I want to help you," Merlin said. "Do you remember your dream? The sparkling city? I want to help you build it."

"And what if I just want to be left alone to find my own way?"

"Then I'll wait," Merlin said.

Arthur didn't like the answer, but he respected it. He sat back down at the fire and nodded his head.

"Go ahead," he said. "Ask your question."

Merlin asked no question but instead continued, "The abbot told me about your part in the attack. He claimed you killed over half of the raiders all by yourself."

"That isn't really true." Almost unconsciously, Arthur shuddered a bit at the memory.

"Oh, don't be modest. You have a talent for war. That may be useful. There have been rumors of war in the west for a long time. I believe that now it has started in earnest."

"What does that have to do with me?" Arthur asked.

Merlin looked at Arthur with a sudden keenness and intensity. His eyes flashed a golden color that held something new, something different, within it, long enough to be noticed but not long enough that Arthur was sure of what he saw.

"Maybe everything," Merlin said.

CHAPTER SEVENTEEN

"What do you know of the Atals?"

"Only what the monks taught," Arthur said. "I'm not even sure if I believe them."

"I will tell you their story," Merlin said. "Perhaps the monks did know it and tell it well—I cannot say. They worship the same creator, but human understanding is murky at best. We do not have reliable memories.

"The Bright Ones are Celestial beings, the Most High's first creations. After this world was made, they saw that it was good and desired to dwell here."

"They left the heavenly realms for this?" Arthur interjected, gesturing at their surroundings somewhat skeptically.

"Yes. My experience is that many long for something other than what they have," Merlin said. "Some are only happy if they wander and discover new places. Perhaps their reasoning was along those lines. Or perhaps, as some have postulated, they found humans to be so enticing that they gave up their place in the heavenly realms to join us here."

"It's a bit hard to believe," Arthur said.

"That's because you're young, Artici. You haven't experienced love. It is a singularly wonderful thing. I was in love once, but that is another story. Whatever their reason, the Bright Ones came and carved out a home for themselves at the far western edge of this world. They look very like us, only they are perfect. The Atals have no flaws, no sickness; they do not grow old or die."

"They're immortals?"

"Some would say so," Merlin said. "But they can be hurt and even killed. They are just as frail as humans when faced with the sword."

"Do they wield magic, like you?"

"They do, but not like me," Merlin said. "I have mastered magic that allows me to control matter, like this fire."

He raised a hand, and a tongue of flame jumped from the campfire to his palm. It flickered there, turning blue, then green, and finally back to yellow, before jumping back to the campfire. Arthur tried to seem indifferent, but he had to admit the trick was impressive.

"The Atals call it enchantment, because I take control of something with magic," Merlin explained. "But that is just one form of the craft—there are many more. I can achieve some feats in other fields, but I have only the one true skill. The Atals, on the other hand, can easily wield it all. They can even pass into the heavenly realms at will. I studied with them for years, and I still don't have a full grasp of their capabilities. Needless to say, they are powerful."

"Can you enchant people?" Arthur asked. "Can you make a person do what you want with magic?"

"All magic comes from the Most High," Merlin said, "and all magic has the capacity for good and for evil. To take control of another sentient creature and bend it to one's will is possible, but it is a perversion of magic. The Most High created people with the capacity to choose. Some call it free will. It is a divine right, and to take that from someone is the darkest form of magic."

"So you don't enchant people?" Arthur said.

"Never," Merlin said sternly.

"All right—I just wanted to be sure," Arthur said.

He felt guilty for insulting the wizard, but at the same time, he needed to know, a compulsion that often beset him. Jon had taught Arthur that when he had this urge, it was best to come right out and ask any questions he had.

"When humans came to Atlandia, it wasn't long until the Atals took some as their mates," Merlin went on, his gaze still holding Arthur's. "The children who resulted from these unions were neither Atal nor human."

"The Farkians," Arthur guessed.

"Not entirely—not all of the children were evil. But these offspring did have powers to varying degrees, and it wasn't long until some began to resent the abilities of the Atals. Fighting grew more and more common. The Atal-human hybrids were not immortal, and when they turned on their forebears, they did so with murderous intent. The Atals have no kings, nor any other rulers, but they began as one to banish the heirs of their mortal affairs. Their offspring left Alal and moved south, founding their own realm. The Farkians have ever sought to replicate the power of the Atals. Their efforts, in most cases, have been dark shadows of the magic their forebears possess.

"Magic, Arthur, is intended to be used to create. You will see the cities of the Atals, I'm sure, and understand better then. They have created wondrous places. With their powers, they can heal, grow, and more. Some claim that all creative works that the common folk have developed originated with the Celestials. This, I think, is a misestimation. Even the Atals answer to a higher power: the core of their magical abilities springs from the Most High, who created the entire world. So too is our own creativity less a mere a reflection of the Atals and more dependent on the ultimate source. Music, poetry, painting, carving—it is mankind's attempt to imitate his creator."

"What does any of this have to do with me?" Arthur asked.

"The Farkians have failed to replicate the power of the Atals. I believe they will instead try to take it from them."

"*Take* magic?" Arthur said. "Is that even possible?"

"It is, and I believe it would have deadly consequences," Merlin said. "Many Farkians hate the Atals. They will destroy them all if given the chance."

"I still don't see what that has to do with me," Arthur insisted.

"I told you who your father was on your eleventh birthday," Merlin responded.

"You told me what he was," Arthur corrected.

"Yes—your father was an Atal. Their mating with humans has become rare. It isn't forbidden, but the consequences in many cases have proven to be dire. Most of the Celestial folk have chosen not to continue their relations with humans. But I have no doubt that you have Atalian blood in your veins—I have felt it. With a little help, we shall discover how deep and strong those roots inside you are. The first step is finding your father."

"Stop," Arthur interrupted, dropping a few more dead branches onto the fire. "This is ridiculous. Whoever my father may or may not be, I won't waste my life chasing him down. He had every chance to come to my mother. He didn't because he didn't want to. There was probably some shame in what they did, if what you're saying about the Atals and the Farkians is true. The last thing I want to do is go to another place where I'll be seen as some kind of abomination. No, I'll stay here."

"Here? You aren't anywhere. Why would you stay here?"

"Because here I know what to do. I know how to find food and water, how to make a shelter, and how to make fire. The forest has everything I need."

"It doesn't have people," Merlin pointed out.

"Even better. It turns out most people don't like me," Arthur said bitterly.

Merlin waved that thought away dismissively. "Don't judge the world by the people you knew in the monastery. It takes a certain type of person to live a life devoted to the Most High. Some have a great love for their creator, but most others have demons in their lives from which they are trying to escape. Abbot Gryald understood that many were jealous of you."

"Odd that he did nothing to help me," Arthur said.

He laid back against the saddle and looked up at the stars through the branches overhead. Pulling Jon's cloak tighter around his shoulders, he tried to let the tension in his body go. For a long time, he had imagined leaving the monastery and what he might do when he was out in the world. Never in his wildest dreams had he considered going in search of his father. While he didn't want Merlin to be right, he couldn't deny that the idea intrigued him.

"Facing adversity is something we must all learn to do," Merlin said. "From what I've heard, you will rise to the occasion when it is needed."

"I had no choice," Arthur said.

"We always have a choice," Merlin said. "Have you ever seen a tree growing from the side of a cliff?"

Arthur had, although some part of him didn't want to admit it. He missed Jon, missed his mother, and couldn't understand why the only person in his life he couldn't seem to lose was Merlin, a wizard who spoke in puzzles. Arthur found that he didn't mind the company, but Merlin spoke as if they were close friends, when in fact Arthur hardly knew Merlin at all.

"I guess," Arthur finally said.

"Those trees sprout from a cliff, where there is hardly any soil, yet somehow they thrive. They have faced adversity and could have crumbled, but instead they choose to live. What will you choose, Arthur? Will you grow, or will you shrivel? Whatever you may feel now, we do all have a choice. Remember, free will is a divine right."

Arthur didn't answer and closed his eyes. While he accepted the company, he didn't always like talking with Merlin: the wizard was full of riddles and word games. Part of him wished that Merlin would just go away—the other part feared that he would.

"I suppose you've decided to go to sleep," Merlin said. "I shall join you."

Arthur waited a few minutes before looking across the fire to where Merlin sat. He didn't lie down or cut himself a bed of evergreen boughs. Instead, he curled up in his voluminous robes and slept.

For a long time, Arthur lay still, listening to the crackle of the fire, the wind whispering through the trees, and the steady breathing of his guest. He was tired, but sleep wasn't going to come easily to Arthur. His mind had been filled with a possibility that he had never considered. What if his father was alive? What if they could find him? What good would it do to Arthur anyway? He was a capable woodsman and as strong as most grown men. He had no need for a father, yet the possibility that his father might be found left Arthur with an intense ache.

He wrestled with the decision for hours before arriving at a conclusion. The moment he settled in his mind what he would do, he drifted immediately to sleep, finally at peace with his choice. Finding his father might be impossible, but Arthur would at least know that he had tried.

Just like the last night he had spent with Merlin the wizard, Arthur dreamed again of the beautiful city, the high castle, and the mysterious woman, more vividly than he had ever dreamed before. It was almost realer than life itself: he could feel the stone of the parapet he leaned on under his hands and the warm embrace of the woman. The tinge of fear at the darkness on the horizon stayed with Arthur even after he woke up.

"Tea?" Merlin asked when Arthur opened his eyes.

The sky above them was soft pink. The birds were

singing loudly in the trees, and nearby, Thunder nickered softly.

"Sure," Arthur said.

"You've made a decision, I'd wager." It was hardly a question.

"What makes you say that?"

"You were sleeping," the wizard pointed out. "More often than not, a person has to settle in their mind what they want before they can sleep."

Arthur got to his feet, stretching his muscles and rubbing the sleep from his eyes. He shrugged as he took the cup of tea that Merlin held out.

"I don't have anything better to do," Arthur said.

"Than what?"

"Than go with you, riddler."

Merlin frowned. "I thought I was being straightforward enough."

"Ha!" Arthur snorted. "Don't play games with me. You like to remain mysterious—Jon told me that much."

"He was insightful," Merlin said with a slight smile. "But I'm not trying to deceive you. I sometimes struggle to make my meaning clear."

"Then let me make sure I have it: we'll be going west? To find my father?"

"Into Atal, yes," Merlin affirmed.

"Then I'll go," Arthur said. "With you, I mean."

"Very good," Merlin said. "You won't regret it."

Arthur hoped that he wouldn't, but he had his doubts. What if they found his father and he didn't want anything to do with Arthur? Or what if they found him, and he wasn't an Atal? Would Merlin still want to travel with him? Arthur didn't know. What he did know was that he had a purpose, which felt better than roaming aimlessly.

He took a long pull from his water skin and walked over to Thunder. The horse pushed his head onto Arthur's shoulder. He wrapped his arm under the horse's head and rubbed the broad jaw.

"What say you, Thunder? Are you ready for an adventure?"

The horse lifted his head and neighed.

"That settles it," Arthur said. "We're in."

"Then we must move—there is no time to waste," Merlin ordered. "We have a long journey ahead."

CHAPTER EIGHTEEN

"I s that all?" the woman asked.

"We have no other captives," General Haylek said.

The general was a huge man, his muscles magically enlarged to such proportions that his head seemed too small for the gargantuan body. His black hair was greasy, and his pointed teeth were too large for his thin lips to hide. He wore a heavy curved sword on a belt around his waist and little else—only a vest laced together with leather thongs over his massive chest—despite the cold wind blowing in off the ocean.

"I need more," she said.

"Then we shall find them," the general said. "I'll prepare a hunting party now."

"No," she said. "The humans aren't strong enough. I need Celestials."

"That is a different matter," General Haylek said. "They have repulsed our raids."

"Perhaps it is time for more than raids," the woman said.

Unlike Haylek, she was thin and rather plain. Her blond hair had a reddish tint against her milky pale skin. She wore a fur-trimmed gown that clung to her body, accentuating her exceptionally thin frame. The bones in her shoulders and around her neck stood out as if she were starved. In contrast to her sharp appearance, she moved with grace and swiftness. With a light step, she crossed the room and lifted a crystal goblet filled with dark red wine. After taking a drink, the wine colored her lips, and her eyes flared golden for a moment.

"We can't risk all-out war," General Haylek insisted. "We aren't ready."

"They are powerful, I'll concede that," the woman said. "Still, we have the advantage in numbers. Besides, they don't know war. Our people have spread across the world, learning all there is to know about battle."

"Not enough have returned."

"You cannot wait forever, General. What we're doing is too important."

"I concur, but if we act too quickly, we might lose too many fighters. Once we begin, we cannot stop until we have killed them all."

"Are you saying that we don't have the strength?" the woman asked.

"No, my queen—only that if we are weakened by the battle, we will be vulnerable."

"Vulnerable to whom? The humans? They can do nothing, fools as they are."

"But they outnumber us."

"They can't stop fighting among themselves long enough

to be a threat," she retorted. "Believe me, they are weak and easily frightened. One show of power is enough to send them into a panic."

"If you are certain." General Haylek was obviously not convinced.

"I don't need them all—just a few. I'm close to solving this riddle, General. When I do, no one will stand in our way, not even the Celestials."

"Then I will find some for you," he said, bowing before her. His body was so big that he could hardly bend, and his bow was stiff and clumsy.

"Good. Get me what I need, and your reward will be great."

"As you wish." Haylek turned and lumbered from her chamber.

The woman looked out across the city of LóArc from her fortress, a tall, dark monolith that dominated the city. Below, in their homes made of stone and timber, her people went to and fro. They were aware of her, but only a handful had actually seen their queen; they might not have liked what there was to see.

Mora ap'Drayd was a necromancer with immense power over the dead and practiced the art of forging new life forms. She couldn't yet summon life from nothing, but she could take it from one being and transfer it another, or create revenants of the dead with souls she captured. Her tower was full of her experiments, creatures cobbled together from the human slaves her raiders captured. Many had animal features, and others multiple limbs. She could give them life, but the humans were weak. Few could process the change without going mad. Those that had died were forever altered by her power, which held them in complete sway as mindless servants with no will or initiative. They were useful, but they had to stay in close proximity to her at all times. For what she hoped to accomplish, Mora needed powerful beings who could adapt to the changes she made in them and carry out her commands across great distances. Once she perfected her dark designs, she would conquer not just Farkia, but also Alal, and the human realms too. She would build such strength that no one could stop her. From each fallen army, she would raise new soldiers, each with but one aim: to fulfill her every desire.

She leaned against the wall, still looking out across the city. It was a filthy mire, the streets littered with sewage. Alas, her followers were not powerful. Most were several generations removed from their Celestial forebears. Still, they all had a spark of magic, and they were united in the desire to destroy the Atals. Mora had no doubt that it would happen. Unlike the Celestials, the Farkians had grown in strength. They worked diligently to hone their power, driven by the singular belief that the Atals held secrets that would give them immortality.

Deep inside, Mora harbored the fear that they might be wrong. What if immortality wasn't a power to be learned and adapted, the way she taken her magical skills and developed them to fit her needs? It wasn't a pleasant thought, and it fueled her determination ever more. If she couldn't live forever as the ruler of the world, then she would watch it burn.

After indulging her machinations for a few moments, she returned to her table, a large slab of obsidian. She took her goblet and swallowed a gulp of the dark red liquid. It burned down her throat and spread heat through her limbs. She felt the magic inside her flare with a sudden brightness, and she turned to the wooden table where her current creation lay. It was a man, stripped and lashed to the table. A heavy blanket stitched with silver thread in familiar designs covered the man from his ribs to his knees. The change came at the shoulders. From the collarbones upward, the man's head was missing, and the shaggy head of a bear was being magically fused to his body.

She held her hands over the man and began to chant, letting the magic inside her flow out and mend the flesh together. Soon, her new warrior would be ready for a living spirit—but not a weak one. She needed someone strong, someone who could survive and accept the life she willed upon it.

Right now, the blood-soaked, stinking bear head would frighten no one. The mouth hung open, revealing a stiff, dry tongue that flopped to the side, and the eyes were glazed and dark. Soon, however, it would come to life, a savage creature of strength and ferocity that would paralyze its opponents with fear. When that happened—when she could create this army of preternaturally fortified beasts with the single-minded purpose to carry out her bidding—she would be unstoppable.

Thus would rise the age of her dominion. From Atlandia to the silk weavers across the world and through the deserts where the people covered their faces from the sun, the name Mora ap'Drayd would be known and would be feared.

CHAPTER NINETEEN

Arthur rode from the forest across a series of hills. Merlin had gone ahead, flying to the village of Ivy Leaf, which was more of a trading center than an actual village and populated solely by tradesman. Arthur had visited the village before on a trading trip with the priests and Jon Longarm and found it to be a good place to get supplies. The brewer there was a woman who made a fine ale—according to Jon, at least, who wouldn't let Arthur drink any. There were the usual blacksmiths, cobblers, weavers, and so on, but there were also merchants with goods from places all across Atlandia. By the time Arthur arrived, Merlin had purchased himself a horse and its tack. He had enough food to last them a week in the wilderness, along with extra blankets.

"It took you long enough," Merlin said. "I've done most of the work myself."

"Sorry," Arthur apologized with a grin. He had taken his time ambling along with Thunder. "I saw no need to hurry."

"It's getting dark out. We might as well spend the night. You deal with the horses—I'll secure us a place at the inn."

"Sure." Arthur stepped forward to take the reins from the wizard.

Ivy Leaf had a small livery. The stableman who took their horses promised to look after them and also their supplies. There was only one inn, the Climbing Vine, which lived up to its name: it was covered with bright green vines that grew up the sides of the stone building. Before stopping there, though, Arthur had a different destination in mind. He needed more arrows and a sword, and he knew of a trader named Horace who sold weapons. Arthur had spent time admiring them in the past. Horace claimed to have the finest weapons from the best smiths in all the realm. Arthur wasn't convinced, but he could have spent hours looking at the myriad designs and feeling their weight. When he approached Horace's stall, the older man saw him coming and spread his hands wide.

"Arthur, as I live and breathe," Horace greeted him. "It does me good to see you. Word is there was a raid on the monastery. I heard there were dozens killed."

"The raiders," Arthur said. "And Jon, I'm sorry to say."

"Jon Longarm?" Horace was visibly shocked to hear the news. "I can't believe it."

"He held the gate," Arthur explained. "He died protecting the place he loved."

"That's the way he would have wanted it," Horace said. "But he'll be missed here, I assure you—aye, he'll be missed. What brings you to the Leaf, then?"

"It's time to move on. Without Jon, I couldn't stay at Byth El."

"You're of an age, I suppose," the trader said. "I take it you've come for a sword."

Arthur nodded. "I need something quality, Horace. Not the flashy junk you push on most people."

"You wound me with your words, young man," Horace said, although he clearly wasn't offended. Like most traders, he loved to bandy back and forth. There was an art to bargaining, Jon had taught Arthur. "Everything I carry is top of the line."

"I'll be the judge of that," Arthur said.

"And you've coin to part with?"

Arthur patted the pouch on his belt. The coins inside clanked together.

"What I have costs more than a few coppers, Arthur," Horace warned him.

"For the right weapon, I can pay the price," Arthur said. "Let's see the goods."

Horace slipped into the interior of his stall and reemerged with a long bag. He set it on the counter and untied the straps.

"You're in luck," he said. "I just got this lot from a merchant traveling from Walot. They have good smiths there and fine steel."

He pulled open the bag to reveal weapons of varying sizes and shapes. Horace pulled out a short, curved sword with a brass cross guard and a round pommel.

"Look at this beauty," Horace said, holding it out to Arthur. "Perfectly balanced. A fine weapon if ever I saw one."

Arthur took the sword. It was a one-handed weapon, and he couldn't argue about the balance, but it was a thick blade made for chopping and hacking. The entire sword was twice as heavy as Arthur thought it should be.

"It's too short," Arthur said. "You'll have to do better than that. Maybe one of the other traders has better goods."

He turned as if he were going to walk away, but Horace, grinning happily, grabbed his arm.

"Wait, wait, there's more," Horace said.

He pulled out a sword that was much like the one Arthur had taken from the leader of the raiders. It was a little longer than the first sword, with a steel cross guard that curved upward. The blade was angled from hilt to tip. The edges were fine, and the one-handed weapon was much lighter than the first, but it still wasn't what Arthur was seeking.

"I'm looking for a sword, Horace, not a toothpick."

"A man of discerning taste," the trader remarked. "And here I took you for a common fool."

Arthur was starting to worry that he wouldn't find what he was looking for. He preferred a longer weapon, one that he could wield with two hands. Most fighters learned clumsier sword strikes, relying on their shields to stop an opponent's counterattacks. But Arthur didn't fight with a shield, since he could move faster than most grown men, so he liked a weapon with reach that could slash and thrust more elegantly.

"I feel that you are trying to cheat me, old man," Arthur warned. "Should I take my coins elsewhere?"

"Only if you want inferior goods. A weapon must match

the bearer, and I think maybe this is what you're looking for."

He pulled out an unassuming broadsword. It had a leather-wrapped handle and a plain brass pommel. The sheath was leather over wood. When Arthur drew the sword, however, the steel had swirls and designs etched into it, and a wide fuller ran nearly the entire length of the double-edged blade.

"It's different," Arthur commented, feeling the weight of it.

"Uncommon doesn't mean inferior," Horace said.

Arthur stepped back from the stall and swung the sword. It had reach, but the balance was close to the hilt, meaning that he could use it with one or two hands. The weapon was sturdy without being heavy. Arthur inspected the edge, which was straight until the final few inches, where it angled in to the tip. It was sharp, and the handle felt good in Arthur's hand. He had no trouble knowing how the sword was oriented. The cross guard was steel and widened at either end. He felt a surge of relief.

"It leaves a lot to be desired, but I think it's passable for now," Arthur said, feigning nonchalance.

"It's a rare find," the trader said. "Easily worth four gold."

"Are you insane?" Arthur was flabbergasted by the man's audacity, even as he prepared to bargain. "Four? Really? I could buy two horses for that."

"You could kill a horse with one blow from a sword like that," Horace countered.

"I'm not a butcher," Arthur said. "No sword is worth four gold. I'll give you one gold, one silver."

"Don't insult me," Horace said. "I gave more than that for it."

"I can't help it if you don't know the value of steel."

"Back east, they don't even know how to forge steel," Horace said.

"But we aren't there—we're here, in Atlandia. In this realm, this sword is worth maybe one gold, three silver."

"Three gold and three silver," Horace said. "That's a long blade, Arthur, and the sheath is custom fit."

"Two gold, and not a copper more." Arthur stepped back and waited.

"You are killing me," Horace grumbled.

"Who else is going to give you more?" Arthur asked.

Horace wavered for only a moment more. "Fine, Arthur —we have a deal. Only because it's the end of a long day, mind. Besides, I'll do this favor for Jon. He was a good man."

"The best," Arthur agreed quietly.

He opened his coin pouch and drew the only two gold coins he had inside. He was left with just three silver and six coppers. Fortunately, he still had the coins that Merlin had given him for his birthday all those years ago hidden inside the cloak he had inherited from Jon.

"You drive a hard bargain," Horace said as he took the coins. There was a scowl on his face but a twinkle in his eye. Arthur knew Horace had made out on the trade, but the wily merchant would never admit it.

"I spent a lot of time watching what you do with other customers," Arthur said, as he slid the sword back into the sheath.

"That explains your education," Horace said.

Arthur extended his hand. "I'm staying the night at the inn. Come by and I'll buy you an ale. We'll drink to Jon's memory."

"I'd be honored," Horace said. "See you soon."

They shook hands, and Arthur walked away, feeling as if he was barely touching the ground. He finally had a sword of his own, a real one—not just a hunk of wood carved to look like a sword—not just a practice weapon, or an old, nicked-up length of brittle metal. This was a real sword that he had bargained for and purchased for himself, with money he had earned and saved over the years at the monastery. It made him feel more like a man than anything he had ever done.

CHAPTER TWENTY

Arthur stepped into the inn and looked around for Merlin, who wasn't in sight. The Vine consisted of a common room and a few storage rooms on the ground floor. The kitchen was out back under an awning of thatch, where an old woman kept a kettle of stew over a fire and baked bread in an ancient brick oven. Against the far wall, a staircase led up to the guest rooms. Arthur had never stayed in the rooms before. He and Jon Longarm had either slept outdoors or in the stable, while the priests took rooms inside. It hardly mattered: the inn's common room was its chief feature, where traders and merchants gathered in the evenings and where Arthur sought Merlin now. The long benches were half full, and a bright fire burned in the huge hearth at one end of the room.

Carrying his newly acquired weapon and being careful not to bump into anyone, Arthur took a seat close to the fire. It was warm and a bit smoky in the room, but the smell of hot food, yeasty bread, ale, and pipe smoke combined to create a homey, appealing smell. Arthur leaned against the table, his sword propped against his leg, as he took in the sights and sounds.

"Oi!" an older woman in a stained dress snapped at him. She carried a platter with mugs of ale. "You want ale or wine?"

Arthur thought for a moment, feeling a bit nervous. "Ale?"

"You asking me, or telling me?" the woman said, her face wrinkling as she squinted at him. "We don't serve drinks for free. How are you planning to pay?"

"He's with me," Merlin said, moving deftly through the crowded room. "We have rooms."

"Rooms is one thing, love—ale ain't free."

"Nothing in this world is free, except unwanted opinions. People are always giving them away. We'll have drinks and food as well. I'll take some of your undoubtedly fine wine."

"Ale for me," Arthur added quickly, and with far more certainty than he felt.

The woman eyed Merlin as he pushed past her and settled across the table from Arthur. Obviously deciding to abandon any further argument, she set a mug on the table and moved on.

"I procured two rooms for us," Merlin said. "Did you see to the horses?"

"Yes, they're in the livery, along with the supplies you purchased."

"Looks like I'm not the only one spending coin." Merlin nodded at Arthur's hip.

"I needed a sword," Arthur said, suddenly hoping that the wizard wouldn't chastise him.

"I agree," Merlin said. "Some light armor wouldn't hurt either. Try the ale."

Arthur was a little taken back. He was accustomed to Jon, who always spoke of weapons and war as something to be avoided—not to mention ale. Jon had never let him even taste the brewed drink. Occasionally, Arthur drank wine, but always with water added. It was surprising that Merlin did not second guess his decisions.

He took the mug and gave the ale a sniff, taking in its unique smell. He brought the mug to his lips and sipped. The ale was unexpectedly light and crisp. It burned his throat a little as it slid down into his empty stomach. He could feel the warmth there, but it didn't spread through him the way that wine often did.

The serving woman returned with big bowls of stew, two loaves of bread, a crock of butter, and some cheese. She set the items in front of them, including a glass of wine for Merlin. In return, he gave her a silver coin.

"You want change?" she asked.

"No, you keep it," Merlin said. "Perhaps it will encourage you not to be stingy with the wine."

The woman nodded and hurried away. There were more people coming in, mostly either locals or the traders who spent enough time in the village to be considered local. After briefly watching her tend to the newcomers, Arthur turned to his meal and found he was surprised at the stew. He was used to the food at the monastery, which was good but monotonous. The Climbing Vine Inn turned out to make a spicy stew full of chunks of meat and vegetables, with rice that gave the stew a hearty texture.

Merlin produced a small knife, not unlike the one he had given to Arthur. The wizard was adept at keeping things hidden inside the folds of his robe. He cut into his loaf of bread and began to spread butter across it. They ate in silence for a few minutes until their hunger was curbed. The ale was a pleasant contrast to the spicy stew. When Arthur finished his first mug, the serving woman came by with a pitcher and refilled it.

Soon, Horace appeared. He took his time moving through the crowd, speaking to different people as he went. Upon reaching Arthur and Merlin, he sat down between Arthur and the fire.

"Horace, this is my friend Merlin," Arthur introduced the two men.

"Any friend of Arthur's is a friend of mine," the trader said. "You didn't say earlier, Arthur: what brings you two to this part of the world?"

"We're heading west," Merlin said.

"Byrtan or Bernia?" Horace asked.

"Is one better than the other?" Merlin asked.

"Not in my estimation," the trader said. "But a word of warning, if I might: the wildlands between them are growing dangerous. There's rumors of dangerous beasts in the old forest. I'd go north or south, but not west, at least not directly."

"What sorts of beasts?" Merlin asked.

"The worst kind," Horace said, taking a mug of ale from the serving woman as she made her rounds. "Them ones out of Farkia, I would suspect." He held up his mug. "To Jon Longarm— may he rest in peace."

"To Jon," Arthur said, raising his own mug.

Merlin raised his glass but said nothing as they all took a long drink. Arthur could feel the ale starting to make him lightheaded. When the serving woman returned, he decided he had drunk enough.

"Keep eating," Merlin told him. "The bread will curb the ale's effects."

Arthur tore bites of bread from his loaf and slowly ate. He didn't sop up the remains of his stew, though, for fear that the spicy broth would make him want to drink more. Horace, on the other hand, had no trouble drinking. He finished four mugs before his dinner was brought. The serving woman left a pitcher of ale with the trader's food.

"What sort of trade do you carry on?" Merlin asked.

"I'm open to anything," Horace said. "I've even taken a few furs from Arthur here. Mostly, I deal in foreign goods— weapons, tools, that sort of thing. There's money to be made if a person can take goods from one realm to another. When I was Arthur's age, I was always on the move."

"Do you still travel?"

"Not as much," Horace said. "I've got friends that supply me with more than enough to keep me busy right here in Ivy Leaf."

"But you hear things, I'm sure...news from the five realms, perhaps."

"Certainly, certainly," the trader said. "Occasionally, there is word from the eastern lands, but that has little enough concern for us Atlandians, eh?"

"What do you hear from Farkia?"

"The Dark Realm?" Horace raised an eyebrow. "Mostly the same rumors that we've heard all our lives: murder, betrayal, nefarious magic, that sort of thing. It's naught but rumors. The only thing I can say for certain is that the Farkians have been busy raiding the border."

"My own home is in Avon," Merlin said. "Butan, to be exact."

"Rumor has it a wizard makes his home in Butan, but that's not exactly reliable. I've been there a time or two myself, and I've never seen anything supernatural in Butan. Only unusual thing there is the pink salt they produce—it's second to none."

Arthur listened to the conversation and relished the warm feeling in his stomach. He was happy, relaxed, and full. In such a state, he had no thought of what might come or what might be happening in the wider world. His complete focus, albeit dulled slightly by the ale, was on the men around him. Other traders joined their group, from whom Merlin continued to ask of news. The merchants and travelers who knew Jon paid their respects to Arthur, and there were many cups lifted in the old warrior's honor.

It was a fine evening until a blood-chilling wail arose over the hubbub, a cold, keening cry, beastly and close to the village. Talk in the inn fell silent as the howl reverberated through the building. Arthur was amazed at the sheer volume: it was louder than anything he had ever heard before, louder even than the large building filled with people talking and laughing, over which the howl was easily heard.

"What was that?" Arthur asked.

"Wolves," said one of the traders. "They've been hunting nearby."

"Don't be daft," Horace said. "That was no wolf."

"And you're an expert?" another challenged.

"I'd say it was an anprophos," Merlin said. "A dread wolf."

"What in the bloody hell is a dread wolf?" Horace's round face lost its color.

"It's a magical creature," Merlin said. "A giant, voracious lone wolf. Have any cattle gone missing of late?"

"Aye," said one of the traders, "Fargus lost a milk cow the day before yesterday."

"Who steals a milk cow?" Horace asked.

"And Warryn disappeared yesterday," another merchant pointed out.

"He left town, is all," said another.

"And left all his goods behind?" said the first. "Not likely."

"He's old," Horace said, his voice almost tremulous with fear. "Like as not, he just had an episode and wandered off."

Merlin frowned slightly. "Was he prone to such episodes?"

"Warryn was sharp as butcher's knife," the serving woman said. When Arthur looked up, there were tears shimmering in her eyes. "He wouldn't have left without saying something."

The howl sounded again, wolfish in some ways, but more of a roar than the lonely call of an ordinary canine. The sound was loud enough to shake the thick timber beams of the inn.

"Whatever it is," Merlin said, "it's coming this way."

"What are we going to do?" another of the traders asked.

"There's only one thing to do." Arthur found his voice at the prospect of the fight ahead. "We have to go out and face it."

"The folly of youth," said a trader in a shaky voice.

"That's daft," another pointed out.

Horace shook his head in agreement. "You couldn't pay me to go out there—there's not enough gold in the world."

"Everyone knows you don't hunt at night," said another of the traders.

"A dread wolf can't be found in the daytime," Merlin said. "You'd do better not to hide: once it has found easy prey, it won't leave until there's nothing—and no one—left to eat."

"You're telling us that this beast is going to kill us all?" Horace asked.

"Those foolish enough to stay," another merchant said. "I'm pulling up stakes at first light."

"We can't all just up and leave," the innkeeper said. He was short and bald, with deep wrinkles around his eyes and across his forehead, but he was still trim and strong. He didn't seem as frightened as the others.

"Dell's right," Horace said. "You never solve a problem by running away from it."

"That's not true," said one of the merchants. "I'm living proof that leaving town can solve all sorts of problems."

"Let's stay focused," the innkeeper said. "What do we need to face this thing?"

Merlin looked at Arthur, who felt some fear but even more excitement. He had run down wild boars that weighed three times as much as he did; in his woodland excursions, he had come across bears and wolves alike. In those times he had felt fear, but also elation as the deadliest hunters in the woods gave him a wide berth. He could tell by the almost amused look on Merlin's face that he too was excited.

"Spears," Arthur said.

"And torches," Merlin added.

Horace put his arm on Arthur's shoulder and leaned in close. "You don't have to do this," he murmured. "No one would judge you for staying put by the fire."

"I'll go," Arthur said.

"Of course he will," Merlin said. How he had heard Horace's whispered warning, Arthur couldn't tell, but the wizard was up to something. "In fact, Arthur and I will be ones to face the beast. The rest of you need only to come and watch."

"He's crazy," said one of the merchants.

"Crazy or not, let's take it—we have to do something," Dell said. "Someone get the lad a spear. I'll get torches."

A deep, menacing growl reverberated through the inn. Several of the merchants and traders dropped to their benches in fear. The serving woman grabbed hold of Horace's arm.

"Strap on your sword, Arthur," Merlin said. "We have work to do."

CHAPTER TWENTY-ONE

Arthur fastened his new sword to the wide leather belt he wore. The merchants, traders, and craftsmen of the village were lighting their torches. From out of the back room, Dell brought out a long boar spear with an angular metal blade. A foot from where the blade started, there was bar of metal that protruded from either side of the shaft to keep the animal from charging toward the bearer.

"Will this work?" Dell asked, holding the weapon out to Merlin.

"Ask him," Merlin replied, pointing at Arthur.

"Don't you need a weapon?" Horace asked the wizard.

"Not me." Merlin smiled again. "I'm the bait."

"He's crazy, that one," declared the serving woman, who was still clinging to Horace. It was obvious they knew one another on more than a merely professional basis.

Arthur could feel his blood pumping hard through his

veins, the same feeling he had experienced when he caught sight of the raiding party approaching the monastery, only there was no accompanying sense of desperation at the prospect of losing his friends. There was also only one wolf, compared to the dozens of raiders he'd singlehandedly faced; how hard could this be?

"Here you are, lad," Dell said.

"Thank you." Arthur took the spear from the innkeeper. It had a good balance and had obviously seen plenty of action, based on the stains of blood on the upper shaft. This gave Arthur confidence: a new weapon might shatter, but one that had been tested in the hunt was reliable. He reached up and checked the edge of the spearhead. It was sharp enough, although not honed to a razor's edge. Fortunately, a boar spear didn't need to be too keen. It was better to have a strong, sharp tip with slightly dull edges, otherwise the weapon might cut through the animal's flesh and allow it free to gore the hunter before it died.

"It's perfect," Arthur said.

"You've used one before?" Horace seemed surprised.

"Many times," Arthur confirmed. He wasn't trying to exude confidence, but he couldn't contain his excitement.

The creature outside roared again. The common room of the inn was growing smoky from the torches. It was time to face the beast, whatever it was.

"Follow me," Merlin said.

He went to the door and threw it open. At this time of year, the nights were cool, made to feel even cooler by Arthur's hot blood thrumming through his veins. The air felt good on his skin. He held the spear with one hand and checked his sword, which slid easily from the shaft. He hoped he didn't have to use it, but if he did, it was there.

"Better hold that thing ready," Horace said. He was standing behind Arthur; his lady friend had remained in the Climbing Vine. "Even with all these torches you can't see a..."

His voice trailed off as they came around the side of the inn. From the light of the torches, two yellow eyes glinted. Whatever the creatures was, it appeared to be big. The light from the torches didn't reach the beast itself; only its eyes reflected the light.

"Spread out," Merlin hissed.

The locals didn't question his order, and Arthur couldn't help but marvel at the authority the wizard commanded. He and Merlin were in the center of a semicircle. The light from the torches filled the space with light.

"That's a magical creature," Merlin said softly.

"You're sure?" Arthur asked.

"Positive. I can feel the magic that sustains it."

"You mean someone conjured it?"

"Now isn't the time for questions," Merlin said. "It won't fear the fire from the torches. When I summon my own power, it will be drawn to me, into the circle of light. The rest is up to you."

"Any tips on how to kill it?" Arthur asked.

"Stab it through the heart or cut off its head," Merlin said as he stepped back. "And don't die."

"Thanks," Arthur griped, but he couldn't help but grin.

His will to live was strong, but he couldn't resist the call of battle. It didn't matter that his opponent was an animal— Arthur realized that he loved to fight. He had the momentary worry that perhaps loving battle wasn't healthy, but the time for moral considerations ran out when the dread wolf moved into the light.

Arthur couldn't see it, but Merlin was behind Arthur, using his magic to levitate a few stones to float in the air at chest level. The dread wolf seemed almost hypnotized by the floating stones and moved slowly and steadily forward. The creature had a massive head, with huge jaws big enough to bite a man in two and uncanny yellow eyes. The shoulders were high, easily as tall as a war horse, and thickly furred with a dirty gray pelt. Ropy lines of slobber hung between the huge pointed fangs, which were as big as a soldier's shortsword.

"Good luck," Merlin said.

Arthur didn't dare take his eyes off the big animal as he contemplated what he should do. The fur that ringed the beast's neck would be hard to penetrate. Then again, if he tried to drive the boar spear into the dread wolf's chest, he would be exposed to the creature's jaws. He needed to hit it from the side, and with force. If the beast's gaze remained fixed on Merlin, it might give Arthur the chance to attack its flank. He was just about to start moving slowly to the side, but before Arthur could take more than a single step, the stones Merlin was levitating flew over the young man's head and hit the dread wolf on its snout.

The creature yelped in pain, then suddenly rushed forward. Arthur saw the creature's jaws open, felt a hot, rancid blast of the beast's breath—he dove to the side. Fortunately, the beast wasn't trying to catch Arthur. Behind him, he heard the flutter of wings just before he hit the ground. Arthur managed to roll over his shoulder and find his feet quickly, but he had dropped the spear. There was no time to consider what he should do next. The only way to stay alive against the dread wolf was keep moving. He drew his sword as he ran. The animal's rear leg was exposed, and Arthur attacked, putting his weight and momentum behind the slash.

Unlike the spear, his new sword was sharp to the touch. Arthur didn't chop with the blade—instead, he swung to connect and then dragged the blade across the dread wolf's leg, just the way Jon had taught him. The animal loosed a howl of pain and rage. Arthur didn't have to look back to know it was turning to find him, intent on ending the threat. The sword had cut well, but the beast's shaggy fur acted as a buffer. A shallow cut was all the damage Arthur had managed, and it had turned the dread wolf's attention on him.

Arthur never stopped moving. He ran toward the other rear leg, hoping to land a cut there too. The wolf lashed out with a wicked rear kick. Arthur nearly dodged it, but one edge of the wolf's hind foot caught his shoulder and knocked him off his feet. Arthur rolled immediately to his knees and was on his feet as the creature turned to face him. There was only one option left. The wolf growled, its head lowered and hackles raised. Arthur raised his sword over his head, holding it carefully with both hands. The dread wolf eased forward and Arthur backed up slowly, keeping the distance between them the same.

It didn't take the creature long to realize it couldn't sneak up on Arthur. Instead, it gathered its rear legs under it and sprang. At the same instant, Arthur heaved his sword straight at the creature, sending it twirling straight at the beast, which had opened its huge mouth. Arthur jumped to the side and ran for the boar spear as the sword sank into the creature's open mouth. The blade ripped into the tongue just as the dread wolf's jaws snapped closed. Perhaps it was already in the act of biting down, or maybe the pain from the sword slashing its tongue caused its mouth to close in a reflex. Either way, when the creature closed its mouth, it caused even more damage. Blood spewed as the beast roared and rolled on the ground, trying to dislodge the sword. It came up on its feet and shook its head from side to side. Blood, spittle, and chunks of its tongue flew out as the wolf recoiled and writhed from the pain.

The sword flew free just as Arthur scooped up the boar spear. He was still running as the dread wolf choked on the blood in its mouth. It barked and coughed, momentarily distracted. This was all the advantage Arthur needed. He charged the beast from the side, leveling the spear. When he was only a few steps away from the dread wolf, Arthur leaped forward and thrust the weapon with all his strength, puncturing the wolf behind the shoulder. The blade bit deep but missed the creature's heart. It tried to turn its head to snap at Arthur, but years of carrying buckets full of water and loads of firewood—not mention his thorough training in combat arts—had given him the strength of a full-grown man. He didn't see his eyes flash with gold, although the villagers did, as his Atal blood gave him strength to shove hard on the spear. It didn't go deeper, but it pushed the dread wolf off its feet.

Arthur had seen a horse break its leg and remembered vividly the way the creature thrashed wildly. The dread wolf was bigger than most horses—its forelegs certainly were longer than a horse's, and its paws were lined with claws. He jumped back, running away from the beast. The dread wolf fell onto its side, the legs raking air, the beast's terrifying roar cut off by the blood it choked on.

He looked around, trying to find his sword, but it was too close to the dread wolf. The beast got slowly to its feet. It was clearly hurting: blood streamed from its severed tongue, enough that the yellow teeth and black lips were stained with it. The creature turned its head, bit down on the boar spear, and, with a sudden jerk, yanked it from its body. It might have survived if the spear had dropped to the ground beside it, but the weapon went spinning away from the creature and right toward Arthur. It hit the ground and rolled across the grassy expanse. The dread wolf growled before charging forward. Arthur snatched up the spear and stood his ground.

When the creature drew close, it slowed, fear causing it to hesitate. Arthur jumped forward to meet the beast, slashing up with the spear. The dread wolf darted back too late: the spear's tip caught the end of its nose and left a ragged gash. Once more, the wolf shook its head as blood flew. Some of the hot liquid splashed across Arthur, staining his clothes. He drew back the spear but kept moving forward. The wolf jumped, leaping high into the air over Arthur. It was a stunning sight, but Arthur didn't wait to see what the beast would do. Instead, he chased it down and stabbed the dread wolf in the back of the leg. The spear sank deep and lodged in the creature's bone. Instinctively, it kicked, the motion flicked the spear up. Arthur was still holding the weapon and was flung into the air. He landed face down on the dread wolf's haunches, his arms and legs spread wide, and clung to the beast's fur as it bucked in response to its latest hurt.

After regaining his balance and presence of mind, Arthur managed to free his dagger from his belt and stabbed down hard into the creature's back. The blade cut down between the bones of the dread wolf's spine and severed the nerves that controlled the beast's hind legs. It dropped to the ground; Arthur had just enough time to leap free as the creature rolled over.

The crowd was cheering now, and their shouts of encouragement broke through Arthur's intense focus on reacting to the beast. There had been no time to plan his attack or consider the fear that still roared in the back of his mind. The cheers of the villagers brought him back to his senses to realize that, astonishingly, the fight was nearly over. The dread wolf, bleeding and lame, tried to crawl away, but Arthur recovered his sword. He moved quickly back to the creature's side and stabbed deep into the gaping wound left by the boar spear. The magical creature didn't try to fight back. It threw its head up, gurgling gruesomely, then dropped to the ground in a violent collapse. Arthur jerked his sword free and backed away as the dread wolf shuttered and twitched, the forelegs pawing at the air, the rear legs lying twisted underneath it.

Arthur heard a flutter of wings, and when he turned, Merlin was standing behind him, a look of pride on his face. The villagers began to move closer, shouting and cheering, the light from their torches showing the savage dread wolf in clear detail. It was a huge beast, clearly dead. Arthur felt his own body suddenly grow tired and shaky.

Merlin wrapped an arm around his shoulders. "Excellent," the wizard said.

If there was more, Arthur didn't hear it: the tumult of the crowd drowned the wizard's words. The villagers thronged around Arthur. He couldn't make out what they were saying, but they were excited. The group moved back to the Climbing Vine. A mug of ale was pressed into Arthur's hand, and he was suddenly aware of his thirst, deep and savage. He turned the mug up and gulped down the ale as people clapped him on the back. Merlin gave him his moment of victory, then escorted him up the stairs to his room.

"What's going on?" Arthur asked.

"You need a bath," Merlin said with a chuckle. "You're quite grotesque."

Arthur's head was swimming too much from fatigue and ale to protest. The wizard took Arthur to a room with a large brass tub. There was already warm water in it, with more being heated by the innkeeper. Merlin took the clothes that Arthur stripped off. The young warrior eased himself into the tub.

"That's going to hurt come morning," Dell commented.

Arthur looked down at his shoulder, already purple from a deep bruise where the dread wolf had kicked him. He hadn't even been aware of it until that moment.

"He'll live," Merlin said.

"Should we burn those clothes?" the innkeeper asked.

"No—just soak them for a few hours and then scrub out the blood," Merlin ordered.

"Happy to do it," Dell replied. "But I doubt we'll be able to get the stains out."

"We don't want them out." Merlin glanced at Arthur. "It's his badge of honor."

Arthur washed himself and then climbed out of the bath to dry off and don a robe that Dell had left. Merlin indulged Arthur with some more ale only after Arthur had a full mug of water. Then, with his thirst slaked at last, he was shown to his room, a small affair with just a bed and a three-legged stool. He could hear the villagers down in the common room. There was laughter, shouting, even a chorus or two belted out. Merlin left the room dark and closed the door.

Arthur lay on his bed, listening to the sounds of joy issuing from below. It was the best feeling he had ever known. The only memory that came close was that of his childhood bedtime ritual with his mother; he could still faintly remember his mother singing to him at night. He couldn't remember what she sang—only that the sound of it filled him with peace. Somehow, the uproarious jubilation echoing from the common room below was even better. Perhaps it was because he had played a part in their joy, or at least he had turned their fear into hope. Whatever it was, it made him happy to hear it.

Arthur drifted off to sleep with the certainty that he had finally discovered what he wanted in his new life: to give people the same gift of life and renewal as he had to these villagers by slaying the dread wolf. If he could find a way to beget that same feeling in other people, he would do whatever it took.

CHAPTER TWENTY-TWO

"Your man is a hero!" a trader shouted as Merlin descended the stairs to the common room after seeing that Arthur was safely in bed for the night.

"Have a drink!" the serving woman said. Her cheeks were red, and she was actually smiling as she pressed a flagon of ale into his hand. It was a pleasant change.

Merlin couldn't help but be impressed by the difference in the villagers' demeanor. They had gone from trembling, terrified cowards to victors celebrating as if they had killed the dread wolf themselves. Their elation was surprising in its intensity—Merlin had only seen people so happy at festivals and holidays. They were almost drunk on happiness, and most, it appeared, were getting drunk off ale and wine.

Horace entered the common room with the boar spear and Arthur's sword. Merlin hadn't known why Arthur would need it, but when he had seen the weapon propped against the young man's knee a few hours earlier, he'd had a premonition that it was a good and proper thing, like seeing someone in fine clothes that fit them well. Arthur with a sword was as natural a combination as bread and butter.

"Here it is," Horace shouted, holding up the boar spear. "Where shall we hang it?"

"A weapon like that needs a name," a merchant called out.

"Wolf's Bane!" someone shouted.

"That's it! That's the name," Horace said, carrying the spear to the fireplace. "Wolf's Bane."

The crowd set cups on the mantel, and Horace propped the spear on them.

"To the Wolf's Bane!" someone in the crowd shouted, holding up their mug of ale.

"I'll drink to that!" another voice cried.

"Hear, hear!" the crowd chorused.

Merlin made his way to Horace and took possession of Arthur's sword. Inwardly, he marveled at the way the crowd told and retold the story. Each person had a different perspective on the battle, but it was clear that they all thought of Arthur as a hero.

It hadn't really been Merlin's plan to build Arthur into a legendary figure. When he'd volunteered them for the fight, he had merely wanted to see what Arthur was capable of. Now, as in the skirmish, he saw that it was possible to spread the young man's fame far and wide. Merlin, after transforming to his falcon shape, had watched the battle, ready to intervene and save his young friend, but Arthur hadn't needed it, so natural was he with the sword and spear. Of course, it helped that his Atal blood made him stronger and faster than a common-born person. Merlin had felt the surge of magic that flooded through Arthur when he struck the dread wolf down.

He retired to the corner with his ale and Arthur's sword, a plan forming in his mind—one that, he thought, might lead to Arthur's vision. It certainly wouldn't hurt; at least, Merlin didn't think it would. The wizard had no desire to make Arthur into something he wasn't. Nor did he long for power or influence, but, like most magical people, Merlin was drawn to the workings of the supernatural, the unseen forces at work in the physical world that his sensitivity to magic helped him to recognize. He had sensed something about Arthur even before he was born. Perhaps it was human intuition, but he liked to think that his magical acumen gave him a sixth sense, a magical perception that sometimes bordered on precognition. Whatever it was, he was convinced that powerful forces were arrayed around Arthur. The boy's future was certain to be monumental, and Merlin wanted to stay close—to be part of something that would change the world. He wanted to help the young warrior accomplish whatever the Most High set before him.

The crowd at the Climbing Vine had shown Merlin the way forward. He would be Arthur's advisor and friend, there was no doubt about that. He had bonded himself to the boy before Arthur was even born. But it wasn't merely an attachment: it was an obligation to serve. It seemed obvious to Merlin that the natural next step was to stoke the spark of Arthur's fame. The story of his battle with the dread wolf would grow. Ivy Leaf was a village of merchants and traders, always on the move: they would carry the story, and the name of Arthur, to every realm in the land. Merlin then would fan the sparks into a flame that would offer light and hope wherever Arthur went.

He looked at the sword, which had been cleaned in a rush. There were still traces of the dread wolf's blood on the metal, especially around the blade guard. He held his hands over the weapon and chanted softly. In the common room, filled with a raucous crowd of those who were convinced they had just seen with their own eyes the work of a great hero, no one heard or paid the wizard any attention. Merlin's power, along with the blood of the magical creature, poured into the sword. Along the blade's fuller, words appeared: *Es Kali ap'Bur,* the Atal for 'the hand of division.' The blade guard transformed from plain metal to what seemed to be brightly polished silver. The wavy lines and whirls in the steel of the blade became more pronounced, and the pommel changed from a simple, round device to a shining silver wolf's head.

Merlin slid the sword back into the scabbard and took a drink from his flagon of ale. They were on the verge of something big—he couldn't see it, but he could sense that it lay ahead. His Atal tutors had taught him to pay attention to signs and the way magic could warn him of danger or opportunity.

Magic...a complex gift he'd learned, and one that rarely went unnoticed. He thought it strange that none of the locals seemed to notice or care that he was a wizard. It was likely that when the dread wolf attacked, they were focused on Arthur. The boy was oblivious to the fact that his stature and good looks drew people to him. Next to Arthur, Merlin was but a shadow—and that was just fine with the wizard. Knowing that people paid him little heed when

Arthur was around gave him the freedom to act without being noticed.

Eventually, Horace recalled the wizard and lumbered over. He was well into his cups, and his words were slurred. Merlin liked to drink, but he hated to lose his composure: it was humiliating, not to mention dangerous.

"Ah, can you believe it?" Horace said, sitting down beside Merlin. There was ale foam in his mustache, but the trader didn't seem to notice.

"Believe what?"

"That we're still alive," Horace declared. "I've never seen anything like it, you know. I still can't believe I was foolish enough to go out there. That beast could have killed us all, and would have, I dare say, if not for Arthur. I've known the lad for some time, and I've always felt he was special."

"Indeed?" Merlin asked.

"Aye, he's got a gift, that boy. I'm proud to call him a friend. In fact, 'twas I who sold him that very sword."

Merlin waved his hand in the air. It left a trail of golden flecks, magical dust. Horace was drinking, his large flagon of ale covering most of his face as he sucked down the crisp brew. When he lowered his mug and inhaled, the golden dust was sucked into his nostrils.

"You never sold Arthur a sword," Merlin said casually, barely even loudly enough for Horace to hear it. "You don't know where he got the weapon."

"Hm? What's that?" Horace asked.

"I was asking," Merlin said, raising his voice, "if you knew where Arthur got that incredible sword of his."

"No idea," Horace said, waving a hand. "But believe me, I know weapons. That one's not made by human hands. No, sir, that's something else—a magical sword for a great warrior. Not just anyone could wield it."

"I agree." Merlin couldn't help his satisfied smile.

"You know that creature was as big as a horse," Horace explained.

"You don't say," Merlin said drolly.

"And absolutely ferocious," Horace went on, as if Merlin hadn't been there at all. "I was terrified, truly, but not Arthur. He stood tall in front of the beast. It was the bravest thing I've ever seen."

The story was growing without Merlin even having to try. Soon, it would be the stuff of legends, and Arthur's fame would grow alongside it.

CHAPTER TWENTY-THREE

Arthur woke early. He was tired, but his bruised shoulder kept waking him up whenever he moved. Eventually, as the sun began to shine through the small window, he decided it was time to get up. He found his clothes neatly folded on the little stool. It bothered him that he hadn't heard anyone come into his room.

He checked Jon's cloak, which he hadn't worn to fight the dread wolf. It was still hanging on a peg on the wall, with his little pouch of coins hidden in the interior pocket. As he pulled on his clothes and boots, he noticed the sword he had purchased from Horace leaning against the wall. Immediately, he saw that it was different: the pommel was silver and had a savage wolf's head carved into the precious metal. He pulled the blade from its scabbard. It was the same weapon, yet it had been changed. The designs in the metal were more pronounced, and the blade guard was dazzling to look at—Arthur had never seen silver polished so well, such that it had almost a mirrorlike finish. He studied the words that had been engraved in the fuller of the blade. It was the same silvery lettering that he remembered from the scrap of vellum where Merlin had written his name. He had no idea what *Es Kali ap'Bur* meant, but he liked the way the silvery characters seemed to flow like liquid before his very eyes.

Replacing the sword in its sheath, he strapped it to his belt. His dagger and knife were there too. He felt better with his weapons in place and opened the door. The smell of stale spirits, wood smoke, and sickness was pungent in the air. The locals had celebrated hard, and clearly many were paying for it. Arthur felt fortunate that he wasn't, but he realized that the ale had robbed him of his awareness in the night. He preferred to sleep lightly, just in case something got close to him in the darkness. Knowing this, and seeing many of the townsfolk nursing bad hangovers, made him resolve to abstain from ale in the future.

"Good morning, Arthur," Merlin said as the younger man reached the bottom of the stairs. "How are you feeling?"

"Fine," Arthur replied. "A little sore, maybe."

"That's good. We should be on our way."

"Already? Are we in a hurry?"

"Not more than we were yesterday, but some fresh air would be welcome," the wizard said.

Arthur wrinkled his nose as the smells somehow intensified. "I can't argue that point."

"You get the horses—I'll procure our breakfast. We can eat as we ride."

"Fine." Arthur headed for the door. The odor in the Climbing Vine was worse on the ground floor, but the moment he stepped outside, a bracing wind carried the stink away. Autumn was upon them. The evergreens of the great forest didn't turn colors or lose their leaves, but the cooler air was a sure sign that winter was on the way.

Stretching his legs felt good. He walked in large strides and rotated his left arm as he went. Unfortunately, the bruise on his shoulder couldn't be healed with simple stretches, and even moving his arm made it ache, but he knew he would live with it. The bruise didn't seem any worse than the beatings he used to get sparring with Jon in the monastery.

At the livery, he found their horses, tack, and supplies, but no stableman. Arthur checked their hooves himself, just as Brother Haymore had taught him. Satisfied that the horses were healthy and their shoes were in good shape, he saddled both animals. He had their bridles in place and was loading supplies when the stableman appeared. It was clear at a glance that the man was sick.

"Too much ale?" Arthur asked with a grin.

"Too much and then some," the man said. "The whole world is spinning."

"I'm sorry to hear that," Arthur said. "How much do we owe you for looking after the horses?"

"No fee," the man said. "No, sir, I should be paying you. I saw you fight that monster last night. If not for you, we'd all be in grave trouble. I'll be telling my grandchildren that I kept Arthur's horses one day."

Arthur murmured something polite, not sure what else to say, and led the horses out into the sunlight. The stableman shrank away from the bright light and obviously preferred to stand in the shadows of the stable, leaning against the door post and shading his bloodshot eyes.

"Farewell," the stableman called as Arthur climbed onto Thunder's saddle.

He gave the stableman a little wave and clucked his tongue to get the horses moving. Arthur was glad they would be eating on the road, as he was anxious to depart. There was nothing finer than riding through the country on a cool, beautiful day.

Merlin was waiting beside the main entrance to the Climbing Vine. Horace was beside him, looking dreadful as he clutched his stomach. The trader's hair was sticking out, and his skin had a sickly green cast to it. Merlin walked over to Arthur and handed up a small sack. From within, Arthur could smell the aroma of bacon and freshly baked biscuits. He pulled out one of the biscuits and took a bite.

"How can you eat on a morning like this?" Horace asked in a shaky voice.

"To be young again, eh, Horace?" Merlin said. He had just the slightest trace of mirth in his voice, but Arthur picked it up.

"These biscuits are delicious," Arthur said. "Would you like one?"

"No," Horace said, waving a hand at him rather desperately.

"It was good to see you," Arthur said, as Merlin climbed into the saddle of the horse he had purchased just the day before.

"You could stay, you know," Horace said. "The pelt on that creature should be yours by right."

"We will leave that to you," Merlin said. "Although I dare say that it will be an odorous task if left too long."

Horace looked like he might be sick to his stomach right there, but he managed to control himself. Arthur turned Thunder and gave the horse a gentle nudge.

"So long, Horace," Arthur called.

"Farewell, Arthur," Horace replied. "May you have safe travels and return soon."

"You're a popular man in this village," Merlin noted as they rode side by side.

"It was good to do something for them," Arthur said.

They rode past the carcass of the dread wolf. It looked almost deflated, as if it had been full of air that had leaked out during the night, and not nearly as large or ferocious as it had seemed the night before. The mangy fur hung from the creature's body. Flies buzzed around it, and the odor of decay was noticeable.

"Do you need a trophy?" Merlin asked, although he didn't slow down at all.

"No," Arthur said. "But I saw what you did to my sword."

"All I did was prompt the magic that already filled the blade," Merlin said. "The anprophos blood added to that. I really had nothing to do with how it affected the weapon."

Arthur grinned. "I'll take the trophy of a magic sword."

"It is not really a magic sword," the wizard said. "No more than you are a wizard. But you have magic inside you. From your father's blood, I would say. Did you feel it last night?"

"I felt...strong," Arthur said. "At times, supernaturally strong."

They rode out of the little village and moved along a trail through the forest. It soon turned northward, and Merlin stopped. Arthur reined in Thunder and looked at the wizard.

"What now?" Arthur asked.

"This road runs north, into Bernia," Merlin said. "Or we could go south through Byrtan and into Avon, and perhaps spend the winter in my home in Butan."

"I do not care where we go," Arthur said. "My only thought is to see as much of Atlandia as I can."

"Then we shall see all of it," Merlin said, with the faintest hint of a smile.

Arthur couldn't help but wonder what the wizard was up to. He seemed to have a purpose that he wasn't sharing with Arthur. He had certainly been quick to push Arthur into fighting the dread wolf. Since the outcome had been good, despite the bruise to his shoulder, Arthur felt great satisfaction about their night in Ivy Leaf. For the time being, he decided it was acceptable to follow the wizard's lead. He was a free man, even if he was only sixteen and not really a man yet; with no ties to anyone or anywhere, he could go wherever the wind took him. That was just fine with Arthur —in fact, it felt like the best life he could imagine.

CHAPTER TWENTY-FOUR

They were camped by a wide stream, clear and swift over a bed of stones the size of Arthur's head. He had spent the afternoon catching fish, which they cooked over the coals of their campfire. Merlin made flatbread sweetened with blackberries they had found earlier in the day.

They were nearly a week out from their stay in Ivy Leaf. To Arthur's surprise, the wizard had let him take the lead on their journey and set the pace. Arthur was taking his time, foraging through the forest as they traveled southwest toward Byrtan.

The flatbread was a perfect complement to the smoky, salty fish, and they had eaten their fill. As night fell, they spread out their blankets by the fire, cushioned by the grass along the riverbank, which was thick and soft. They built up the fire and settled in for the night. Arthur gazed up at the stars, listening to the fire crackling and the river gurgling. It was peaceful and helped him deal with the bout of deep grief he was feeling, as often he felt when he thought of his friend Jon Longarm. There were moments, especially at night, when he couldn't shake the idea of Jon's body moldering in the ground outside the monastery from his mind. It was a terrifying thought, even if he understood that Jon was beyond thinking or feeling. At times, he woke up after dreaming that he himself was being buried alive.

Arthur was trying to think about something less morbid when a bird flew into their camp. They were in the woods surrounded by wildlife, but normally the fire kept most animals at bay. Arthur wasn't alarmed, but he was surprised. He sat up and looked over, just as the bird, a common swift, morphed into a tall, thin woman with black skin. She looked regal, her hair plaited intricately in tiny braids, her big eyes looking around the clearing and settling on Arthur.

"Viocee." Merlin was awake as well. "What a surprise."

"I have news," she replied, holding Arthur's gaze.

Merlin gained his feet and moved swiftly toward the woman. Arthur stood up as well. His weapons were on the ground near his bedroll, but he didn't feel threatened, just curious.

"News is always welcome," Merlin said. "What transpires beyond the mountains in Alal?"

"Raids," Viocee said. "A group of travelers was taken."

"In Alal?" Merlin asked in disbelief.

"That is what we believe," Viocee said. "They were ambushed. We found blood on the trail. Their belongings were left untouched."

"You think they were taken captive," Merlin said. It

wasn't a question; he was merely thinking out loud. "I didn't expect them to move through the mountains."

"No one did," Viocee said. "The Farkians' power has grown. Their boldness is appalling."

"I concur," Merlin said, spreading his hands in a placating gesture. "Why have you come to tell me this news?"

"The elders gather in Atland. You have been summoned by the council."

"The council wants me?" Merlin said. "My obligation was fulfilled. I'm not sure what I can do for them."

"Who is your companion?" Viocee said, nodding at Arthur.

"Oh." Merlin turned. The look on his face wasn't quite one of distress, but the mirth that usually lit up his features was gone. "This is Arthur. We are traveling to Butan together."

Viocee pushed past Merlin and approached Arthur, who had just dropped a few more branches onto the fire. The flames caught immediately, and the light increased. She had a narrow face, but a wide mouth with full lips. She smiled as she approached.

"And his true name?" Viocee asked.

"He can speak for himself," Merlin said.

Arthur felt a strange feeling, as if he had met the woman before. He knew he would have remembered such an occasion: there was a mysterious and unearthly beauty to her, not just because her skin was so dark, nor because her body was unusually thin. Arthur's own mother had grown painfully thin when the sickness took her, and he remembered her bones protruding as if there was nothing beneath the skin but a skeleton. Viocee was even thinner than mother had been, but there was no sign of sickness. Her body was graceful and strong, and very different from anyone Arthur had ever met.

"Will you share your name with me?" Viocee asked.

"I was cautioned against sharing my name when it was given to me," Arthur said, omitting that it was Merlin who had given him both the Atal name and the warning.

"It is obvious that we are kindred," Viocee said. "Was it your mother or father that gave you their Celestial blood?"

"I never knew my father," Arthur said.

Viocee turned and looked at Merlin. "Why are you hiding him, Errol? What mischief are you up to?"

"I'm not hiding him," Merlin said. "Arthur grew up with his mother, and more recently with the monks at Byth El. We have only just begun our travels."

"He should be brought to the High City, where his heritage may be made known."

Arthur couldn't be sure, but he felt that what the woman meant was more along the lines of a test of his worth, rather than an education about the Atals.

"If that is his wish," Merlin said. "Arthur is his own man."

Viocee turned back to him. "The Most High has marked you. I cannot see his purpose or design, but that much is clear."

"Thank you," Arthur said.

"I ask again: will you share your name with me?"

"Maybe once we get to know each other better," Arthur said.

"Sadly, I must depart immediately," Viocee said. She turned to Merlin. "We should go now."

"I understand," Merlin said. "Give me a few moments to gather my things. Why don't you have a bite of our flatbread? Arthur, if you could assist me..."

Arthur nodded and walked over to where Merlin's bedroll was laid out. The wizard didn't carry many things and always seemed to produce whatever he needed from his voluminous robes. Merlin joined him, squatting down and whispering so that Arthur had to strain to hear him.

"I have to go," he said. "There are dangerous happenings in Atal. I regret leaving you on your own."

"I'll be fine," Arthur said, although he didn't really feel it. He hadn't expected to, but somewhere along the way, he had begun to depend on Merlin. The wizard was pleasant to be around, deeply knowledgeable, and skilled in interesting ways. Their conversations, especially in the evenings, were something Arthur had begun to enjoy. At the monastery, he was taught so much, yet no one wanted to talk about what they were learning outside of the tutoring sessions. The monks looked down on Arthur, as if his status as an orphan meant he couldn't possibly have anything of interest to talk about it. The other friends of the monastery simply didn't want to talk with Arthur about anything.

"Good," Merlin said. "I'll return as soon as I can. In the meantime, I want you to continue to Avon. Stay on your guard and skirt the salt marshes until you reach Butan. I have an estate on the Black Lake. If you reach it before I return, wait for me there."

Arthur nodded tersely, trying to fight the inadvertent feeling of irritation he couldn't help but feel. It was impossible not to think that Merlin thought so little of him that he would rush off at the first opportunity. On the other hand, Viocee was an imposing person. Not sharing his name with her had been difficult. Merlin too was certainly acting strange around her. Perhaps, he told himself, there was more to Merlin's behavior than he currently understood. There was plenty about the wizard's life that Arthur didn't know. Still, he couldn't shake the feeling that he was being abandoned all over again.

Arthur began rolling up the blankets, but he watched as Merlin tightened the belt around his robes. He walked toward Viocee, who had taken them up on the offer of food. She pulled the bread apart delicately. Her long, slender fingers were adept, and she made eating with them look elegant.

"I am ready when you are," Merlin said.

Setting the bread aside, Viocee pulled a thick strip of fish meat from the nearby bones and held it in her hand. "I too am ready," she said, before turning to Arthur. "It was a pleasure to meet you."

"It was a pleasure to meet you as well," Arthur replied. "Safe travels."

Viocee nodded, then, in one quick motion, she tossed the strip of fish meat high into the air. As it flew up, she jumped and transformed into the common swift, catching the meat in her beak as it fell. As Arthur watched, she glided over the river, tilting her head back and gobbling the last bite of fish.

"I will return," Merlin promised, before he too dissolved before Arthur's eyes, morphing into a small falcon that rose quickly and followed Viocee.

"And I guess I'll just...travel by myself," Arthur muttered, returning to his bedroll.

The stars overhead were bright, and the warmth of the fire felt good, but Arthur couldn't hold back the desolation that swept over him. He had come to realize that he didn't like being alone, and yet it didn't feel safe to trust anyone. So many people in his life had left unexpectedly or even died. There were times when he wished he would have died instead. The monks and priests at the monastery gave beautiful homilies about being in the presence of the Most High when a person died, which sounded much better than being left behind to grieve for those who were lost.

Arthur had trouble sleeping that night. The fire burned low, unable to assuage the cold night air, and then clouds rolled in. An hour before dawn, a cold rain began to fall. Arthur got to his feet in the predawn darkness to fumble through his pack and find the old rain gear he had purchased with Jon a long time ago. The waxed leather would keep the rain off him, mostly. For nearly an hour, Arthur marched back and forth across the little camp to stay warm. The cold had seeped into his body as he tried to sleep, and the rain was only making things worse. Try as he might, he couldn't stay dry. As dawn broke, he packed up the rest of their belongings, mounted Thunder, and began to ride.

The rain turned to sleet. It stung his exposed skin and eventually forced Arthur to take shelter under the branches of a huge fir tree. There was no dry wood, no way to make a fire. He huddled under the tree between the two horses, trying to stay warm. When the weather broke in the afternoon, Arthur chose to lead the horses. He didn't feel like walking, but it was the best way to stay warm. He walked until dark, slogging his way through the woods. It felt like a miracle when he came to a small village just after sunset. It didn't have a proper inn, but it had an alehouse that allowed travelers to sleep on the floor. The horses were taken in by a local with space in a small stable. Arthur stowed his gear in the corner of the alehouse and sat as close to the small hearth as possible. For a few coppers, he was served a dinner of boiled potatoes, rubbery carrots, and stale bread. The ale was sour, not crisp like the ale in Ivy Leaf, and Arthur was happy that he wasn't offered more after his first pint.

The locals were poor farmers who didn't trust visitors. They kept to themselves, which Arthur didn't mind. He stayed by the fire, trying to warm his clothes. When the locals left, he hung his blankets and his second set of clothes near the fire, in the hopes that they might dry by morning. The floor was made of rough planks, but the fire was bright and cheerful. Arthur, exhausted from his cold journey, managed to sleep for several hours. Miraculously, the next morning, his clothes were dry; after changing into them, he felt like himself again. Even better, the brewer who operated the alehouse shared a pot of porridge with him. They ate in silence, but when Arthur left, his mind was clear, and his stomach was full of warm food. The sky outside was clear, and Arthur felt certain it would be a better day.

Seeing to his horses, Arthur set out from the village, expecting to reach the edge of the forest shortly after. Merlin had talked of Byrtan as being a land of rolling hills and open pastures. After over a week in the forest, open land sounded like a nice change. But in his haste to leave the forest, he stopped paying such close attention to his surroundings—to the slight crunches of leaves not made by animal feet, to the clinking of metal buckles, to the nearly imperceptible, but still audible, mutterings of human voices. All of the warning signs escaped his notice.

This was how Arthur ran right into a group of bandits, who quickly surrounded him. There were five outlaws: three on horses, one riding a mule, and one on his feet holding a pitiful bow with a warped arrow on the string.

"What have we here?" one of the bandits said.

"A wealthy traveler," said another. "He has one too many horses."

"Never met a man who could ride two at once," sneered the first.

They laughed, revealing missing teeth. The men were filthy and arrogant. With his sword at his side, Arthur was ready to stand his ground if it came to it.

"I'm not looking for trouble," Arthur said.

"Not too many folk are," said the most talkative outlaw, a heavy man with a gray in his beard. "Unfortunately for you, one might say trouble is our trade. Climb down off that horse."

"No," Arthur said.

"There's five us," the man with the gray beard said. "Get down, or we'll take you down. Don't make no difference to us."

The bandit with the bow drew the arrow back. It was pointed in Arthur's direction, but he could tell that the youth didn't know how to use the weapon, just as he knew the warped arrow wouldn't fly straight. He drew his sword but laid it across his thighs.

"I'm not a dandy," Arthur said. "If you come at me, you'll

pay for it with blood. I can promise you that. Now stand aside!"

He gave the last order with a loud voice. Two of the bandits actually took a step back. The man with the gray beard waved his sword and called to the archer.

"Take him out."

Arthur didn't move as the arrow shot past him. It wasn't even close. He knew what was coming: one wrong move, one miscalculation on his part, and it could cost him his life. Even with that knowledge, he couldn't help but smile as he kicked his heels into Thunder's flanks and raised his sword into the air.

CHAPTER TWENTY-FIVE

The flight was long, but it could have been worse. Merlin could sometimes soar for hours just on the currents of air, and he was lucky that the winds favored them. Viocee was tireless and pushed the pace hard as they traveled west. They flew through the night and the next day. On the second afternoon, Merlin was at the end of his strength when the gleaming White City, as Atland was sometimes called, became visible in the distance. The sight of their destination was enough to carry Merlin on.

They didn't waste any time circling the huge castle at the heart of the city. It was made of polished white limestone with silver fixtures, and Merlin had only been inside a time or two. Viocee led the way. She hurtled toward the ground and transformed from her bird form at the last second, yet made it all look simple and graceful. Merlin landed before transforming. He morphed back into a man on his knees and could hardly find the strength to rise.

"Errol ap'Tunnar Foyl of Avon, welcome," a kind Atal man said, approaching him and lending the wizard a long, powerful arm.

"I was...summoned," Merlin said, his throat so dry that his voice was a whisper.

"Yes, and you have responded admirably," the man praised him.

Merlin didn't say that Viocee had given him no choice. He could have stopped, he supposed. The way to the White City was known to him. At the time, it hadn't occurred to him.

"I am Deelti," the man said. "Let me help you."

He snapped his fingers, and a common-born woman appeared. She was slender, dressed in all in white, and attractive, but in comparison to the Celestial folk, a regular person seemed second-rate. The woman brought with her a tray holding a single crystal goblet of dark red wine. Merlin took the drink and thanked her with a nod of his head.

"Our guest requires sustenance as well," Deelti said.

The woman hurried away, and Merlin took a sip of the wine. It tasted rich, a medley of flavors combining like the instruments of a symphony as it flowed over his parched tongue to revive and warm him. As the heat spread through his body, he felt his strength returning as well, along with his perpetual astonishment at the standards of the Atals. There was nothing normal about the Atals or their works— they never accepted anything less than perfection. From the clothes they wore to the wines they made, everything was of the highest quality.

Fruit, bread, and cheese were presented as Merlin was

shown to a tall white chair. The woman set the food on a white table and slipped away without a word. Merlin knew that common folk came to Atland for a variety of reasons. As a boy, he had come looking to learn the secrets of magic. Others came just to be near the Celestial folk, since it was a close to walking with the Most High as a person could get. Despite this, the Atals still remained a mystery. They held their secrets close and rarely spoke plainly, even to the people who committed their entire lives to serving them.

Merlin wondered briefly, as he began to eat, if Arthur's mother had been a servant like the one who brought his food. Had she come to live among the Celestials only to find love that could never be? He didn't know, and his chance to ask had long passed.

"There are details you should know before the high council meets," Deelti said. "Change is upon us."

"Is that the prevailing thought?" Merlin asked.

Deelti stopped pacing and looked at Merlin. His gaze was penetrating, but the one ability the Atals didn't have was telepathy. The tall Celestial couldn't read his mind.

"It has been said that you are perceptive. Now I see that it is true," Deelti said. "No, we are divided between those who hold to the old way and those who embrace the change."

"Is the change that you speak of the end of the Atals in the land of the living?"

Deelti inclined his head. "Our folly with the common folk will eventually lead to that inevitable conclusion."

"So you want to know if you should fight," Merlin guessed, his mind revived by the food and drink. He shrugged off the fatigue from more than fifty hours of constant flying. There were times in his life when he marveled at the magic he experienced with the Atals. At the moment, the news of the council was more pressing than the joy he found in their magical abilities.

"What do you want me to do?" Merlin asked.

"You have spent time in Farkia. The council will want to know what you believe will happen in the days ahead."

Merlin nodded, and Deelti gave another long, piercing stare. Merlin knew his host wanted an answer, but Merlin needed time to think. The Atals came from a different time and place than the world Merlin knew, and their knowledge and abilities were correspondingly vast. They could have been the lords of the world, had they so chosen, but instead refrained from any involvement in the world of men. Merlin had always found that strange, although he knew they believed their time in the mortal world would come to end at some point—not that they would die, but that they would pass on to a new place. The very thought frightened him. Most wizards believed that once the Atals were gone from the world, magic would disappear as well, and so would dawn an age of men without the wondrous intervention of the Most High.

"I will be ready," Merlin said.

Deelti's lips pressed together in a thin line, not quite a frown. His facial features were still bright, but Merlin recognized the look of disappointment on his host's face.

"I must make preparations." Deelti moved as if to leave. "The council will convene soon. Viocee will come for you."

"Thank you."

Deelti left the room, which was really an open portico. Merlin turned back to the meal that had been prepared for him. He ate it all and finished the wine just as Viocee appeared in the doorway through which Deelti had left.

"It is time," she said softly.

Merlin rose to his feet and followed her. They passed through a series of rooms and came to a wide staircase. At the top, Merlin was presented at a set of double doors.

"Errol ap'Tunnar Foyl," Viocee said in a loud voice as he walked past her.

The council chamber was in the tallest part of the castle, with floors of polished stone and arched walls open to the elements. Merlin could see out the city laid out below and the dark blue sea beyond. Eight Atals, four male and four female, sat in tall, thronelike chairs. In fact, the council chamber would have been the envy of any king in the common world: their palaces were hovels compared to the White City of Atland. The Celestials had built their home on the westernmost tip of a peninsula. It stood surrounded on three sides by water like a gleaming gemstone.

Another common-born sorceress was already in the council chamber. Sursi was the name Merlin knew her by, although she also had an Atal name that she had never shared with Merlin. He was an enchanter, while Sursi was an animage with the ability to commune with animals. A bright green serpent coiled around the upper part of her left arm, and a spotted leopard with white fur and dark spots lay at her feet. On top of her head, her dark hair was pinned in a messy pile like a nest. Merlin could see a large, furred spider gazing out of her hair, its rows of eyes glossy black.

There was also a man with black robes and very dark skin. He wasn't Atal, but, like Arthur, it seemed to Merlin that one of the man's parents most likely was. The man sat on a stool near one of the thrones.

"We are all assembled," a male Atal named Tierti said. "Let us begin."

Merlin walked toward the semicircle of thrones. He took up a station beside Sursi, but not too close. La'Rish gave Merlin an amused smile; obviously, he knew they would push for the Atals to begin leaving. In his mind, what happened among the mortals was beneath them, even if the Atals had sired some of those mortals themselves. Merlin also recognized Aawyzi, eldress of Newspan, and Nor'Kai, the elder of Mizlof. He had spent time in both of their cities. Tierti was known to Merlin only by reputation, and the sixth member of the council—presumably the eldress of Glomee—he didn't know at all.

Cold air was blowing in off the sea. It was late in the year, and Atland would soon be frosted with a coating of snow. The sun, reflecting off the polished white stone, filled the chamber with light. The Atals didn't seem affected by the cold in the winter or by the heat in summer, but they were creatures of the light. Everything they built captured and maximized the sunlight by day. At night, they used candles and crystals to magnify the light, even when they rested, which was usually just one day out of seven.

"There is nothing to discuss," La'Rish said. "Our time has come."

"That is not a decision for you to make," Aawyzi said calmly. "The Farkians have grown bolder, but not more powerful."

"This world had been our home for a long time," Tierti said. "We owe the children of man our assistance."

"I do not share your view," La'Rish said. "We are travelers, sojourners on this world. It was never intended that we would stay."

"No one is arguing that point," Nor'Kai said. "The issue at hand is the constant raiding by the Farkians. They have a powerful sorceress in their midst. What are we to do about it?"

"It is time that we hear from our guests," Tierti said. "Sursi, what have you seen? What have the animals told you?"

The leopard growled softly as Merlin turned his attention to the woman beside him. She was out of reach by several paces, but Merlin still felt slightly threatened by her, as well as the animals she traveled with.

"I have seen magical beasts," she said. "Dark magic stirs in the south, and the Farkians are behind it."

"What kinds of beasts?" Deelti asked.

"Dragons, dread wolves—and worse, beasts that are part human, part animal. They prowl the dark places, growing in power." Sursi's voice was surprisingly deep and gruff.

"Fostus," Tierti ordered, "give us your report."

"A group of Farkians contacted me seeking my assistance. I refused them," the unknown man, who Merlin gathered was an alchemist, said. "They seek weapons of war: eternal flame, poisons, seeing stones—that sort of thing." He grew quiet and hunched on his stool.

"Errol, what can you add to this council?" Tierti asked.

Merlin gave his answer a moment of thought. The council already knew about the danger from the Farkians.

He needed to tell them something that would convince the Atals stay and fight.

"You know I have long warned of this growing darkness," Merlin said. "Their raids, down the coast and through the ancient forest into the Avon, have only increased over time. Now they have begun raiding up the coast as well."

"It is so!" Nor'Kai exclaimed. "But those raiders were repelled."

"Those raiders were merely testing your defenses," Merlin pointed out. "They intend your destruction and that of every common-born man, woman, and child."

"The enchanter tells us what we already know," La'Rish said. "If the Farkians intend our destruction, then we should begin our transition."

"Not all of our people feel as you do," the last Atal to speak in the council said. She had brown skin and brown eyes, framed by glossy black hair that hung in straight lines to either side of her face.

"Jai'Doll speaks truth," Tierti said. "This is our home, and all that was promised to us."

"The Most High will give us another," Deelti insisted.

"None here can fathom his will," said Aawyzi. "We would be poor stewards of the gift he has already bestowed upon us if we leave the Farkians to run wild over the land."

La'Rish shook his head. "We are not warriors. We have no choice."

"There is always a choice," Tierti replied.

"If I may," Merlin spoke up. "There is a way that might satisfy you."

Tierti nodded his head. Merlin took a breath to steady

his normally unflappable nerves. He was about to make a promise he couldn't deliver—not on his own, at any rate. But it seemed like the best solution, and, if his intuition was right, it was the reason why he was there in the first place.

"You could form an alliance with the people of Avon, Bernia, and Byrtan," Merlin explained.

"That is folly of the highest order," La'Rish said, the playful smile that usually graced his features gone. "This is not our world, nor our problem to deal with."

"How can you say that?" Aawyzi was aghast. "The Farkians are the children of our indiscretion."

"Speak for yourself," Deelti snapped. "I have had no such indiscretions."

"Arguing amongst ourselves and laying the blame will not solve this crisis," said Tierti. "I believe Merlin's suggestion may be the way forward. Unity is a power that is not easily overcome. We all know the terrible red dragon's divisive plans."

Merlin felt a shutter at the very thought of the red dragon. He was only whispered of by the Atals. He was once one of them, the most powerful of all, but his hatred of the Most High's affection for mankind drove him insane. He became a beast of destruction so fearsome that many Atals refused to even speak of him.

"He is far from here," Nor'Kai pointed out. "The dragon is obsessed with corrupting the children of men."

"The seeds of his rebellion have been sown here," Jai'-Doll countered. "Hate, fear, division, and the need for control are beginning to spring up."

"We are not the defenders of this world," said La'Rish.

Tierti shook his head. "Weeds exist in every garden and choke the flowers if they can. To tolerate one is to invite many. I think there is merit to Errol's plan, but such an alliance would take time and someone to lead it."

"There may be someone," Merlin said. "A young man I have watched from before his birth. He is a link between the Atals and the common folk."

"Indeed?" Deelti asked sternly. "I thought it was agreed that we would no longer entertain such dalliances."

"Who is this person?" Sursi asked.

"He is called Arthur in the common tongue," Merlin said. "He has only just begun to realize what he could achieve."

"Arthur," Tierti said, as if he were trying out the name to see how he liked it. "If he has gained your trust and respect, Errol, this is a promising development."

"Too little, too late." La'Rish seemed utterly fed up with the course of the conversation. "There is no time for an alliance, and I have no stomach for war."

"If you wish to leave these shores, that is your right," Tierti said. "For now, I would meet this Arthur and consider the possibility that the Most High is at work in this plan."

"I agree," Nor'Kai said.

"And I," added Aawyzi.

"That is three." Tierti nodded across the room. "What say you, Deelti?"

"I am undecided," the other replied. "But I see no reason not to meet this Arthur."

"I too reserve judgement," Jai'Doll said.

"Am I the only voice of reason?" La'Rish demanded. "This council has grown overly reckless, if you are all thinking of delaying our departure. I have seen the blood of our people spilled out on the rocks. It will take more than just words to change my mind."

"He has a point," Deelti said. "If this Arthur is strong enough to unite us, then perhaps he must prove his abilities."

"Prove how?" Merlin asked.

"Some of our people were taken captive," La'Rish said. "Six innocents, the same number as this council. I would be convinced if he rescued our people."

Merlin felt a shard of icy fear pierce his heart. Arthur was a natural-born fighter; he was also intelligent, capable, kindhearted, and still so very young. The last thing Merlin wanted was to send his young friend into Farkia. Humans might not see that he was part Atal, but the Farkians would. If they couldn't turn him to their side, they would kill him.

"Interesting," Tierti said.

"My lords," Merlin interjected, "I understand your desire to save your people, but sending Arthur into Farkia without an army would be to throw away our best chance to save Atlandia."

"These others may judge a man by his words, but I judge a man based on his actions," La'Rish insisted. "There can be no other way to test this Arthur. You said yourself he is our offspring. For all we know, he could be spy sent from Farkia to lead us astray."

"Your pessimism does not serve you, brother," Tierti said. "However, this plan solves two problems at once. Let your man show us his value, Errol. If he is as capable as you claim, we will ally our strength to his."

Tierti struck the floor with a staff. The boom of the

wood on the stone echoed through the chamber and ended the council.

Just like that, the die was cast.

CHAPTER TWENTY-SIX

When Jon had trained Arthur in the ways of the sword, the older man had taught Arthur to respect life and to avoid hurting others. Arthur therefore took no pleasure in that aspect of battle. While he didn't like the idea of maiming and killing, though, he couldn't deny the thrill of the fight.

As his horse leaped forward, two of the bandits fled. Thunder was not a warhorse, but he was still big enough to trample a man. One of the remaining four bandits had a wooden club and raised it block the slash that was coming from Arthur's sword. The blade struck the wooden club and sent it flying from the bandit's grasp. It flew into the adjacent man, opening a gash above his eye and knocking him senseless. The man who had dropped the club drew a small knife, but by that point, Thunder was past him.

The gray-bearded talker reeled back, holding his short-sword in front of him. It wasn't just the archer who was unskilled in the combat arts: Arthur could tell that none of the bandits were trained with weapons. The gray-bearded man held his weapon incorrectly and was moving away from the fight. The fourth bandit, a large man holding a length of metal chain, swung it at Arthur's head. The young man swayed in his saddle, avoiding the chain, and then righted himself. He had to lean over Thunder's neck to reach the man with his sword. Arthur jabbed the tip of *Es Kali ap'Bur* into the shoulder of the bandit, who shouted in pain and fell back. The short cut was perhaps only deep enough lacerate the muscle without reaching the bone, but it bled excessively.

Arthur slowed Thunder as the gray-bearded man continued to back away. Arthur moved in a methodical fashion. First, he wiped the blood from the tip of his word and sheathed it. Then he pulled his bow from where it was tied to his saddle under his right leg with a quick release knot. He brought the bow up with one hand, the other selecting an arrow. Horace had supplied Arthur with a dozen good arrows, some with plain bodkins, but the one Arthur drew had a steel broadhead point. It was triangular in shape, the edges slightly serrated to cut easily through flesh and cause the most damage. It was meant for a big animal, but the bandit saw the weapon and lost his composure. He turned and ran.

In one fluid motion, Arthur nocked the arrow, drew it back to his cheek, and fired. He could have let the bandit go, since the band of outlaws was no longer a threat to him. It didn't matter: they would be a threat to someone else, and Arthur's sense of justice made it imperative that he stop them from continuing to harass other innocents. If the outlaw had turned and dashed through the trees, he might have escaped, but instead he ran straight down the path. Arthur's arrow flashed through the air in a heartbeat and sliced deep into the outlaw's leg. The man fell with a scream. His sword was flung into the bushes as he held his wounded leg with both hands.

Arthur turned Thunder with his knees. He hadn't found many opportunities to ride in the monastery, but occasionally he had taken the horses out for exercise. The priests usually preferred to ride in the wagon when they made their trips into the surrounding towns, but after a few years, Arthur had begun to ride alongside Jon when the priests took their trips. Between those trips and the experience he'd gained since leaving the monastery, Arthur had become a natural in the saddle. Thunder obeyed him instantly, turning around in the middle of the path.

Arthur could see that the man with the knife, the same fool who had attacked him with a wooden club, was surreptitiously trying to steal Merlin's horse, which was carrying all of their supplies—it was easier to ride Thunder with his meager belongings on the other horse, which he had been leading with a rope. When he saw that the bandits wouldn't stand aside, he had dropped the rope, leaving the other horse behind him; the outlaw had decided to take the easy target when Arthur had ridden past and begun taking out the other bandits.

"Stop!" Arthur ordered, pulling another arrow from his quiver.

The bandit looked up and started to lead the horse off the path. *Enough was enough*, Arthur thought. It had been his intent to let the outlaws live, and he had thought that giving them a beating was enough punishment for trying to rob him. As he drew back the arrow, he realized that wounding the bandit might not be enough. He brought his palm to his cheekbone, aiming and releasing without a conscious thought. The arrow flew true and hit the bandit in the back just before he stepped behind a massive fir tree. There was no scream of pain, no sign that the outlaw was even injured, other than the halted steps of the horse he had been leading. Arthur gave Thunder a gentle nudge, and the horse trotted forward. When Arthur reached Merlin's mount, he could see the outlaw lying dead on the ground. The arrow had pierced his heart, killing him instantly.

Arthur dismounted from Thunder, stepped over to the bandit, and nudged him with his boot. The man didn't move. His head was face down in the wet dirt, his hand still clinging to the horse's lead rope. Arthur put one foot on the man's back and took hold of the arrow right above the bloody stain on his filthy shirt. He had to pull hard to retrieve the arrow, but, unlike the broadhead that had wounded the gray-bearded man, the bodkin came out with enough effort and didn't cause any additional damage.

After wiping the blood from the arrow on the dead man's clothes, Arthur pulled the pack horse's lead rope from the outlaw's hand and moved back to the path. Three of the outlaws were still on the ground, one knocked unconscious while the other two moaned and writhed in pain. He began leading the horses toward the gray-bearded man. Arthur was only a few paces from him when the bandit archer, younger than the others, stepped from the trees. Arthur tensed, but the bandit didn't have a weapon. Instead, he held up his hands in surrender.

"How'd you do that?" the boy asked.

"Training, practice, and some irritation," Arthur retorted. "I suggest you leave and find something else to do. This bunch is finished, and next time, you'll end up just like them."

"Please," the gray bearded-man cried, "don't kill me."

"Why not?" Arthur asked, as he drew his short knife. "You were fine with killing me."

The outlaw tried to push himself away with his good leg, but it was no use. Arthur leaned over the man and hit him hard on the side of the chin. His head snapped to the side, then back to center. His eyes rolled up and his body arched stiffly for a moment.

"Did you kill him?" the boy asked tremulously.

"No," Arthur said, "though I've no doubt he deserves it. Is he your father?"

"Not him." The boy shook his head. "My da died when I was a baby. My mother sold me to Harkyn, and Harkyn sold me to him. His name's Garr."

Arthur pulled the belt from around Garr's waist to wrap it twice around the man's upper thigh, above the arrow wound. He pulled the belt as tight as he could and fastened it. The arrow had cut through and lodged in the muscle on the outer side of the outlaw's leg, so there was no way to pull it out without ruining the arrow. Instead, Arthur cut the skin and muscle between the arrow and the side of the man's leg. It left a long gash but had pierced no arteries or veins; the man would live, if he was lucky. Arthur cleaned the arrow as best as he could on the unconscious outlaw's clothes and checked to make sure it was still straight.

"Could you teach me?"

Arthur looked up at the young archer, a little surprised. The boy was a few years younger than Arthur, but much smaller. The skin on his face seemed thin and brittle. Arthur had seen other youths who looked that way when they arrived at the monastery. Jon said they were half starved.

"Do you like being an outlaw?" Arthur asked.

The boy shook his head, seemingly sincere. Arthur considered the request. Jon had made Arthur teach those interested in learning archery at the monastery. He knew he could teach a person to shoot with a bow, but true mastery took practice and time. Still, the boy seemed eager, and Arthur knew what it felt like to be abandoned. He didn't want to ever cause that hurt if he could help it.

"What's your name?"

"Drust," the boy said.

"Can you ride?"

"I don't know," he said. "I've never tried."

"We'll walk for now," Arthur said. "Come on."

Arthur took Thunder's reins and led the horse. He gave the other horse's lead to Drust, who followed along beside Arthur. The young slave looked back often, and seemed frightened, but Arthur got the impression the boy wasn't afraid of him. His fear came from what he was leaving behind.

It didn't take them long to reach the edge of the forest, where the trees gave way to rolling hills. The sky overhead was slate gray and thick with clouds. It felt to Arthur as if it might start raining again.

They stopped long enough for Arthur to retrieve some bread and dried fruit from his supplies. He gave the food to Drust, who looked at Arthur with wide-eyed gratitude but stuffed his mouth before he could actually utter a thank you. They walked for nearly two hours before finding the remains of an old shelter, nothing more than a few rotting posts, the bones of one wall, and part of a roof. From the looks of it, travelers used the structure to camp. There was a firepit dug and lined with rocks, surrounding an area filled with old ash. Arthur saw to the horses, while Drust searched for firewood. The hills were dotted with trees: oak, maple, willow, and pine. They weren't as dense as the forest and not nearly as tall as the massive fir trees, but they provided enough wood by way of broken limbs to build a suitable fire. With water from a nearby spring, Arthur started boiling a pot of rice.

Drust curled up on Merlin's slicker by the fire and fell asleep before their dinner was ready. Arthur let the boy sleep. It was clear he was exhausted, and since they had a little shelter, Arthur was in no hurry to push on. A soft rain began to fall. Their wood was damp but burned well enough. Arthur sat on his own blanket, propped against his saddle, his feet stretched out by the fire that popped and hissed from the rain dripping through a hole in the roof of the ancient shelter. It wasn't a perfect place, but Arthur was dry and out of the rain. He leaned back after stirring his pot of rice and wondered, briefly, what Merlin was doing at that very moment.

CHAPTER TWENTY-SEVEN

After the council meeting, Merlin had been taken to a guest room, where he immediately went to sleep. When he woke a few hours later, sleep still clung to him. In a desperate attempt to wake up, he splashed water on his face and ate a bowl of wonderfully seasoned vegetables that had been left by his hosts. Merlin wasn't sure how the Atals did it, but they had mastered the art of cooking hearty vegetables in a way that was both savory and filling.

He left his little room with some regret, wishing he could have slept twice as long, but there was no time. The need to return to Arthur and tell him what they were committed to was a heavy weight on his shoulders. Merlin had no way of knowing how his young friend would feel. Arthur had a good attitude about most things, but he still didn't trust Merlin. Going into Farkia would be dangerous enough—trying to rescue the captured Atals would add a whole new level of difficulty. Even if they could pull off an infiltration, there was no guarantee that the Celestial folk hadn't already been killed. What would Merlin do if all they could bring back to Atland were the bodies of the slain? Perhaps more importantly, what would the council do?

Snapped to wakefulness by these concerns, the wizard was hurrying down a corridor, his mind going over the many things he needed to do, when he almost ran into Tierti.

"You are leaving?" Tierti asked, as if he didn't already know.

Merlin had discovered long ago that the Atals were always aware of what took place within the walls of their dazzling abodes. Merlin nodded.

"May I speak to you for a moment before you go?" Tierti asked.

It wasn't really a request, but Merlin didn't begrudge the head of the council. Had Tierti wanted to leave Atlandia and the Farkians for the humans to deal with alone, he easily could have. Most, if not all, of the Atals would follow the will of the council, even if many of them feared leaving.

They stepped into a room with a huge window over-looking the sea. Tierti went to the window and leaned on the wide, stone sill. Cold, salty air flowed in, and Merlin wrapped his robes closer around his shoulders as he waited for his host to speak.

"Leaving is still an option," he said after a long pause. Merlin wasn't sure how to respond, but Tierti explained before he had to. "But I fear we have been here too long. My people have become part of this world, or perhaps the world has become part of us. Either way, I would prefer not to push them into doing something they do not want to do. Tell me about this Arthur. Do you know his true name?"

"I do," Merlin said. "I bonded with him before he was born."

"Indeed? What prompted you to bond with an infant?"

"I cannot say entirely," Merlin admitted. "I could sense greatness in him, for one thing. We seemed to be thrust together by the Most High. His mother was fragile, and there was something about her…"

Merlin watched as Tierti's gaze drifted for a moment. There was a look of bittersweet emotion on his face, like he was caught in a memory.

"I have known women like that," he said.

Merlin wasn't sure exactly what the head of the council meant by his statement. Was he saying he understood what Merlin's sentiment, or was he implying that he had known intimately women who made him feel the same way? It was impossible to know. Unlike humans, Atal body language was often hard to read..

After a short beat, Merlin shrugged. "I suppose it was all those things together."

"Tell me about his mother," Tierti said.

"Her name was Cryslov," Merlin said, watching his host for clues about why he was asking about a common-born woman. "She was waiting for the father of her child to come for her."

"Waiting where?"

"In Byrtan, across the salt marshes. She settled in Lontown."

"The gateway to the world," Tierti commented absently. "Have you ever crossed over to the east?"

"No, although I have heard stories of the people who dwell in those lands."

"They are godless," Tierti said. "Unrefined. Some call them barbarians or savages, but they have not been blessed with knowledge of the Most High. Lontown is as far as one could get from Alal, wouldn't you say—as far as one could get while still in Atlandia, at least."

"Perhaps," agreed Merlin, who had never thought of it that way before.

"Is it possible that she wasn't waiting, but rather hiding?"

"Anything is possible. That's not what she told me, nor what she told her child."

"There are truths too dark to believe, even about ourselves," Tierti said. "You speak of her in the past."

"She died," Merlin said.

Tierti didn't move or speak. He stood like a statue, unreadable, for several seconds. Merlin wasn't sure how to react and hesitated to move too quickly. If the wizard spoke to break the tension, would it somehow diminish his standing with the Atal?

"How long ago?" Tierti finally asked, his voice quiet.

"Seven years," Merlin said.

"I see. Thank you, Merlin—I look forward to meeting this Arthur," Tierti said, before suddenly turning on his heel and leaving the room.

It was a departure abrupt enough that it took Merlin by surprise. He stood in the bright room, wondering what had happened. The cold wind continued to blow in from the sea, carrying with it, Merlin thought, some moisture, and an edge of chill sharp enough pierce him.

The cold air got Merlin moving again, back to the

balcony where he would transform into his falcon form and begin the long journey back to Avon by way of Farkia. Before he reached the balcony, however, a voice called to him. Merlin turned to see Deelti striding toward him, a staff in one hand.

"Tierti wanted you to have this," Deelti explained. "It is powerful and may be useful in your efforts to rescue those taken by the Farkians."

He held out the staff. It was smooth and white, fashioned from some exotic wood the wizard couldn't identify. The butt was slight larger than the shaft, and at the head, the wood spread apart into seven branches that grew around a dark purple crystal. As soon as Merlin touched the staff, he could feel the power humming inside, although he couldn't hear it with his ears. The power from the staff flowed into him, and whatever remaining fatigue clung to Merlin was flushed away. He felt strong holding the staff, such that even his thoughts carried more certainty.

"It is a precious gift," Merlin said.

"Yes," Deelti agreed. "Use it wisely. Bring our people home."

"I will," Merlin did not quite believe his own words, and yet he felt in that moment as if he could do anything.

"Farewell," said Deelti. "May the Most High speed you on your way."

Merlin inclined his head a little. The need to get into the air was pressing on him. He turned, hurried toward the balcony, and transformed mid-step. The magical staff, along with his other possessions, simply became part of him; he couldn't explain how it worked, only that it did. A gust of wind off the ocean lifted Merlin high into the air. He didn't even have to flap his wings to sail away from the White City. It dazzled behind him, the polished stone contrasting with the deep blue sea. But Merlin only had eyes for what lay before him: a long and dangerous journey, but one that would affect the future of Atlandia. Of that, he had no doubt.

CHAPTER TWENTY-EIGHT

The morning sun rose bright on a clear day after the rainstorm that had forced Arthur and Drust into shelter. They moved south, stopping at a small village where Arthur was able to buy Drust new clothing. The boy had been in filthy rags that were too large and threadbare, with raggedy holes in some places and puckered patchwork in others. Worse still was their stench, which lingered on Drust. Arthur forced the boy to bathe, then dressed him in wool breeches, a thick shirt, and a cloak. Drust was a little timid at first and looked almost distressed in the new clothes. Over the following days, however, as he got used to Arthur, he opened up more and more.

The boy was a helpful addition around camp: he gathered firewood, assisted with the horses, and never complained. It was obvious that he was happy to be away from the bandits. Still, some habits died hard—Arthur noticed him hoarding food, even though Arthur made sure there was plenty. He began teaching Drust how to ride a horse and the proper technique for shooting a bow. They took their time traveling and camped out, rather than staying at the inns in the towns they passed through. Drust seemed nervous in these towns, as if he expected someone to take him from Arthur and force him back into slave labor with the bandits. Arthur knew it wouldn't happen, but Drust couldn't be convinced. To him, every adult was to be feared; he acted as if even Arthur's kindness might be hiding a nefarious motive. He learned not to sneak up behind Drust or make sudden movements when the boy was close.

On the third day, they reached Éire, one of the larger settlements in Byrtan. Flanked to the north and south by swampland, the city itself was built on a sloping hill that served as the central trade route through the marshes. They reached the city late in the afternoon. Their supplies were running low, and Arthur decided to stay at an inn called the Dogwood. It was a big establishment, with its own stable for patrons. As they got settled, Drust and Arthur ordered food and refreshments. The inn had warm apple cider, slow-roasted pork ribs, potatoes and onions fried in bacon grease, and bread made from cornmeal. They ate their fill, tossing the rib bones to a pair of hounds that lay stretched by the fire. The main floor of the inn was comfortably large, with round tables and low-backed chairs, as well as a huge fireplace that dominated one wall. The patrons were served by young women who flirted with every guest. Wine and ale flowed, pipe smoke filled the rafters, and the aroma of roasted pork mingled with the sweet smell of pumpkin cakes, which were served with fresh cream. It was nothing short of an oasis.

Drust was finally starting to relax and take a second helping of the hearty food when two men in dark cloaks came in. Arthur didn't notice them at first: he was sitting low in his seat, his feet stretched out toward the fire to better enjoy its heat, which paired with the warm cider served with fresh cinnamon. He was thinking of what he might do once they reached Butan. It was possible that Merlin could be gone for months, perhaps years. Arthur decided he would give the wizard a week, and then he would push on. Traveling soothed Arthur's restlessness, and there was so much more of Atlandia to see.

His idle planning was cut short when Drust stiffened, his face frozen in a mask of horror. Arthur turned to see what had frightened the boy. The two men in dark cloaks were big, at least as tall as Arthur but thicker through the chest. Their heavy, fur-lined cloaks accentuated their massive shoulders and hid the swords they carried. Arthur saw them adjust their weapons as they took a seat near the door.

"Who are they?" Arthur asked.

"D-d-don't know." Drust was audibly shaking.

His reaction, and the lie inherent within it, caused Arthur to raise an eyebrow. "It seems like you do."

"They're Harkyn's men," Drust said. "Swordsmen."

"Who is Harkyn?" Arthur asked.

"Harkyn," Drust said, as if Arthur was stupid. "Lord of the North Marsh. He's a slaver."

Suddenly, Drust's fear made sense. "I understand. But they're not here for you."

"I ran away," Drust said. "Do you know what they do to slaves who run away?"

"No one is doing anything," Arthur said. "No one is looking for you."

It was no use: the boy was terrified. Arthur would have liked to stay by the fire longer, sipping the hot apple cider, but that simply wasn't an option. To stay would be torture to Drust, and Arthur would never do that to the boy.

"Let's go up to our rooms," Arthur said.

"Can't," Drust said. "If we stay, they'll catch us."

"They're not chasing us," Arthur said calmly as he got to his feet.

The big men in dark cloaks hadn't even looked their way. Arthur picked up his sword and his cloak, which were laid out on the unoccupied chair at their table. His other weapons were up in their room, but he couldn't even imagine leaving his sword behind. It was part of him; to leave it would be like going out naked.

Arthur was just about to take Drust by the arm when another man stood up. He wasn't one of the men in dark cloaks, but rather a short, heavyset man with a dark red stocking cap over his balding head and large ears. He looked almost comical and approached Arthur with a smile. There were nearly forty guests in the inn's noisy common room and several serving maids moving among them with pitchers of ale and jugs of wine. No one was paying attention to Arthur and the fat man as he approached the tall young man by the fire.

"Leaving so soon?" the fat man asked.

"We've had a long day," Arthur lied, thinking the man wanted their table by the fire. "You can have our table."

"I don't want the table, friend—just a word."

The fat man sat down at the table across from Drust, who was trembling visibly.

"Excuse me?" Arthur said.

"Sit down, lad," said the fat man. "No need to make a fuss. You've overstepped your bounds, but I can remedy that."

Arthur looked up and saw one of the dark-cloaked men staring at him, and it suddenly all made sense. They weren't alone in the inn. Arthur couldn't possibly know who was a traveler and who was part of the crew that worked for the slaver. It didn't make sense to Arthur that they would cause such a fuss over one boy, yet he knew they were trapped by violent men who wouldn't hesitate to kill him.

His heart began to pound in his chest from the anticipation of a fight and the deep fear that innocent people could get hurt. Surrounded within four walls, he felt trapped, like a boar that has been hemmed in by spears. He dropped his cloak into his empty seat and sat back down, keeping his sword across his knees.

"There, that's better," the fat man said. "Why'd you run, Drust? There was no call for that."

"I thought Garr was dead," Drust said.

The fat man made a noise with his mouth: *tsk, tsk*. "Don't lie, now. You're caught, and lying will only make things worse."

"I don't know who you are or what you want," Arthur said. "But you need to leave."

"Is he the one that got the jump on Garr's crew?" the fat man asked, still speaking to Drust and ignoring Arthur.

Drust nodded. Arthur was beginning to get angry, but the fat man finally turned to him.

"Harkyn respects talent, so he's giving you two choices," the fat man said. "You were defending yourself, but you killed his nephew—shot him in the back with an arrow. That's a debt that has to be paid. You can leave your sword and all your coin on the table and walk on out of Éire tonight. We'll take your horses, too, and call things even. Or you can join Harkyn's crew yourself—turn this whole debacle into something positive for everyone. There's always work needs doing by capable men."

"I don't take lightly to being threatened," Arthur warned.

"It's not a threat," the fat man said. "It's an offer, and I suggest you take it, boy. You're in way over your head here."

"All of this because of a slave?"

"Oh, no, we don't much care about Drust. It's the debt he's carrying that means something. See, around here, when a man owes something, he pays it."

The fat man wasn't looking at Arthur, but rather steadfastly fixed his gaze on Drust. All the same, Arthur felt the tension rising, so when the fat man tried to slap him without warning, the young warrior was ready. Arthur was to the side of the fat man, who twisted in a fast lunge, but Arthur was faster. Speed, Jon Longarm had told him countless times, was more important than strength. Fortunately for Arthur, he was both faster and stronger than the fat man. He caught the man's wrist before the blow struck. This was lucky: the fat man was wearing a ring with a wicked little barb on the inside, which, Arthur had no doubt, was either dipped in poison or had a clever little way of injecting it into the target on impact, like the fangs of a viper.

The fat man's eyes widened in surprise when Arthur caught his wrist. He immediately tried to pull a knife from his belt, but once again, Arthur was faster. An open-palmed strike to the fat man's temple knocked him senseless and sent him toppling over backward with a crash. At the same moment, the two big men in cloaks stood up. Arthur stood too, drawing his sword from its scabbard. He held the weapon with two hands as the patrons around the room scrambled from their seats. Many hurried to leave, but nearly a dozen stood and drew weapons of their own. Arthur hadn't realized how many of Harkyn's men had surreptitiously thronged the room. The men in dark cloaks had been a distraction, and he really was trapped.

"Drust," Arthur said, knowing that no matter how skilled he was with a sword, he couldn't defeat a dozen men, "get behind me."

The boy obeyed. The room cleared of patrons, but no one attacked. Arthur wondered if perhaps it would better to go on the offensive. If he could take a few out before the others reacted, he might stand a chance. Before he could make up his mind, a tall man with a braided beard and golden hoops through his ears stepped in from the back room. He stood tall as he walked past the fighters assembled around the room. Calmly, he glanced at the fat man on the floor in front of Arthur and shook his head.

"Not many men get the jump on Chubb," the man with the braided beard said. "That sort of talent is rare."

"Who are you?" Arthur asked, still weighing his options.

"Harkyn is my name. And these fine gentlemen all work for me," he said, his braided beard swaying. "Now, like it or not, you're in a pickle—and all over a boy who broke the one immutable law in my enterprise."

"Because he left a life of squalor and depravity?" Arthur spat.

"No, I can't say I agreed with the way Garr made his living or treated the people in his employ."

"But Drust wasn't his partner," Arthur pointed out. "He was a slave."

"Precisely: slaves don't run away. I guarantee that young Drust there is aware of this fact. He might not have shared it with you, but that's the way this works. Now, you can give me the boy and we'll call it even, despite the loss of my nephew. He was a dullard, and no one would argue that. You and I can let bygones be bygones. We'll even sit down and have some of this establishment's fine ale together to discuss your future. There's coin to made by a man with your skills. Look at this as an opportunity. If it's young boys you like, that can be arranged...just not Drust."

Arthur felt a wave of revulsion at the insinuation that he would harm a child. He glanced at the men on either side of Harkyn. None of them had moved, and each one was armed. If they rushed him, he could stop some, but not all. He needed another way out of the fix he found himself in without handing over Drust, which simply wasn't an option. Arthur had no idea what life was like as Harkyn's slave, but he knew from the way Drust acted that it was a fate worse than death.

"Drust isn't mine," Arthur said slowly. "He chose to follow me when he could have done anything he wanted."

The boy, Arthur realized, also clearly had more to his story than he had shared, although that was his right. Still, it didn't make navigating the current situation any easier.

"My slaves don't run," Harkyn reiterated, his voice growing cold. "He knows that. Garr still lives, and he had an obligation to help his master, not flee the first chance he got. I've a reputation to uphold, myself. People buy slaves from me because they know my people don't run—ever. If they do, they have me to contend with.

"That's enough talk. You step aside, or this will get bloody."

Arthur wasn't sure what to do. Unfortunately, his chance to surprise the men working for Harkyn had passed. All he could do was take them as they came. He wished the inn wasn't so crowded with tables and chairs, but that might play into his favor as well. His sword and long arms gave him the reach advantage over those closest to him. He hoped his speed and decision-making would prove greater than theirs as well.

"You want Drust?" Arthur challenged. "You'll have to go through me."

Suddenly, the door burst open, and everyone looked to see who it was, including Arthur. It wasn't a man that came through the door—it was bird. A falcon with brown and gray feathers flew in. There was a flutter of wings before Merlin stood up. He looked fierce, his hair and beard sticking out across his head and face at odd angles. His robes were wrinkled and unkempt. In one hand, he held a white staff. There was an expression of intense anger on his face.

"What the devil is this?" Harkyn bellowed.

In reply, Merlin tapped his staff on the floor, and the fire from the hearth roared out into the room. It flowed up and over Arthur's head, split in two, and stretched from one end of the room to the other. The fire floated in midair, slowly pressing the warriors back, away from Arthur and Drust. Only Harkyn stood in Arthur's way.

"If you have an issue with Arthur, then I suggest you get on with it," Merlin said. "But it should be a fair fight, so the rest of us will just watch."

One of the warriors decided to try to duck under the floating wave of fire. He moved quickly, but an invisible force threw him back into the wall so hard he dropped to the floor, unconscious. A look of fear crossed Harkyn's face. Although clearly a powerful man, and likely one unused to being dictated to, it was probable, Arthur realized, that he hadn't been on his own in a fight for a long time. Arthur decided it was time to press his sudden advantage.

"Release your claim on the boy and step aside," Arthur commanded. "Drust goes free, and you promise to never bother him again."

"I won't do that," Harkyn snarled.

"Then come and take him," Arthur said. "That is your choice."

Harkyn drew two thin, sickle-shaped swords from his belt, a solid set of one-handed weapons. Arthur hadn't even noticed them under the slaver's cloak.

"Wouldn't be the first time I've had to deal with matters myself," Harkyn said. Then he charged at Arthur with a fury and speed that was completely unexpected.

In his sparring sessions with Jon, Arthur could always see the angles of attack. It was like a dance, and he was good at anticipating his partner's next move. But Harkyn wasn't a swordsman: he didn't control his body to use his sword to its advantage. He was a crazed fiend, intent on hacking Arthur to pieces. As Harkyn leaped over Chubb, who was still unconscious on the floor, Arthur slid to the side, avoiding the slaver's first chop. One sickle-shaped sword slammed into the wooden surface of the table and wedged there. Arthur brought his sword up defensively and moved one step to his right, expecting Harkyn to turn and continue the attack, but instead he released his grip on the sword in the table and rushed toward Drust. Arthur snatched up a chair and hurled it at the slaver as Drust fled into the corner of the room, where he dropped to the ground and curled into a ball, raising his arms to cover his head.

The chair hit Harkyn a glancing blow, but it was enough to slow the slaver. Arthur rushed to intercept him as Harkyn turned to defend himself. With a feint to his right that forced Harkyn to bring his remaining blade up to block from that side, Arthur slid left. Harkyn was focused on Arthur's sword, which he held out with his right hand to distract the slaver. His left hand shot forward. Harkyn was expecting a blow and tried to jerk back, out of reach.

But Arthur didn't hit him—instead, he grabbed the slaver's braided beard. One tug pulled Harkyn off balance. He stumbled forward, trying to hack at Arthur, but Arthur brought his own blade down. The metal hit with a clash and slid down toward the hilt. Harkyn's curved blade caught on Arthur's shining cross piece just above the handle, but the slaver's weapon had no such defensive device. Arthur slashed his blade across the slaver's grip. Razor-sharp *Es Kali ap'Bur* severed three of Harkyn's fingers.

The slaver screamed in pain, and the sickle sword went flying. It looked like the fight was over. Arthur even released Harkyn's braided beard as he reared back, trying to escape Arthur and the terrible wound.

It was a mistake that almost cost Arthur his life.

CHAPTER TWENTY-NINE

Once again, Merlin was tired: he had flown for three days straight. He'd spent most of the first reaching Farkia, where he spied on the growing army of darkness. There was no doubt that someone was using terrible magic. Many of the Farkians had power, but few were strong enough to bend magic to their will. Instead, it seemed that they were lending their strength to someone who had taken control of their efforts. Merlin couldn't see who and didn't stay long enough to discover the leader of the Farkians, but he saw the mutilated, nightmarish creatures that were fruit of their evil efforts. It was a perverse twist of the Atals' power to use magic to create. Merlin saw common folk waiting in cages, while others were mutated into savage half man, half beast creatures that were clearly insane, left only with the desire to kill and destroy.

After leaving Farkia, Merlin had crossed over Avon in search of Arthur. The young man was easy enough to find:

Merlin could feel Arthur's growing power. The glow of his Atal blood made him stand out in the crowds of common folk. Merlin had just discovered the Dogwood Inn and was searching for a place to land and transform back to his human self when he saw the patrons come streaming out. When Arthur wasn't among them, he knew his friend was in trouble.

Making a grand entrance, Merlin had regained his human shape, the staff that Deelti had given him clutched firmly in his hand. A surge of magic, partly from the staff and partly from his own anger at seeing Arthur surrounded, flowed through Merlin and banished his fatigue. He summoned the fire and pinned the warriors to the walls, leaving Arthur to deal with the leader of the group, which he seemed to be doing quite well. When Arthur severed the man's fingers, Merlin thought the fighting was over and almost released his hold on the magical fire.

They'd both misjudged the slaver—Harkyn wasn't finished. As he stumbled back, clutching his wounded hand to his chest, his other drew a throwing knife. It was a plain piece of metal, well balanced, with just a simple metal handle. It spun toward Arthur and narrowly missed his face as the young warrior dodged to the side.

Merlin saw the blade coming and knew instinctively that it would hit him. He had drop his hold on the fire to stop the blade; the moment the fire vanished, which it did as quickly as a candle under a puff of breath, the inn fell into a furious chaos. Arthur charged forward and thrust his sword straight into Harkyn's leg, just above the knee. The slaver howled as he fell, and the youth hidden in the corner screamed, causing Arthur to jerk his sword free and spin.

The young warrior was a sight to behold as he ducked under a diagonal chop from one of Harkyn's men and slashed another in the stomach.

Harkyn sank to the floor, and two of his men rushed to his aid. The hulking warriors in dark cloaks drew thick-bladed swords and advanced on Merlin. He backed up, acting as if he were frightened, then used his magic to fling the throwing knife that had clattered to floor at the warriors. It flipped end over end, unnoticed since Merlin hadn't physically cast the weapon. The knife sank into the neck of the warrior to Merlin's right, and the big man dropped to his knees. His massive sword drove straight down into the wooden plank flooring. He leaned on the weapon, holding it with one hand, while the other tried to stem the flow that was gushing from the wound in his neck. His companion glanced down nervously as the wounded man coughed and sputtered blood, eventually toppling onto his side.

The rest of the fighters converged on Arthur, who whirled like a violent tempest. He jumped onto a table, kicked a chair into one of the men, and dodged another's swipe at his feet. From the elevated position, Arthur's long arm and equally long sword made him difficult to reach. He wounded two men before someone dove to the ground and hacked at the leg of the table. The table tipped forward, and Arthur used the momentum to fling himself away from the back of the room. His sword took the head of one of the fighters as he fell. The head flew up into the air and then landed on the wooden flooring with a thump. Arthur, on the other hand, landed on one side, rolling smoothly over his shoulder and coming back up on his feet as if by magic.

At the other end of the room, the last big warrior raised his sword over his head, as if to cleave Merlin in two. Luckily, magic wasn't the wizard's only strength, and in a smooth, strong motion, he lashed out with the butt of his staff. The thick wood thumped into the warrior's groin so hard he dropped his sword behind him and doubled over. Merlin drove his knee into the man's face with all his strength. Pain exploded in the wizard's knee, but the warrior's nose was broken. He bobbed up from the impact, blood running from his nose as if a dam had broken inside his head, and then fell face first onto the floor.

With his helpers carrying him, Harkyn was trying to escape. Merlin gave a solid magical push using the strength of the staff, and the trio crashed to the ground as if they had run headlong into an invisible wall. Harkyn was moaning and cursing, his men scrambling to escape. One drew a dagger and moved toward Merlin, who brought the butt of his staff up again to hit the dagger from the man's hand and send it flying upward. Before the man could react, Merlin caught the dagger with his magic and drove it back down. It dropped, point first, into the back of the man's neck with enough force to cut his spine. The man crashed to the ground.

His companion was dragging a screaming Harkyn toward the door. Merlin went to intercept him when the warrior with the broken nose grabbed his foot. The wizard fell hard and had to kick the wounded warrior away. When he looked back up, Harkyn and his accomplice were gone.

Arthur was still fighting four men. They had learned to respect his speed and the reach of *Es Kali ap'Bur*, but their combined cautious efforts were forcing the young warrior back. If he committed to one, the others could flank him. No one saw Drust, who had gotten to his feet and found the sickle sword Harkyn had dropped when Arthur severed his fingers. The boy attacked one of the men from the rear, chopping with the sickle sword. The blade tore the man's hamstring. He cried out and fell to the side, into one of his companions. Capitalizing on the distraction, Arthur kicked one man in the chest and almost simultaneously drove his sword into the stomach of the other. The weight of the wounded man pulled him backward, off Arthur's sword. With their advantage lost, the last two men fled. One ran toward the kitchen; the other scrambled to get back on his feet, but Drust bore down with the sickle sword. It would have been a killing blow, but the man dodged to the side, and the sword bounced off the wooden wall.

"Don't kill him," Arthur warned the boy.

Drust looked at Arthur with menace in his eyes. He clearly wanted vengeance, but he didn't disobey Arthur, who gave the order in a commanding voice.

"Harkyn fled," Merlin said, getting to his feet.

"He won't be back," Arthur said.

"But he won't forget you, either," Merlin said. "I leave you for a few days, and you anger an entire gang of killers?"

Arthur shook his head. "It's a long story."

"You can tell me on the road. Go fetch your things—we're leaving."

"Drust, get the horses," Arthur told the young boy, who ran off.

Arthur stepped over to the fallen warrior in the dark cloak that Drust had hoped to kill. The man looked resigned to his fate, but Arthur didn't kill him, either.

Instead, he tilted the man's bloody chin up with the toe of his boot, then bent low, looking into the man's blackened eyes.

"We are letting you live," Arthur said. "If you or your master come after us again, we will not be so merciful."

The man nodded. Merlin stood up and looked at Arthur, who was watching him.

"Well, what are you waiting on?" Merlin asked. "Go get your things."

"What are you going to do?" Arthur asked, a look of mistrust on his face, as if he expected the wizard to kill the wounded the moment the young warrior left the room.

Merlin grinned. "I'm going to get something to eat."

CHAPTER THIRTY

They left the inn by the light of torches ignited by fire Merlin conjured. In this way, they left Éire in the dead of night, with Drust riding behind Arthur. Once they were out of the town, they took the southern road that skirted the salt marshes. As Arthur told his tale of fighting the outlaws and taking in Drust, Merlin couldn't help but think of the night he had met Arthur's mother and fought off the huge snake. The world was not a safe place— there was a freedom in its wildness, but also danger.

Safely out of town, Drust fell asleep leaning against Arthur. The fight had been traumatic for the boy. Merlin had heard of Harkyn and knew his reputation: he bought children from people in debt and sold them to anyone who had coin, no matter their desire for the innocent children. Harkyn also had a name for scaring his slaves into obedience, no matter what their masters forced them to do. A slave bought from Harkyn never ran away, or so it was said. Drust was the exception to that rule, but having dealt the slaver a savage blow, Merlin couldn't help but hope they might have ended his evil trade.

"If he lives, he will look for vengeance," Merlin warned Arthur.

"Your point?" Arthur asked.

"Just that mercy may be a virtue we cannot afford," Merlin said.

"I do not turn away from violence," Arthur stated firmly. "But taking a life is not something I will ever do if I can avoid it."

"It may be your life that pays in the end, or that of someone you love. Something to think about."

They made camp a couple of hours outside of Éire beside a freshwater creek that flowed into the marsh. It was only a few hours before dawn, but they were all exhausted. Merlin lay down cocooned in his robes and slept soundly.

When he awoke, a fire was burning higher than they needed, but the smoke kept the troublesome gnats away. They weren't in the salt marshes, but they were close enough that the foul creatures that made the swamps their home were an annoyance. The sun was up, and so was Arthur. He looked tired, but that was no surprise.

"Will you tell me what the Atals wanted?" Arthur asked as soon as Merlin was sitting up and looking around.

Arthur had a pot of oatmeal boiling over the embers at the edge of the fire. From his supplies, he had taken some raspberries, which he was stirring into their morning meal. Merlin rummaged through the hidden pockets of his robes and produced a small vial of salt. He handed it to Arthur and leaned back.

"The Farkians have kidnapped some of the Atals that dwell in the mountains."

Arthur looked surprised. "The Farkians? I thought you said the Bright Ones were too powerful for the Farkians?"

"I said the Atals are the most magically powerful beings in Atlandia, and that the Farkians are their offspring."

"Like me," Arthur said.

"No, not like you," Merlin corrected. "You were raised by your mother in Lontown and by the monks at Byth El. The Farkians were raised in Alal and despise common-born folk."

"Because of the power they inherited?"

"Perhaps," the wizard conceded. "Their jealousy drove them to do wicked things and continues to entice them into perverting the magic they control."

"Like what?"

"From what I saw recently, they are using their power to create beasts that are part human and part animal. It's an abomination not just in a physical sense, but also to the true nature of magic. You see, the magic that the Atals possess is a creative power. Think of it like a farmer who takes raw land and cultivates it: he spends his time and energy making things grow. That is what the Atals' power is like."

Arthur wrinkled his nose. "And the Farkians use that power to kill?"

"To kill, to steal, to destroy—that is the legacy of their power. They are driven by jealousy and resentment. Hatred has hardened their hearts and turned the light of the Atal blood into darkness."

"Is that my fate?" Arthur looked concerned. "Will I become a tyrant no better than Harkyn?"

"No," Merlin said firmly. "Everyone has a choice in life. You have many gifts and abilities, but they don't define you. It's what you do with those gifts that make you who you are. Do good with your gifts, and you will be accepted. But be careful, Arthur: it only takes a single decision to ruin the legacy of an individual. Evil will always seek to destroy you, so you must be stronger than the evil around you."

Arthur thought about that for a while, and Merlin didn't interrupt the young warrior's thoughts. The wizard could see that Arthur had a grand future. He was already an extremely talented warrior, and he was still just starting to recognize all that he could become. Soon, all of Atlandia would be talking of his heroic deeds. Men of all walks of life would flock to his banner, and Arthur would know real power. What he did then would define his life and color the way he was remembered.

"The Atals want your help to rescue the captives?" Arthur asked after stirring the oatmeal.

"The Atals need a reason to resist the Farkians," Merlin said. "And to do so, they need allies."

"Like you. That makes sense."

"Not entirely like me," Merlin said. "What they need is an alliance with men. They need an army to fight."

"Why? They're powerful wizards. What would they need an army of common-born men to do?"

"They are powerful, but they are not violent. Remember, their magic is a creative force. They can no more use it to destroy than the trees of the forest could march to war."

"Is your job to raise an army, then?" Arthur asked.

"They want to know if mankind will stand with them," said Merlin, as he contemplated how much he should actually tell Arthur. It wouldn't do any good to overwhelm the young man with the idea of building an alliance around him, who, although mature for his age, was still just sixteen years old. His Atal blood had given him size and strength, but the idea of leading an army into battle might be too much, even for him.

"Makes sense," Arthur said. "There are more common-born folk than Atals. Still, Merlin, that doesn't really explain why they sent for you."

"They sent for me because they need someone to rescue their people," Merlin said.

"They want you to do it?"

"They want *us* to do it," Merlin said. He couldn't help but feel a little guilty. Thrusting Arthur into a conflict between Farkia and Alal might be his path to greatness, but it was still a dangerous road. If Merlin was wrong, they might both die in the attempt to rescue the hostages. Worse still, they might succeed and have the Atals turn their back on the alliance. Merlin didn't want to risk their lives for nothing. Despite this, he was hopeful that the venture might yield the results he wanted. Leading the alliance between men and Atals made perfect sense. Arthur had one foot in each world; he could bridge the gap between them.

"Us?" Arthur said as he started to ladle out bowls of oatmeal. "You mean me as well? That's crazy."

"Maybe," Merlin said. "But I would not turn my back on those in need."

Arthur looked up at the wizard, suspicion in his eyes. "Don't do that. Don't try to manipulate me, Merlin. I know you better than that. You didn't help my mother when you could have. You didn't help Jon."

"I came back to you as soon as I could," Merlin said. "I had obligations to fulfill."

"Maybe this mission to rescue the captive Atals is another part of your obligation, but it isn't mine."

"Arthur, I don't mean to push you."

"Look, I'll help—but don't treat me like a fool," the young warrior warned. "Tell me what's going on. I can take it."

"Fine." Merlin knew when he was beaten. "I'll tell you everything. Not now—it isn't something we can cover over breakfast, and we need to start moving west if we're going to attempt to rescue the Atals."

"What about Drust?" Arthur asked.

"From what you've said, he's useful. We'll take him with us. Not all the way, and certainly not into danger. Perhaps we'll find a home for him along the road ahead."

CHAPTER THIRTY-ONE

They purchased another horse in a small village later that day. Drust had no skills on a horse other than holding on. But his mount followed Arthur's without any direction from Drust, and they made good time, reaching the west fork of the great forest by nightfall.

The following day, they crossed the forest and found a place to ford the Albion River into Farkia. It was the last boundary between Avon, which was occupied by men, and Farkia, a land reserved for the offspring of the Atals. Gone were the rolling hills and lush landscape. Farkia suffered the effects of the dark magic that its citizens practiced. There were no farms, no pastures with cattle grazing. The soil was rocky and dry, fit only for weeds and scrub brush. What trees grew there were gnarly and stunted. Water was hard to find and sometimes tainted.

"Where are we going?" Arthur asked, as the barrenness of the landscape began to weigh on him.

"There are clans gathering at a place called LóArc," Merlin said. "I can't be sure that the captives are there, but that's where I am inclined look first."

"What's your plan?" Arthur said. "Do we simply ride into town?'

"No, that would be a mistake," the wizard replied. "You could blend in, but Drust and I would stand out."

"I wouldn't think that a wizard and a boy would be so remarkable," Arthur commented.

"We are only of note here because we have no Atal blood," Merlin explained. "You do—in fact, you are what the Farkians call 'high caste,' because your father was an Atal. Most of the Farkians are low caste, with many generations between them and the Atals. They generally have physical strengths, but no magical powers. There are some middle caste with weak magical gifts. For a while, the Farkians tried to breed more power, mating high caste individuals in the hopes that their offspring would have greater powers. To my knowledge, that effort failed."

"This caste system...did they learn that from the Atals? How was society structured before the Farkians left Alal?"

Merlin looked impressed, if cautious. "Their common-born parents lived in service to the Atals. It's a bit difficult to explain." Merlin looked at Arthur, clearly hesitant to share everything he knew.

"Go on," Arthur urged him.

"You were born with your mother and raised with common folk," Merlin said. "As a result, you think of yourself as a human. The first Farkians, on the other hand, were raised among the Atals. They saw the difference between their parents, in both knowledge and abilities. Most longed to be like their Celestial parents."

"That makes sense."

"Yes, of course; but in time, they realized they weren't Atals and never would be. They couldn't do the same things. Their power and their works were poor imitations of that of their Atal forebears. They aged and sickened. Even so, most felt superior to their common-born parents and longed to replace their Celestial forebears. When it was clear they could never rise to the heights that the Atals had attained, they grew jealous. Many believed that the Atals were hoarding the secrets to their superior magical powers. Eventually, their frustration and resentment grew into full-blown hatred."

"But they have their own country now—their own space to live in and do as they wish."

"All they wish for," the wizard explained, "is to crush everyone around them. Their particular focus is on the Atals. They resent the beautiful cities the Atals have built and the peaceful societies of the Bright Ones. Once the Atals have been driven from the world, they will turn their focus to the east and the common folk they hate just as much as their Celestial counterparts."

"Because it's the common blood that keeps them from the power they're after," Arthur pointed out. "What a shame."

"Indeed," Merlin replied. "The Atals have great wisdom and could enhance the world of men. Yet they are not perfect, and many among them look down upon humanity."

"We are both created by the Most High," Arthur said.

"As powerful and peaceful as they are, why should they bother with such feelings?"

"This world was created for man, and the Atals are just temporary visitors here. For some among the Celestial folk, there is resentment that a people so weak could be given a gift as precious as the world."

Arthur thought about it. He could see both sides— which perhaps made sense, since he was half human and half Atal. He didn't feel different than any other common person he knew, though. His skill with a sword and bow came not from a natural gift but from hours of training. Even when his abilities matched Jon Longarm's, Arthur had continued training on his own, often spending hours every day in the forest building on his skills. Arthur didn't feel superior to anyone, but nor did he feel inferior. Everything in the human world was new and interesting to him. He relished the freedom to go where he wanted and do what he wanted. Perhaps the Farkians couldn't understand that because they had experienced the Atal society in all its supposed perfection.

That evening, they stopped at a cave that was carved into the side of a bluff. It was a deep recess into the hillside, large enough for the three of them and their horses. Merlin told Arthur and Drust to stay put while he morphed in his bird form and scouted the surrounding countryside. Drust saw to the fire, gathering enough dead brush and twigs from an old tree nearby to keep a small fire going most of the night.

Arthur went to the horses. Checking their hooves and brushing them down after a long day helped to calm his nerves. Farkia was a strange place. He couldn't say what it was exactly that made him uneasy, but there was something about the land. It felt ill, diseased—tainted. Left to his own devices, he would have left as quickly as possible, and Drust felt the same.

"I don't like it here," he said when Arthur returned to the fire.

"In the cave?"

"In this land," Drust said. "Why would anyone live here?"

"I don't know," Arthur admitted. "But we won't be here long. Tomorrow, you'll stay here with the horses while Merlin and I take care of something."

"I don't like that, either," Drust said. "I can fight."

Arthur smiled. "I know you can."

The boy had kept Harkyn's sickle sword. Merlin had even crafted him a half sheath so that he could carry the weapon on his belt. It wasn't much more than a leather loop, but the crooked sword wouldn't slide into a traditional sheath. There hadn't been time to begin teaching him to use the sword, but if Drust stayed with them, Arthur knew he would have to learn at some point. The wildness of the world required that a person know how to defend themselves.

"We aren't here to fight anyone, Drust," Arthur said, knowing the excuse sounded as lame as it felt. "We're going to rescue some people."

"The Atals," Drust said. "I've been listening."

"Of course you have," Arthur said.

"And you won't just stroll in and take them without a fight," Drust said. "I'm not daft. Please, Arthur, don't leave me behind."

"We aren't," Arthur said. "But we're dealing with sorcerers. It's complicated, but they would recognize you as being common born."

"What does that mean?"

"It just means you're innocent."

"Won't they recognize you?"

"Merlin doesn't think so."

"Because you're like the people here?"

The question was innocent enough, but it hung like a dark cloud over Arthur. Merlin had tried his best to explain who the Farkians were and why they hated the Atals. The wizard insisted that Arthur was different, yet he also expected the Farkians to see him as like their own. It didn't make sense to Arthur. In the back of his mind, fear was worming its way into his subconscious. Perhaps he *was* like the Farkians; perhaps the blood of the Atals in his veins mingling with that of a human would make him evil.

"I suppose," Arthur said. "I never knew my father."

"Me either," the boy said. "Then my mother sold me to Harkyn."

"Mine died and sent me to a monastery."

"We're the same, then," Drust said.

Arthur nodded. "Tomorrow, you'll stay here with the horses until we return."

"With the captives?"

"I hope so," Arthur said.

"But what if you don't? What if you don't come back?"

"Then you'll take the horses and ride back east, just the way we came."

"Harkyn will send men for me," Drust said with a sadness that was heart-wrenching.

"No," Arthur said. "Harkyn may not have survived. If he did, his men will have given him the warning. They'll want nothing to do with us. You'll be fine—and you'll have three horses. Sell two of them, and you'll have enough money to get started somewhere. You can make a life for yourself, Drust. That's the truth."

"I've never had any coin of my own," the boy said wonderingly.

Arthur pulled the little coin pouch he kept on his belt. It had a few silver coins and twice as many coppers. He tossed the pouch to Drust. "Now you do."

They ate and tried their best to sleep, but the ground was hard, and no matter what, Arthur couldn't escape the sharp edges of rocks poking into him. He tossed and turned as Drust did the same.

Arthur had more bothering him than just the discomfort of the present conditions. The idea of fighting the Farkians unnerved him. Normally, he enjoyed a fight. He hadn't shied away when the raiders attacked the monastery or when the dread wolf preyed on the village of Ivy Leaf. Even when he was surrounded by Harkyn's men in the Dogwood Inn, he hadn't dreaded the fight. Now here he was, afraid, and no amount of denial could change that fact.

Merlin returned just before dawn. Arthur heard first the flutter of wings and then the footsteps of the wizard approaching. Their fire was tiny, with just a few little sticks left burning. It was no more light than a candle in a large room.

"We're close," Merlin said.

"Are the prisoners there?" Arthur asked.

Merlin nodded as he knelt by the fire and extended his

hands. The flames grew, and so did their warmth. Arthur had no idea how the wizard made the fire bigger and brighter than the fuel ever could have done, but somehow his magic fed the flames.

"Two are dead already," Merlin said. "I'm not sure what the Farkians are doing, but it is foul magic. The bodies of the dead were carried out of the little village and hacked to pieces."

"Why?" Arthur was aghast.

"More arcane rituals, I suppose," Merlin said. "Some of the Farkians are no more than brutes. They might even believe that eating the Atals could give them some of their power."

Arthur shuddered with disgust. He had read scrolls in the monastery detailing the savage beliefs and rituals of the people living beyond Atlandia's borders. Cannibalism wasn't unheard of, nor were the ideas of other gods that required sacrifices from their followers. The monks at Byth El called them false gods and taught that the Most High was the one true deity, but if Merlin's instincts were right, it was likely that the Farkians were godless savages.

"What are we going to do?" Arthur asked. "I doubt they'll let us stroll into their village and just take the captives."

"Actually, the Atals are being held in a pit outside of the village," Merlin said. "They're guarded by a few middle caste Farkian warriors."

"That can't be," Arthur said. "Surely they would use their magic to escape."

"If they could—but the Farkians are keeping them

drugged. We'll go in, take out the guards, and revive the captives, hopefully without anyone being the wiser."

"You know what it sounds like to me?" Arthur said. "A trap."

"Perhaps, but what other choice do we have?" Merlin replied wearily.

He began tracing in the air with one finger. A dazzling light filled the space. It grew brighter and brighter, before suddenly transforming into a floating image of a city as seen from the air.

"This is LóArc," the wizard explained.

Arthur could see dozens of rock huts with sod roofs clustered around a stone tower. The streets were mud, and there was filth and decay all around. The people moving through the dark streets were hard to make out, but Arthur could tell they were larger than common men.

"Someone—I'm not sure who—controls the tower. I could feel their presence," Merlin went on. "The magic they wield is powerful and probably produced the creatures."

"That sounds ominous," Arthur commented as the image shifted.

"Beyond the village is a series of pens and cages," Merlin said. "The dark magic from the tower is transforming prisoners into the hybrid creatures. The transformation destroys the person and leaves only the mind of a beast."

"How many?"

"Dozens. Someone is building an army with no care for whoever these creatures are set loose on," Merlin continued, and the magical image changed again. "On the opposite side of the village is a group of pits. It's where the captives are held, Atals and common folk both—even some of the Farkians are held captive there."

"The sorcerer in the tower is experimenting," Arthur said. "On their own kind, it seems."

Merlin nodded again. "There are sentries to the north, but we're coming from the east, which is to our advantage. Besides, I'll be the one to deal with the guards and rescue the Atals."

"What am I going to be doing?"

Merlin waved his hand, and the image fluttered apart like a thousand dazzling sparks from a multicolored bonfire. His eyes twinkled almost as brightly. "Creating a distraction."

CHAPTER THIRTY-TWO

Arthur followed the directions that Merlin had given him. The village came into sight less than an hour from the cave, where Drust was watching the horses. Merlin was somewhere above, and Arthur envied him. On the ground, dust rose up in every breath of wind. His feet ached from the rocky, uneven ground, and the harsh sun shined down unrelentingly. The hardpacked earth seemed to both absorb the heat and reflect it back up at him simultaneously. The strangest thing was that just a few days ago he had been cold, with chilling autumn winds reminding him that winter was on the way.

Eventually, Arthur met another person. The Farkian was tall, like Arthur, but thicker through the neck and chest. His face was odd, too, with a blank expression. He paid Arthur no heed as they passed one another. The stranger lumbered with a heavy gait, plodding along. The only interesting thing about the

Farkian was the way he made Arthur feel. There was tingling sensation in the pit of Arthur's stomach and quickening of his blood, followed by a sense of empathy he'd never felt before.

It took an act of will to lower his head and keep moving. Eventually, he came to the town itself. It was a few hours after dawn, but the town was almost empty. Arthur had never been in a settlement where no animals were kept and the workmen weren't busy in the morning. It seemed more like late night, when people were finally heading home from the taverns and inns to sleep off the ale they had consumed. He moved through the narrow streets, avoiding the worst areas of grime, and made his way to the tower before anyone spoke to him.

At the entrance to the tall, round structure, a hulking Farkian stood guard. It was obvious that he was more intelligent and alert than the other Farkian Arthur had seen. He wasn't as tall as Arthur, but he was heavily muscled and had a long-hafted war axe beside him. The butt of his weapon was on the floor, and he leaned against it like the axe was a staff, one hand at the top between the double crescent-shaped blades.

"Who are you?" the guard grumbled.

"Artici," he said, using his Atal name to avoid suspicion. "I'd like to see the person in charge."

"The person in charge?" the Farkian said with a chuckle. "Fat chance of that. Besides, you don't want to see her. She's a cruel one, and no doubt about it."

"I've got news," Arthur said, following the script that Merlin had given him. "From Dorn."

"General Haylek's who you want to see," the guard said.

"He's in charge. Mora ap'Drayd is too busy with her craft to come out of the tower and do the dirty work."

"Word is she captured a group of Atals," Arthur said.

"She didn't do it," the man said angrily. "General Haylek's who gets things done around here. You see him."

The Farkian stepped aside, and Arthur went into the tower. He could feel a difference inside. It wasn't just the lack of light or the strange smells: there was a hum of magic to the entire structure. Incense was burning on a table in the middle of the dark room; despite that, Arthur could still smell the sickly smell of decay. The building was circular, with a staircase running along the outer wall that started directly across from the doorway. There were several floors above the ground level, and a hole through the center of the floors above allowed the smoke and aroma from the incense to rise up. There were several Farkians with weapons near the bottom of the stairs, who looked up as Arthur entered.

"General Haylek?" Arthur inquired.

Several of the soldiers pointed up and paid Arthur no heed as he started for the stairs. Perhaps intruders were simply unheard of in Farkia. Arthur knew that in the eastern lands of men, Farkia was spoken of with a shudder of distaste, although Arthur had never met anyone who had actually been there other than Merlin.

The other explanation for the ease with which Arthur was given entrance was his Atal blood. It was an idea that sat uneasily with him, since Arthur had no real connection to the Atals—only times when he felt things that he knew common-born folk didn't feel. He'd experienced that tingling deep inside when he met the first Farkian outside the village. Perhaps these guards simply saw another of their kind, which made Arthur nervous.

But not as nervous as the third possibility, which was that his presence was expected and he was walking into a trap. If the Farkians knew he was coming, they would be ready. For all Arthur knew, Merlin could be serving him as a sacrificial lamb so that the wizard could rescue the Atals. All Arthur knew for certain was that no one questioned him, and he still had his weapons. If he walking into a trap, whoever waited to pounce would have to be wary.

On the second floor was a table laid out with food, mostly smoked and salted meats, the type that could last for days or even weeks without going bad. There were a few Farkians lounging in that room as well; Arthur paid them no heed, and they in turn ignored him. Continuing up, Arthur found three men on the third level. They were standing around a table looking at a map. One was the biggest individual Arthur had ever seen, both taller and wider than the young warrior. Muscles stood out all over his body, inhumanly large. He also had a huge sword strapped to his back.

"General Haylek?" Arthur asked.

"That's me," the big man said, looking up. "Who are you?"

"Artici from Dorn. I have news."

"News from Dorn is no news at all. What are those cowards complaining about now?"

"I was instructed to give my news to the person in charge, Mora ap'Drayd."

"She's busy. Leave your message with me," the general insisted, "and be on your way."

Merlin had given Arthur a small glass vial filled with

powder that would billow dark blue smoke when the vial was broken. The tower had windows opposite the winding staircase. Arthur's task was to break the vial near one of the windows and get out of the village as fast as possible. Somewhere in the distance, Merlin was watching for the smoke that would signal him to begin his task of freeing the hostages. Of course, once the alarm sounded, Arthur would have to do more than run: he would have to fight his way out of the tower and possibly out of the town. Arthur hadn't seen many Farkians, but that didn't mean they weren't there.

Arthur stepped off the staircase and moved over to the table. He was closer to the window, which gave the only real light in the room. The general and his lieutenants were near that source of light, but not blocking the window. Arthur was fumbling in his satchel, trying to appear deeply incompetent. From the looks of disdain on the faces of the soldiers, he was doing a convincing job.

"Hurry up!" General Haylek barked. "We haven't got all day."

Arthur turned suddenly when a woman's voice startled him. It was different from the others, almost melodic. It awoke a sudden tingle deep inside, the same way he felt when riding a horse at a full gallop and making a jump.

"What are you fussing about down here?" she asked.

There was no impatience or anger in her voice—it was almost teasing. The woman was painfully thin, her tight, fur-trimmed gown clinging to her bony body. Her fair hair had just a touch of red, and her skin was incredibly pale. Despite her frail appearance, she moved with strength and grace. Arthur had seen dancers with a traveling show in one of the towns visited by the priests; he remembered how they moved, as if their feet barely touched the ground. Mora had the same graceful movements.

When she saw Arthur, she froze, halfway down the stairs. He in turn couldn't take his eyes off of her. *It couldn't be…*

Arthur had spent most of his adolescence with monks who rejected any form of vanity, but mirrors were necessary for shaving. Jon had owned one, and Arthur had been fascinated by it. He had spent hours staring into the mirror when Jon had first showed it to him on one of their trips. Arthur therefore knew what he looked like, and his resemblance to the woman coming down the stairs was undeniable.

"This bumbling fool has news from Dorn," General Haylek declared. "But he can't seem to give us the message."

"Leave us," Mora demanded.

Although her voice was soft, it carried an authority that surprised Arthur. General Haylek had an irritated look on his face, but he didn't argue. His lieutenants followed him. When they were gone, Mora descended the staircase and walked over to Arthur, who felt paralyzed.

"Who are you?" she asked.

"My name is Artici," he said. "From Dorn."

Mora smiled. "We both know that isn't true. We are bonded, you and I. The blood that runs through your veins also runs through mine. Can you feel that?"

"I have a message," Arthur managed to say.

His voice was feeble. The air was still inside the tower, and Arthur's throat was suddenly very dry. Standing was difficult on legs that were suddenly shaky and weak. It was as if the woman was looking right through him and seeing the little boy who had lost his mother.

"It must be our father's," Mora went on. "My mother died giving birth to me. She would have been much too old to give birth to you, anyway. But we are different. The gifts are not the same, nor are they equal."

"You're the witch," Arthur said.

Mora turned and began walking around him. Arthur could feel her presence, like body heat, although she was much too cold for that.

"I am a visionary," she replied. "Our father is limited, and I am not. Did he send you?"

"No," Arthur said. "I've never met him."

Mora sneered slightly. "You are better off for it. He was a beast—a wolf in sheep's clothing, so to speak."

"And you want to kill him?"

"Does that bother you, Artici?"

"Killing someone is never the answer," Arthur insisted, quoting Abbot Gryald, who had so often reminded him of the axiom.

"But you have killed," she said. "I can see that. Violence radiates from you like heat from the sun. Yes, you have the physical gifts I was denied. Look at you: a perfect combination of Atal and human."

Arthur had the vial of powder in his hand and had to force himself not to squeeze it too hard for fear that it might break. Some part of his brain was telling him to run, but another part was begging him to stay. He wanted to know more about his father, and yet he was repulsed by the woman who claimed to be his sister.

"I wish I had more time," Arthur said.

"We have time," Mora countered.

"No," Arthur said, as much to himself as to her. Denying the desire to know Mora, to be close to her, was difficult.

"Yes."

Arthur felt a tingle of magic behind the word as it slipped into his ears. The thought flooded his brain. She wanted him to stay—to be part of her. But what did he want? He couldn't remember, couldn't think straight. She was bewitching him, and he was almost lost. The only thing he could do, the last act of defiance to her magical will, was to throw the vial.

He flung it toward the window with a flick of his wrist, but Mora saw it. She caught the vial with her magic before it hit the stone floor and broke open. Arthur felt the intense desire to obey Mora evaporate like fog in the sun. Her focus had left him and was on the vial.

"What treachery is this?" she asked, her voice no longer light and playful.

The glass vial floated up between them into the light from the window. Mora's face was pinched in concentration and anger. This was his opportunity to act—perhaps the only one he had. Arthur drew his sword and slashed it across the space between them so quickly that Mora didn't have time to cast another spell. Arthur wasn't attacking her: the blade struck the vial and shattered it. She was immediately obscured in a cloud of blue smoke that spread through the room and billowed out the window.

Arthur followed the slash with a break for the stairs. The smoke roiled around him as Mora screamed, not in pain but absolute fury. Arthur bounded down the stairs, and her voice trailed after him.

"Kill him!" she screeched.

General Haylek and his lieutenants turned to see Arthur hurtling down the stairs. Only one was close enough to try to stop him, but Arthur was too fast. He slashed with the long sword, careful not to chop the way Jon had taught him. The last thing he could afford was for the sword to get wedged in a body. He let the blade bite then slid it; *Es Kali ap'Bur* connected with the Farkian's chest and sliced across his stomach in a spray of blood. The Farkian dropped to the ground, trying to hold his opened guts together.

The distraction had begun. Arthur hadn't failed, but he hadn't escaped yet. He had to get clear of the tower, then out of the village, and finally somehow, some way, find his way back to the cave without being followed or caught. Still, Arthur couldn't help but smile. He was in mortal danger, but he thrived under the pressure; and the fight of his life had only just begun.

CHAPTER THIRTY-THREE

Merlin saw the blue smoke immediately with his acute falcon eyesight. Perched atop a scrub pine on a hill, he could see the sentries, the prisoner pits, and, in the distance, the village of LóArc with its tall, stone tower. Merlin waited for a few moments to see what the sentries would do. Half were sent to investigate, leaving four to guard the pits.

It was impossible to work magic in his falcon form. He took to the air, glided down over the pits, and landed on the ground. The sentries paid no attention; clearly, they weren't magically sensitive, else they would have noticed his approach. It was indeed fortunate that many of the lower caste Farkians were too many generations removed from their Atal forebears to retain any magical power. Merlin transformed back into his human form but stayed low, squatting on the ground.

Using his magic, he levitated dozens of fist-sized stones

and sent them flying at the sentries. Nearly half of the stones missed or only landed glancing blows that were easy shaken off, but the rest hit with the intended effect. All four sentries were knocked senseless. As soon as the guards were down, Merlin moved to the edge of the pit. It was nearing midday, and the sun was bright overhead, shining down into the prisoner pits. Yet the Atals were all sleeping.

Manipulating fire or levitating small objects was easy enough for a wizard of Merlin's knowledge and experience. Levitating fully grown Atals out of a twenty-foot pit was a different matter, one that required energy and concentration. Merlin focused on the first of the Atals. He had to wrap the body in magic, then lift. Merlin's body tensed, his breathing becoming rapid and shallow. Sweat sprang out on his forehead before he got the Atal out of the pit. The body floated just outside the pit and then to the ground.

The real problem was time. Merlin had to take a moment before doing anything else just to catch his breath and make sure no one had seen him helping the Atals escape. If they had been awake, they could have saved themselves. As it was, levitating them away from the camp would be nearly impossible. Merlin also knew they couldn't get far in broad daylight—they would be too easy to spot. Nor was it lost on Merlin that Arthur was risking his life to give just one chance to save the Atals. He needed to get the Atals to help themselves if they were going to succeed. Merlin decided to see if he could rouse the Atal he had just rescued.

Merlin let his magic flow again, this time searching the unconscious prisoner for what was keeping them asleep. They had been given a powerful sleeping agent, probably in their food or water. It took Merlin a few minutes to isolate the sedative and remove it from the prisoner's bloodstream. Slowly, he began to wake up. Merlin moved to his side and pulled the Atal to a sitting position.

"What's happening?" the prisoner asked, his voice slurred as if from too much wine.

"I'm Errol ap'Tunnar Foyl," Merlin said. "I've come to rescue you."

"Rescue?"

The prisoner was awake, but still reeling from the effects of whatever potion he'd been given. There would be no help from him, and that didn't bode well for the others. Merlin went back to work levitating the next prisoner and got the next Atal to the surface. The first prisoner was still trying to regain his senses.

Merlin was halfway finished raising the third prisoner when a shout alerted him to danger. Unfortunately, Merlin couldn't stop what he was doing without dropping the prisoner. He strained against the gravity that was pulling the unconscious Atal down and got him to the surface. When Merlin broke the spell, his own strength waning, he saw three Farkians with weapons drawn running toward him.

The wizard had to wait for his strength to return and could do nothing but watch as the warriors neared, fear tearing at his insides like an animal caught in a trap. Part of him wanted to revert to his falcon form and race away, but he couldn't leave the Atal prisoners. If he did, their rescue efforts would be for naught, and they wouldn't get another chance.

In the end, mere chance was what saved him. The Farkians made a mistake and got too close to another of the pits, one filled with humans that weren't drugged. From the sounds of unrest issuing from the pit, they knew something was happening but didn't know what. Merlin summoned the power of the staff, making the crystal shine. He swung it and loosed a wave of magic that bludgeoned the three Farkian soldiers right into the pit. Merlin didn't have to look inside to know that the humans had jumped at the chance to finish off their captors.

It took several minutes to get the final Atal prisoner to the surface. Merlin was sweating through his robes and seeing spots by the time he finished. He hadn't pushed his magical abilities so hard in a long time—most spells didn't require such care and strength. There wasn't even time to rest: he still wasn't finished, and in the distance, he could see more Farkians leaving the village to see what was happening at the pits. He wondered, as he stumbled over to the pit where the human captives were held, if Arthur had survived. The young warrior was more than capable, but Merlin's rescue was taking too long. He needed to get away and move to help Arthur.

The first Atal prisoner was finally on his feet, albeit unsteady. Merlin still needed to wake the others and get them moving. He couldn't do that and fight the Farkians. With a sudden wave of inspiration, he looked over the edge of the pit where the common-born folk were being held. The prisoners had divided the weapons from the fallen soldiers and hacked the Farkians to pieces. A rope ladder lay in a pile by the edge of the pit.

"If I let you out, you have to fight," Merlin told them.

"We'll fight," said a skinny man with a scraggly beard.

"Aye, just give us the chance," said another.

They were all filthy and half starved, but they knew

there was no hope of survival if they couldn't get out of the pit—and maybe, Merlin thought as he pushed the pile of rope into the pit, they would rather die fighting. He knew he would. The rope ladder was already fastened to a large boulder, and the prisoners started climbing.

Merlin turned back to the Atals. He couldn't use a spell to hide them, since, unlike the guards, the oncoming masses of Farkians almost certainly had sorcerers among them who would pick up the magic like a beacon, which would defeat the purpose. Distance was what they needed, a chance to get away from the village and give the Atals time to recover.

Merlin set to work on the second prisoner, a female with white hair. While he sifted the potion from her blood, the humans formed a line between the Farkians and him. Merlin didn't know how many were coming or if the prisoners could even slow them down, only that he had to keep working. Even so, he wondered if this effort was already a lost cause. Bringing back just four of the six Atals taken prisoner might not be enough to sway the council, even if the others were dead before Merlin and Arthur had arrived. Merlin shook off the thought as the prisoner awoke and gave her his water skin before moving to the third prisoner.

The sound of weapons clashing got Merlin's attention. He looked up as two Farkians killed two of the human prisoners. The humans were too weak to defend themselves, and the Farkians cut them down easily. There were more humans, however, and they seized the opportunity, attacking the Farkians from both sides and landing several blows before having to retreat. The wounded soldiers did the same.

Merlin was on his fourth and final prisoner when one of the humans, a woman with blood-matted hair, ran to him.

"We can't stop them," she said.

More of the Farkian soldiers were coming. Fighting the large, strong brutes would be difficult for anyone, and even if the Atals hadn't been drugged, outrunning the soldiers would have proven hard, if not impossible.

"Have your people come and help these Bright Ones," Merlin told her. "Move them up over that hill. See the pine tree?"

"Yes," the woman said.

"Get them there. I'll stop the soldiers."

"You will?"

"Yes," Merlin said, rising to his feet.

Merlin was a wizard. It didn't matter that he was tired or that he felt weak—he was the only one capable of buying them enough time to get the prisoners free. Someone had thrown the rope ladder into the third pit, and more common-born folk were climbing out.

"That way!" Merlin shouted, pointing behind. "Get over that hill."

The prisoners got the Atals on their feet and lent them strength to make for the hill marked by the scrub pine. Merlin waited until they passed him, then lifted his hands. Nearly two dozen warriors were racing to stop him and either kill or recapture the prisoners. Merlin closed his eyes and focused his magic.

Of all the environmental features it did have—dry heat, arid air, and more—Farkia wasn't a windy place; but suddenly, a wind picked up, blowing with it a swirling cloud of dust. The Farkians didn't even slow down as the dust cloud grew stronger. Merlin could feel the power of the staff and his own magic stirring the ground. With a powerful swing, he brought the staff down. The butt of the staff hit the ground, and the dust cloud blasted into the onrushing warriors with enough force to knock them off their feet. The dust was so thick they had trouble breathing. Most were on their knees coughing and trying to cover their faces as the dust began to settle.

Merlin had bought some time. Would it be enough? There was only one way to find out. Hastened by urgency, the wizard morphed into his falcon form and chased after the escaping prisoners.

CHAPTER THIRTY-FOUR

Arthur burst onto the ground floor of the citadel, only to run into several soldiers with weapons drawn, not sure what was happening. The shouting from above was growing louder, but they stood frozen with indecision and fear, leaving Arthur a window of opportunity. He leaped toward the first Farkian, a dull-faced soldier with a fighting axe in one hand, and rammed his sword straight through the Farkian's belly, snatching the axe from his hand before the man knew what had happened. As he fell to the floor, Arthur turned and hurled the axe at one of General Haylek's lieutenants, who was charging down the stairs. The axe caught the big Farkian in the leg, severing the muscle and lodging in the bone. The soldier roared as he fell down the stairs.

As the Farkian fell back, Arthur used the axman's body weight to help pull his sword free, and just in time: three more soldiers were closing in on him. Arthur feinted toward the stairs, then bolted toward the doorway, know that he needed to get out of the tower before the call to arms had him trapped inside. The Farkians were all big and power-fully built, but they were also slow. Arthur avoided a soldier's clumsy chop and let *Es Kali ap'Bur* slice across the Farkian's shoulder. Unfortunately, the Farkian didn't even seem to notice and continued to pursue Arthur, who was almost to the door, blocked by a guard.

The soldier behind Arthur gave himself away when he grunted as he thrust his big sword at the young man's back. The guard at the door raised his battle axe, but Arthur ducked to the side. The Farkian behind him missed Arthur and ran his blade into the stomach of the door guard. The guard's long-hafted battle axe came down and split the wounded Farkian's skull. They both fell as another soldier rushed at Arthur.

While Arthur was easily the better warrior, he quickly realized that he would have to deliver critical blows—flesh wounds weren't enough to stop the immense Farkians. Arthur ducked under a slash intended to take off his head and drew his dagger with his left hand. He stepped toward the big soldier and rammed the dagger into his groin. Blood from a severed artery sprayed like a fountain as the Farkian stumbled backward into the soldier behind him. The dagger was deadly in close quarters where his sword was too long, and, being shorter, it was easier to pull free. With one weapon in each hand, Arthur jumped over the body of the guard and through the door of the tower as General Haylek lumbered across the tower's ground floor chamber in pursuit.

Outside, there were at least fifty Farkian soldiers, who

either looked around, bewildered, or stared dumbly up at the copious amounts of blue smoke that billowed from the third-floor window. Arthur wondered what had happened to Mora ap'Drayd. The memory of her filled him with a sense of unease. He had a sister—a half-sister, at least—with the same father, he was sure. They looked too much alike, and there was a magnetic feeling between them. Arthur wondered if Merlin had known. The wizard was too secretive; when there was a chance, Arthur intended to find out.

That, however, was for another time. As Arthur dashed away from the tower, a few of the Farkians realized that he was the intruder and pursued, but most did nothing at all. Arthur slipped between two stone huts, where the Farkians could only come at him one at a time. The first slashed at his head with a rusty sword. Arthur dodged easily, and the weapon shattered against the stone wall. With a quick jab, the tip of Arthur's sword slashed through the Farkian's throat. The soldier staggered back until he was pushed to the ground by the soldier behind him.

Arthur kept moving through the muddy streets, slick and hard to navigate—the huts had been built without any planning. The young man pushed himself to stay ahead of the growing tide of Farkian soldiers in pursuit but made a wrong turn and found himself surrounded in an open space near the edge of the villages. His only path of escape was to climb over the huts, and Arthur wasn't sure the sod rooftops would hold him.

He moved to the center of the open space, turning around, expecting the Farkians to attack from his blind side. They held back, obviously in respect for his speed and skill with a blade. Before Arthur had much time to consider what else might be giving them pause, a strange yelping sound reached his ears. It was unnatural and made the hair on the back of Arthur's neck stand on end.

The crowd parted to let General Haylek step into the open space. His big sword was still on his back, but the look of victory on his face was undeniable.

"Time to die, fool," Haylek shouted.

The crowd, blocking any escape from the area, laughed. They may have feared Arthur's sword and speed, but they were supremely confident in their numbers and in their mammoth leader. Compared to the colossal general, Arthur looked like a little boy.

"Have you come to face me, General?" Arthur said.

"You wouldn't last thirty seconds with me," Haylek snarled. "I don't need to get my hands dirty, anyway—I'm leaving you to the dogs."

More laughter and jeering followed his statement. The howling grew louder. Whatever the creature was, there was more than one...and Arthur didn't think it would be mere dogs.

Arthur didn't know what was coming, but he hoped he could get the general to fight him, since perhaps the soldiers with their howling creatures wouldn't turn the animals loose if their leader might be at risk. Arthur also needed to buy himself time to figure out a way to escape that was more viable than the rickety rooftops, which would be hard to climb up quickly. Perhaps, if he could kill a few Farkians, he could jump off their bodies and reach the rooftops, but the survivors might reach him and pull him down. The risk was still too great to try; instead, he taunted the general, choosing to play a different game.

"Afraid, General? You know you don't stand a chance against a high caste warrior like me."

"I would rip your heart out, pup!" Haylek bellowed.

"Then prove it," Arthur challenged him. He cleared his throat and spit toward the general.

Haylek roared with anger and drew his sword. It was straight, the gray blade as wide as Arthur's middle finger was long. The Farkian general whirled the massive sword around his body as if it weighed nothing.

"I'm going to enjoy softening you up for the dogs. They love the smell of blood," Haylek taunted.

"Show me," Arthur said calmly. "You fat oaf."

Haylek wasn't fat—in fact, he barely had any fat at all on his massive frame—but the insult landed. He snarled and started toward Arthur, holding his sword high. Under different circumstances, Arthur would have gone on the offensive and tried to take out the Farkian as quickly as possible. Now, if he killed Haylek, the others might converge on him, and what Arthur needed more than this victory was an escape route. He held his ground, waiting as Haylek advanced close enough.

Arthur raised his sword, as if he would try to block the inevitable chopping stroke that the general intended to make. Arthur saw a flash of eagerness in his opponent's eyes. Arthur was still holding his dagger in his left hand, and there was probably no way that, even with two hands on his sword, Arthur could stop the powerful blow from the Farkian general. *Just a little closer...*Arthur thought.

He waited until the very last instant. Right as Haylek chopped down with his sword, Arthur spun out of the way. Haylek's downward stroke missed, and he was beginning a backhanded slash as Arthur came around. He could have driven his sword deep into Haylek's side, but he waited instead. As the Farkian's sword came whistling through the air in a level slash at shoulder height, Arthur ducked. The big blade missed him, and Arthur thrust his sword into the side of Haylek's knee.

The general bellowed in pain and hopped back out of reach. For a moment, he lost his balance, but Arthur hesitated again. The howls were closer, the crowd screaming as blood poured from the puncture wound in the general's knee. It wasn't a deadly injury, but Arthur knew it would be painful, and Haylek's big, heavy body was dependent on his knees. The general was never fast, but he was slower than ever with a wounded leg. He screamed furiously and came limping toward Arthur.

All the sword lessons that Arthur had been taught came back to him at that moment. Speed, finesse, leverage, skill— he knew exactly what to do. He didn't wait for Haylek to reach him but charged toward the hulking general, feinting one way and then attacking from the other. Haylek was off balance as Arthur's sword grazed his ribs, splitting his flesh. Arthur could have finished the fight with one blow, jabbing his sword into the gash he'd opened between the general's ribs, but instead he sliced and moved despite the heavy mud that sucked at his feet. As Haylek bent over the cut in his side, Arthur slipped behind him and slashed the wide back. Once again, he didn't cut deep. *Es Kali ap'Bur* was like an extension of Arthur's arm. He slid the sharp blade across the bulging muscles of the general's back, then, moving to his other side, Arthur stabbed the dagger into the general's elbow. The dagger bit deep, cutting muscles and tendon before glancing off bone.

General Haylek lost his grip on his sword and fell to the ground, helpless. The crowd had fallen silent, watching the deadly dance that Arthur was performing and realizing that he could kill their leader. The braying animals were louder. Arthur picked up Haylek's sword, which was heavy and unwieldy. He tossed it away and turned back to the Farkian. Arthur bent low so that only Haylek could hear him.

"They're almost here with the animals," Arthur said.

"They'll tear you to pieces," Haylek said, his voice tight.

He lay on his undamaged side, struggling to get into a position that would lessen the pain. One arm was worthless and one knee injured. The powerful warrior was wounded but not completely out of the fight. He lunged, trying to get his good hand on Arthur's leg, but the young man easily stepped out of reach. In retaliation, Arthur brought the heel of his boot down on the general's outstretched fingers. Two broke on impact, and Haylek wheezed in agony.

"Think about it," Arthur said. "Who will they attack? A warrior on his feet with weapons, or a bleeding Farkian already helpless in the mud?"

The look on General Haylek's face changed from hatred to fear. Arthur had to assume that these were the insane, bloodthirsty creatures that Merlin claimed Farkia was creating. Perhaps the beasts could be ordered to attack Arthur, but he was betting they would fall on Haylek first.

"Call them off," Arthur ordered the fallen general. "Tell

your men to fall back. I'll leave your village, and your people can help you. These injuries can be healed, General, but not if the creatures you are bringing out fall on you."

"I'll find you," Haylek spat. "I'll hunt you to the ends of Atlandia."

"You won't have to go that far," Arthur said. "I'll be around."

Haylek hissed in a frustrated breath before bellowing, "Retreat!"

Arthur stood up, back on his guard, expecting trickery. None of the Farkians had moved, but slowly, at their general's order, they started to slink back.

"Let him go!" Haylek said. "We will finish this fight another day."

There was murmuring among the soldiers, but a gap opened between two of the rock huts. Arthur saw his opportunity and sprinted for the opening. He didn't bother to look back as he ran from the scene of the fight. He knew that Haylek would still send the animals after him. Once he had been helped from the place where Arthur had struck him down, the general would send whatever mutilated creatures were being summoned in pursuit. If they were dogs, they would be able to track his scent. That meant that Arthur couldn't lead them back to the cave where their horses and Drust waited. He needed a place to set an ambush of his own.

He wished that he had brought his bow and arrows, but all he carried was his sword, dagger, and knife. As he ran out past the last of the structures in the crowded village, the arid plain opened before him. If he could take out the creatures chasing him and get back to Drust before morning, they might just be able to outrun their pursuers and escape the Farkians altogether. With the unforgiving plain ahead and a trail of enemies behind, Arthur knew he couldn't drop his guard. They wouldn't forget that he had insulted them, and they wouldn't rest until they had his blood.

CHAPTER THIRTY-FIVE

Merlin pushed the captives as hard as he dared. Fortunately, they weren't being pursued, although Merlin feared that meant the Farkians had Arthur. Once he reached a small wooded area, he let the exhausted captives rest. The Atals were on their feet, but the potion with which they had been drugged had strong aftereffects. The run from LóArc had taken all their strength, and once they reached the shade under the gnarly trees of the small forest, they dropped to the ground and curled up.

The human prisoners weren't in much better shape. They had been starved, and the heat of the afternoon was bearing down on them. The woods were like an oasis, a break from the unrelenting sun, offering softer ground and even fresh water that trickled from a spring and ran between the roots of the trees before flowing out into the sun, where it quickly dried up. The freed prisoners dropped to the ground and began cupping the water with their hands, slurping greedily. Merlin checked the water and was relieved to find that it wasn't tainted.

"We'll stay here until nightfall," Merlin told them. "Try to get some rest."

"Where are you going?" asked one of the humans, a young woman with long brown hair that was tied back in a messy braid. Like everyone else, she was filthy from living in the pit, her skin dark from exposure to the sun and dirt. It hung on her in places from lack of nourishment. Yet her eyes were fiery, and her mind seemed sharp.

"My name is Merlin," he told her. "I'm going to see if the Farkians are following us."

"They can get to us anywhere," said a frail older man. "We're not safe here."

"It will have to do for now," Merlin said. "We all need rest. I'll see what the enemy is doing and return."

"You swear it?" the woman asked.

"Yes," he told her. "I swear."

He walked out from under the trees, which had thick, leathery leaves and branches covered with hanging moss. Once he returned to the sunlight, he morphed into his falcon form and took to the air. By the time he got high enough to glide for a bit, he was exhausted. Using magic always cost him strength, and it had been a long time since the wizard had pushed himself so hard. It came as a relief that there was no sign of the Farkians.

Merlin lapped a long, slow circle above the small woods before he decided he had to go back to LóArc. He had to know if Arthur had survived. The flight didn't take long, and his keen eyes took in the sight of the forlorn-looking soldiers. If Arthur had gone down, it hadn't been without a fight: several bodies were laid out near the pits where the beastly creatures were kept, at least nine Farkians that Merlin could see. He flew as close as he dared to the tower, but there was no sign of the young warrior. Merlin got a familiar feeling from someone inside the stone structure, but it wasn't Arthur.

Merlin turned back. The sun was sinking toward the horizon when he landed and resumed his usual form. Once night fell, he would lead the group in a circuitous route back to the cave where Arthur and Drust were waiting. The humans could continue east, while Arthur and Merlin would help the Atals to return to their homes in the north.

Except when he walked into the woods, no one was there—not even the Atal prisoners.

"Hello?" Merlin called out.

There was no answer. He leaned on his staff as he marched into the woods. The fading sunlight didn't penetrate the woods. Merlin let his magic mingle with that of the crystal at the head of his staff, and it began to shine light around him. Deeper into the woods, the trees seemed older and more twisted. The ground was covered with rotting leaves and crooked tree roots. He moved slowly, his senses alert.

He felt it before he saw anything: something moving—something big and magical. The magic felt ugly and murky, like sunlight shining through a dirty window. Merlin didn't move. The creature, which was beyond the ring of light from his staff, was moving cautiously toward him.

"Who's there?" Merlin asked.

"What's wrong, enchanter?" a voice like a whisper came from the darkness. "Don't you recognize me?"

"Should I?" Merlin asked.

"You always were an arrogant one, Errol. But you are not the only wizard the Atals favor."

"Sursi?" Merlin asked.

Eight gleaming black eyes appeared at the edge of the ring of light—spider eyes, like dark pits that reflected the light from the staff's crystal, higher than even Merlin. Slowly, the creature's full size began to emerge from the darkness. Silvery threads of silky webs began to glow on the spider's huge, hairy body, and two of the dark eyes were alit with a pale green light. It was massive: each of the spider's eight legs was as big around Merlin's body, and the joints in the legs were easily three times his height. The body of the spider was huge, and dark tendrils hung from the pincer mouth.

"You were a fool, Merlin. The Atals are losing strength. A new power has risen and will soon rule all of Atlandia," the spider hissed.

As the creature spoke, more light glowed from its eyes and the silver threads of web that crisscrossed its massive body. Beyond it, lying in the shadows, were the prisoners. They were unconscious, and many were wrapped in cocoons of spiderweb.

"What have you done?" Merlin asked.

"I have ensured my future," the great spider said. "Change is coming. Man's time on this world is at an end."

"You're insane," Merlin said. "Let these people go."

"A spider must eat," Sursi said. "Don't worry, I'll only

take the humans; I'm saving the Atals for the queen in the tower."

"I can't let you take them back."

"You can't stop me," the spider snarled.

Merlin called his magic to swirl around him. He held up the staff in both hands, pointing the crystal at the spider. Light flooded from the stone, blindingly bright, and the spider shrank back.

"Begone!" Merlin ordered.

The spider didn't flee and instead jumped into the tree branches, looming over Merlin. He tried to follow the beast, but the forest canopy was dark with shadows, and the tree limbs shook with the spider's movements until he couldn't tell what was the spider and what was simply a swaying bough. A moment later, the huge spider dropped down almost on top of Merlin. He ran to avoid the snapping pincer and tripped over a thin strand of sticky webbing. It brought him to the ground, the web tangling around his ankles.

"How the mighty have fallen," the spider cackled. "If only La'Rish could see you now, rolling in the dirt. The great enchanter, Errol ap'Tunnar Foyl, the mighty Merlin...you are mine now."

Merlin swung the staff, and bolt of lightning shot up into the trees above. The massive spider scuttled back to avoid the magical discharge, not knowing that it was only an illusion. Merlin didn't have the strength or the power to engage the spider directly. Had there been a fire burning, or some type of object that he could manipulate and use as a weapon, it would have been different, but there was nothing in the forest but brittle wood.

He reached into his robes and pulled out a dagger—delicate, but razor sharp—to cut through the web at his feet and retreat to the prisoners. Some were dead, just dry husks with huge wounds where Sursi had drained them. Others lay on the ground, barely conscious. Merlin could feel the spell that bound them in a dreamlike state. He couldn't attack the spider with his magic, but he could break her spell over the prisoners.

"What happened?" asked the woman in the braid as she sat up.

"A powerful animage had you under her spell," Merlin explained.

Someone started screaming. He understood the grief they were experiencing. It had to be hard to wake up and find a loved one dead. He cut the woman with the braid free as the trees overhead shook. Merlin's time was running out. He handed the woman the dagger and was casting around in search of something to use against Sursi when he saw the pile of weapons the prisoners had taken from the Farkians laying on the ground in a small heap.

"Stay here," Merlin warned before dashing away, leaving them in darkness.

Some cried out—they didn't understand his purpose. They were also scared, since Merlin had the only source of light in the dark wood. The light that gave them comfort also attracted Sursi. She dropped out of the branches into a clearing between the trees.

Merlin braced himself for what he knew was coming. One of the hairy legs swept out and knocked him to the ground. Merlin hit his head on a root and felt two of his ribs snap as he crashed into the trunk of a tree. He lay still for a moment, trying to catch his breath, which had been stolen away by the massive blow. Somehow, he'd managed to hang onto the staff, but the crystal barely glowed.

The spider was moving in. "Now I will see how a wizard tastes," Sursi said.

Before she could pounce, Merlin reached out with his magic and found the pile of weapons, a set of crudely made swords and knives—only some sharp, but all heavy. With the last of his strength, he levitated them and sent them flying haphazardly toward the huge spider, unable to direct them and just hoping they would hit. Merlin nearly blacked out from the effort, but to his relief, he heard the spider hiss and squeal in pain. There was a thump as she fell, then the huge hairy spider began to shrink down, smaller and smaller, until Sursi lay on the ground.

Merlin sat up, feeding what little magic he had left into the crystal. It showered light down on the fallen animage. She was bleeding from several wounds, but not dead.

"Please," she begged, "don't kill me, Merlin."

"Why not? It's no more than you deserve."

"I was forced to do it," Sursi said. "The Atals sent me to Farkia, and I was bewitched by the sorceress in the tower. She stole my power. I was helpless to deny her bidding."

"We always have a choice," Merlin said.

"My choice was to serve her or die," Sursi exclaimed. "Please, I don't want to die. I'm not ready."

"You cannot stay here," Merlin explained. "Not now. We can't trust you."

"I'll leave," she swore. "I promise, I'll go far away. You'll never see me again."

"Go, then; but you will not receive mercy from me a second time," Merlin said.

The truth was he didn't have the strength to kill her. Perhaps he could have lifted a sword or found a knife to cut her throat, but he didn't want to. She began to crawl away, and he limped over to where the surviving prisoners waited. They were weak, too—hungry, exhausted, some nursing wounds of their own. There was no time to recover and no resources to be found. They freed the Atals, got everyone on their feet, and left the woods, with its hanging moss and tendrils of web, behind, although Merlin was certain he would see it again in his nightmares.

CHAPTER THIRTY-SIX

They weren't dogs, not exactly, although they looked a bit like them. These hounds were larger, with wide heads and huge jaws. Fortunately for Arthur, they weren't natural trackers; but they were still too close for comfort.

He had run to a ravine between two jagged cliffs, as good an ambush spot as any. After climbing to the top of the shorter side, about ten feet above the ravine, he saw them coming: three large canines, loping toward the ravine, slobber dripping from the huge fangs that stuck out of their wobbling jowls. Like their Farkian masters, they were thick with muscle. The dogs all had broad chests, huge heads, and skinny legs. He had only been waiting on the short side of the ravine cliffs for a few moments when the animals arrived.

They came running into the ravine, sniffing the ground

and growling. Arthur hadn't done anything to hide his scent, and the dogs reared up on the cliff wall, trying to get to him.

"Hello, boys," Arthur said, drawing his sword.

The dogs howled and scrambled, trying to climb up the cliff but only managing to dislodge dirt and rocks that showered down on them. Arthur knelt and leaned over the cliff face, holding his sword ready. One of the beasts jumped, trying to reach it. At the same moment, Arthur stabbed down with his sword. The blade speared through the dog's open maw. He felt the flesh give way as the blade stabbed into bone. The creature died instantly, its backbone cleaved just below its skull by the blade. Unfortunately for Arthur, the blade wedged in the bone, and the weight of the dog tugged Arthur off balance.

For a moment, Arthur hung out over open space; the next thing he knew, he had tumbled over the edge of the ravine and into the roiling mass of dogs below. His body crashed down onto one of the beasts. Arthur wasn't hurt, but the creature's thin legs snapped under the sudden pressure. Knowing he was in trouble, Arthur rolled to his knees just as the third dog barreled into him.

Arthur was thrown backward and landed hard on the rocky ground with the heavy animal on top of him. It went immediately for his throat, but Arthur caught the beast with a palm strike to its bottom jaw. The oversized teeth clashed together, and the animal was pushed back by the impact. As he struggled to catch his breath, Arthur instinctively brought his legs up to kick out. By the time he realized his mistake, it was too late: the beast latched onto his right calf, sinking the huge fangs into the muscle and scraping across Arthur's shin bone.

The young warrior had never felt such intense pain. He tried to scream but had no breath. He managed to suck in a lungful of air just as the creature began to violently shake its head from side to side. The flesh tore and muscle shredded. Now Arthur screamed in pain, but his hand found the hilt of his dagger. He drew the blade as he sat up and had just enough reach to stab the weapon into the dog's side. It released him and stumbled backward, coughing up blood as it panted.

The dogs were defeated, at a great cost. Arthur was in agony. He reached down with a trembling hand and cautiously probed the bloody wound in his leg. Pain shot through his entire body, and he nearly passed out. It took a few minutes before he was able to sit up and, trembling, get his shirt off. He wrapped it around the dog bite and then painstakingly pulled himself up onto his feet. The sun was going down, and Arthur was less than an hour's walk back to the cave, but he couldn't put any weight on the wounded leg. It was too fragile, too weak, to hold him up, and the sensation when his foot touched the ground was excruciating.

First, he had to gather his belongings. Arthur hopped over to where his sword was wedged in the mouth of the dog, wrenched it out, and leaned against the fine weapon like a crutch—a travesty for such a noble sword, he thought with regret. He also retrieved his dagger from the wounded dog that was bleeding to death. One he left alive, although hobbled with two broken legs, as he limped from the ravine.

Perhaps he had gotten overconfident, and that was why he found himself hurt, and so badly, for the first time in his life. Arthur felt terrible at the thought and even worse when he considered what came next. If the Farkians sent anything else after him, he would be killed. Speed and agility were Arthur's greatest strengths in battle, and the dog bite had robbed him of both. It was a lesson he wouldn't soon forget.

Night soon fell as Arthur dragged his battered body inch by inch by inch across the land, with no sign of more trouble from the Farkians. They had unleashed their hounds and expected the animals to finish him—and had very nearly succeeded. It occurred to him that the Farkians might be too busy dealing with Merlin; Arthur could only hope that his comrade was having better luck while rescuing the Atal captives.

Once the sun set, the land grew cold, and Arthur found he had more discomfort to contend with than just his leg. He wasn't sure how he could sweat and shiver at the same time, but it turned out he could. His right boot was filled with blood that squelched unpleasantly when he moved. Several times, he had to stop and wait for a dizzy spell to pass. Once, he fell hard on his hands and knees, and it took him several minutes to get back to his feet and continue.

Eventually, he saw the cave. A dim, flickering light revealed the small fire that burned within. Slowly, agonizingly, the light grew larger as Arthur drew nearer, but it seemed to take a lifetime just to reach the edge of the cave. When he finally did, he saw Drust sleeping by the fire.

Thunder neighed loudly and the boy sat up, looking tired as he rubbed his eyes. Arthur limped forward and called out.

"Drust," he said, through lips cracked and bleeding. His throat was so dry his voice sounded like the croak of a bullfrog.

"Arthur?" the boy replied. "Where are you?" He couldn't see beyond the light of the fire.

"Over here," Arthur replied. "I need help."

Drust used a small, skinny stick that was half burned already to light the way. He held it like a torch, although the flame was more like a candle.

"You're hurt!" Drust cried when he saw Arthur.

He dropped the stick and ran to his friend, valiantly letting the young warrior lean on him as they hobbled to the fire.

"What do you need?" Drust asked as Arthur slowly eased off his feet.

"Water," Arthur said.

Drust found the water skin and handed it to Arthur. The water was tepid but felt unspeakably rejuvenating as it ran down his parched throat. After quenching his thirst, Arthur asked for food. He ate some stale bread while they cleaned the wound on Arthur's leg. Gritting his teeth, he let Drust pour wine from Merlin's supplies over the wound. It burned so fiercely that Arthur nearly fainted again. They wrapped the leg in fresh bandages made from a spare blanket.

It was nearly dawn when they finished, and Merlin still hadn't returned. Growing more nervous by the minute, Arthur sent Drust to look for the wizard, with the warning that the boy be cautious. As he lay near the tiny fire, looking up at the roof of the cave, Arthur thought about his life. It had seemed to him that nothing could threaten him. In every fight, he'd been faster than anyone he had ever faced. The lessons Jon Longarm had taught him gave him confidence, and he enjoyed the battle, so much so that he had never really thought of what was at stake. Supine on the cave floor, shivering with cold, his leg hurting more than ever, he realized how foolish he had been.

The sound of clattering footsteps roused him from his reverie. "They're coming!" Drust exclaimed as he burst back into the cave. "A whole group of them."

Fear clutched Arthur's heart: there were only four Atal captives. If a group was approaching, it was more likely a group of Farkian warriors coming to finish them off.

"Help me up," Arthur said. Drust pulled him to his feet. "Get the horses."

"But Merlin is coming."

"Are you sure? Did you see him?"

"It's too dark still," the boy explained.

"Then it could be the Farkians," Arthur said.

He was about to limp over to the horses when a falcon flew into the cave. It circled past them, then landed, transforming into the wizard.

"You're alive," Merlin said, relief evident in his face.

"There are people coming this way," Arthur warned him without preamble.

"Yes, I led the captives back here. We have common-born folk as well as the Atals. The Farkians aren't following us."

"You're certain?" Arthur asked.

"Yes, Arthur. You seem upset—tell me what's wrong."

As Merlin inspected Arthur's wound, the young warrior shared what had happened with the canine creatures. People began trickling into the cave, with Drust moving between them, busily fetching water and helping the exhausted captives. Soon, they were forced to move the horses out to make room for the captives.

Merlin had medicinal herbs in his robes that he used to make a poultice for Arthur's leg. Once the wound was bound up again, the pain subsided enough that Arthur finally allowed his growing exhaustion to creep up on him. Through half-closed eyes, he watched the captives and even Merlin settle down to rest as well. After seeing to everyone else, Drust took the longest turn standing watch outside the cave in the pounding sun. At last, Arthur could keep his eyes open no longer and slept deeply and dreamlessly.

He awoke when evening fell, weak but happy that he had gotten some sleep. Merlin was nearby, looking glum.

"What's wrong?" Arthur asked.

"The captives were held using some kind of potion," Merlin explained. "I woke them at the pit and checked on them just now, but they still haven't regained their faculties."

"Maybe they just need time to do so," Arthur suggested.

"Or maybe they never will," the wizard replied. "I've never seen magic like this. I don't know who is in that tower, but they have great skill."

"It is Mora ap'Drayd," Arthur explained. "My half-sister."

"What?" Shocked suffused Merlin's face.

"You really didn't know?"

"Of course not," the wizard said. "Do you honestly think I would have kept something like that from you?"

"I'm not sure," Arthur said.

"How do you know she's your half-sister?"

"I know," Arthur said. "If you had seen her, you would know too. It wasn't just that, though...."

"You felt something. A bond."

Arthur nodded.

"I felt her, too. I knew it was familiar, but I also knew it wasn't you, so I didn't investigate," Merlin admitted.

There was a short silence as this sank in. "What do we do now?" Arthur asked, steering the subject away from Mora.

"You and Drust will take the Atals north."

"What about the rest of these folks?"

"They can make their own way east into Avon. I'll scout ahead and alert the Atals that we're coming."

"And then this will all be over," Arthur said, although his world seemed turned upside down.

"Over? What do you mean, over? Look around you, Arthur. Nothing's over. This struggle is only just beginning."

EPILOGUE

The old man stood up from the little table. The sun was setting out over the ocean, casting his skin in a golden pink color.

"It's getting late," the man said. "I'd better be getting home."

"What about the rest of the story?" I asked. "There must be more. The legend of King Arthur couldn't have arisen just from what you've told me."

"Oh, there is much more," the old man said. His voice was so sincere, as if the tale was more than just a story. "The story of Artici and Merlin is a true saga."

"Then you must tell it," I insisted.

"You really want to hear more?" the old man asked. He seemed a little surprised, but also pleased that I was eager to hear more of the tale he was crafting.

"I have to," I said. The truth was, I felt that it was more than just a desire to hear how the story unfolded—I was compelled to know the truth. Like most people, I had heard of King Arthur and *his round table; I had read books about Camelot and seen the movies. But there was something about the old man's tale, an authenticity that held my attention and demanded more.*

"I suppose I could spare some time tomorrow," the elderly man said. I was once again struck by his strength and vitality despite the obvious signs of age. "Will you be around?"

"I'm not going anywhere," I told him. "I want to know what happened."

"Then meet me by the old harbor fortress an hour after dawn," the old man said. "There's a lot to this story, so we should start early."

I watched him leave. He had a slight limp, but what he lacked in physical fitness, he more than made up for with his vibrant personality. Looking at my watch, I realized I had just spent most of the day listening to his tale. I left money on the table for our drinks and hurried back to my hotel. The hunger to start writing was stronger than ever, and I wanted to get as much of the story written down as I could. Not a single word of this magnetic tale, I promised myself and the old man, would go unwritten. It would live forever in my book.

AFTERWORD

It's probably every author's dream to write their version the great stories, or at least the stories that resonate the most deeply within them. I always knew that I would one day add my version to the pantheon of King Arthur's legend.

The the purists, please forgive my recreation of the entire story. I wanted do something completely different, to tell a version that mirrored certain parts of our world and yet was completely new at the same time.

Please leave a review on Amazon and Goodreads. Tell us all what you really thought of the book, and know that I am grateful to each of you for sharing.

— Toby Neighbors, December 16, 2020 —